COURT INTRIGUE
THE MAN WHO REFUSED TO KNEEL

THE SAGA OF
MORDECAI AND ESTHER

ILAN SENDOWSKI

In service of God.

"A deposed prince struggles to save his people from extinction and brings them durable prosperity."

ISBN: 979-8-89419-476-9 (sc)
ISBN: 979-8-89419-477-6 (hc)
ISBN: 979-8-89419-478-3 (e)

Cover page contribution: Muli Voller
Illustrations: Mark Reeve

THE EWINGS
PUBLISHING

One Galleria Blvd., Suite 1900, Metairie, LA 70001
(504) 702-6708

About the Author

Ilan Sendowski grew up in a picturesque village, where the beauty of nature sparked his curiosity and wonder. He later earned an MA in engineering from UCLA, showcasing his intellect and passion for problem-solving. While working for a defense contractor troubleshooting hardware and software bugs, Ilan pursued a legal career, ultimately becoming both a lawyer and a registered patent attorney.

His analytical skills and legal expertise later led him to explore the Bible, where he applied his tenacious focus on the significance of every word and his rigorous effort to find textual evidence, uncovering hidden insights within its stories. This journey resulted in the publication of two groundbreaking Biblical commentary books, offering innovative interpretations that blend modern perspectives with ancient texts. One of these works has been recognized for its scholarly value and is now housed in 24 distinguished university libraries.

Beyond his professional achievements, Ilan is a devoted grandfather. Inspired by his grandchildren's love for reading, he has crafted captivating heroic tales that have become cherished family treasures, passing down his storytelling passion and wisdom to the next generation.

PREFACE

My mission is to present and preserve the wisdom embedded within biblical stories.

In this work of historical fiction, we look into the biblical characters' hidden events, strategies, decisions, and actions from the Scroll of Esther. Set during the glory days of the Persian Empire, the story portrays a scattered nation of merchants engaged in an existential struggle against a hostile force.

Many readers often wonder, "Why is God's name absent from the Scroll, despite the narrative being filled with miraculous and, at times, even humorous events?" This book seeks to explore that mystery by revealing the wisdom and insight of its main characters. Like a masterful chess game, each challenge is met and overcome, guided by the unseen hand of God, ultimately saving the Jewish people from assimilation or extinction—paralleling the stories of Joseph and Moses in Egypt.

I sincerely hope you find as much joy and inspiration in reading this book as I did in writing it.

CHAPTER 1

"Grandpa, this Scroll of Esther—it's such a funny, miraculous story," my grandson said, grinning. "But why did Mordecai take such a big risk? He could have destroyed the entire Jewish nation!"

"Oh no," I replied, shaking my head gently. "Our ancestors knew its deeper wisdom. That's why they included it in the Bible. Let me share a secret with you—an incredible story I once heard from my own grandfather."

"Tell me!" my grandson leaned forward, eyes wide with excitement.

———≈———

Mordecai, the unspoken king of the Jews, stood alone. Tomorrow, the attack would come. The fate of his people hung by a thread. The mob would descend on them—killing young and old, men, women, and children. Raising his arms to the heavens, Mordecai prayed, "God, help me fulfill my mission for Your sake."

This might be my last day, he thought. *Could I have done things differently?* His mind raced back through the years, a blur of memories flashing before him…

———≈———

"You know," whispered Shimei, Mordecai's grandfather, his frail hand trembling as he pointed at the boy, "one day, you will carry my royal title. I expect great things from you—greater than I ever achieved. I have a plan for you. Power. Leadership."

Power? Leadership? Mordecai wondered, bewildered. I'm just a captive child in Babylon.

"But I don't have friends. None at all," Mordecai protested, his voice small.

"You have me," Shimei replied, his tone steady. "You are special. You see things others miss. Your analytical mind is sharp—your memory, incredible."

"Maybe... but no one else cares. When I ask questions or try to explain things, they walk away and don't come back. Even when I stay quiet, they laugh at me behind my back. They think I'm stupid!"

Shimei placed a reassuring hand on his grandson's shoulder. "I am your friend," he said gently. "And let me tell you something important. People aren't always what they seem. They say one thing, but mean something else."

"I know, but I just don't understand them! How can I lead if I can't figure people out?"

"Humans are not open books," Shimei explained. "To truly understand them, you must learn to listen beyond their words. Watch the flicker in their eyes, the curve of their mouth, the movements of their hands. These silent cues often speak louder than their words, revealing what they try to hide."

"I try to fit in," Mordecai said, frustrated. "I laugh at their jokes, even when I don't get them. But then they mock my laugh—it's too late, too loud, too long. I can't win."

Shimei smiled softly. "You laugh wholeheartedly, but perhaps not always at the right time. In time, you will have many who want to be your friend. And when you rise to lead, they'll make sure you understand them—then, you can laugh as loud as you wish."

Tears welled in Mordecai's eyes. "Thank you, Grandpa."

Shimei's face grew serious. "When I was your age, we were a proud nation in Judea—our promised land. But then King Nebuchadnezzar's Babylonian army came. They captured Jerusalem, looted our treasures, destroyed the Holy Temple, and exiled us. General Nebuzaradan, the Butcher, blinded our King Zedekiah after slaughtering his sons before his eyes. That was our future—your future! Blind, barren, and banished."

Mordecai's eyes widened in horror. "Why weren't you killed?"

"Miracle," Shimei said with a faint smile. "No—I wasn't there. Years before, King Jehoiachin surrendered to Nebuchadnezzar, and many of us dignitaries were taken here to Babylon as hostages. I was just a boy. It saved our lives. God's ways are mysterious."

"Tell me more," Mordecai urged.

At ten, Mordecai was tall for his age, slim, with long black hair that he often flicked out of his eyes. He favored soft, loose, bright-colored clothing, and any wrinkle or button out of place bothered him. Cleanliness was an obsession, and he couldn't bear bad smells. In public, he stood tall with his hands on his hips, trying to look the part of a future leader, though inside, he was lonely.

Early one morning, Mordecai and Shimei walked hand-in-hand along the Euphrates River, watching the merchant boats glide by. Mordecai spotted a half-dried earthworm on the path, carefully picked it up, and tossed it into the grass, wiping his fingers on the dew-covered blades.

"That was kind of you," Shimei observed. "You protect even the smallest of God's creatures."

They continued walking, guessing the contents of the passing boats and their destinations. The green fields along the shore swayed in rhythm with the river's gentle waves. Shimei had taught Mordecai to notice the smallest details: the scent of blooming trees, the hum of bees, the patterns of migrating birds, and even the subtle color changes in the river water. "These," Shimei would say, "are the signs of future prosperity or hardship."

As they walked, Shimei spotted a radiant narcissus flower, the king of the swamp. Gently, he plucked it and handed it to Mordecai. Mordecai brought it to his nose, breathing in its delicate fragrance, and a soft smile spread across his face, his delight unmistakable.

"And?" Mordecai urged, breaking the silence.

Shimei smiled knowingly. "I have a method for success. One day, you'll be ready." He winked at Mordecai.

"You've definitely piqued my curiosity, Grandpa," Mordecai said with a hearty laugh.

"Life is a difficult game," Shimei mused, his tone growing thoughtful. "Timing is everything. Patience is key. My motto: 'Learn, plan, attain gain. Learn, plan shun pain.'"

"Wow... 'Learn, plan, attain gain,'" Mordecai repeated, clearly impressed.

Shimei chuckled, affectionately patting Mordecai's head. As they strolled along, Shimei gestured toward the bustling city before them. "Look at this city—truly magnificent. The towering palaces, the Hanging Gardens, floating in the sky. Learn their secrets, their knowledge. One day, it will serve you well. Knowledge is fragile, Mordecai. Our forefathers built the pyramids in Egypt and perfected the art of mummification. Now, all of that knowledge is lost. Civilizations rise and fall, and when they do, their wisdom vanishes with them. Babylon, too, will crumble someday, likely to fierce nomads. But you, Mordecai—you may have the chance to help build a new empire and carry forward a refined culture to its new rulers. Knowledge will open doors for you, bring you wealth and power."

He cares for me so profoundly, Mordecai thought, his heart swelling with affection. *And I love him, too.*

"Now, listen to me very carefully," Shimei said, his tone suddenly shifting to a grave seriousness. He leaned closer, lowering his voice to a near whisper. "What I'm about to tell you is crucial."

Mordecai leaned in, attentive.

"We are the direct heirs of King Saul, the first king of Israel. God Himself chose him to lead the twelve tribes of Israel. When King Saul and his sons fell in battle, David ascended the throne. But, as he promised to Prince Jonathan—Saul's son—David protected our family. His descendants continued to shelter us, and we repaid them with our loyalty and counsel.

"But as time passed, David's heirs ruled with an iron hand, and our nation fractured, split in two, never to reunite. Years later, King Nebuchadnezzar expelled us—the tribes of Judah and Benjamin—from our homeland, scattering us across his empire like dust in the wind.

"Now you, my only grandson, are the direct heir of King Saul. My heir. One day, you may be called to lead our people. You must be ready to restore prosperity and unity to them. This… this must be your life's mission. An enduring mission."

This is it, Mordecai thought, his heart racing. *He's planting this mission in my mind. He wants me to carry it forward. Can I fulfill it? Will I succeed?*

Shimei's voice softened, but his eyes burned with intensity. "Strong belief in your mission, the willingness to sacrifice, and a burning desire will guide you to success. People will recognize your leadership and follow you. Share that success with them, and in unity, you will prevail."

Desire, effort, join, share, united. Desire, effort, join, share, united, Mordecai silently repeated, the words looping through his mind like a mantra.

Shimei watched him, his expression thoughtful. "I see you're turning it over and over in your mind. Write it down. That will help calm your thoughts and sharpen your focus."

———≈———

Every year during the Passover Seder, Shimei would sternly remind his prosperous family and their guests, "We were slaves in Egypt! Be wise—learn and plan, or you will find yourself a slave again." He would then glance at Mordecai with pride, silently mouthing the words, *"Remember your mission."*

Mordecai would nod, understanding the unspoken weight behind those words. Things haven't changed much. We may no longer be slaves in Egypt, but we are still hostages here in Babylon, under the king's control. Our situation is fragile. I have to watch every word I say, every gesture I make. People read me, even if I can't read them. One wrong move, one careless word, and I'm finished. *We're* finished. I must succeed. I have to save our people.

One day, Shimei brought out a beautifully crafted wooden box. Inside, he revealed intricately carved black and white ivory figurines.

"Wow! What beautiful toys," Mordecai exclaimed, his eyes wide. "Are these armies?"

"This," Shimei said with a knowing smile, "is a game of chess. My father gave it to me when I was a child. He brought it from the East. It's a royal game."

"Why royal?" Mordecai asked, intrigued.

"Because it's a cold game," Shimei replied, setting up the board. "In chess, the only thing that matters is protecting your king," he pointed to the black and white kings, "and feeding your own ego and pride."

"And the other pieces?" Mordecai inquired.

"They're just tools," Shimei explained. "You sacrifice them when necessary to achieve your goal. It's not a game of morality—it's strategy. There's very little luck involved. It's mostly memory and analytical skills. You'll be excellent at it if you practice enough."

"Do you have a strategy?" Mordecai asked, eager to learn.

Shimei chuckled softly. "Of course. When you move your pieces, you're projecting power. Your goal is to make each piece as powerful as possible, controlling as many options as you can." He placed the queen on the board, demonstrating how she commanded the game. "But remember, if a piece takes on too many responsibilities, or gets locked into a single task, you'll lose control of other opportunities. That's why having two or more partners is better than relying on just one."

Mordecai stared at the board, his mind already analyzing the game's possibilities. Every piece mattered—every decision, a ripple of consequences. And just like in life, he realized, one wrong move could spell disaster.

Mordecai grinned. "Is this like real life?"

"To some extent, yes," Shimei replied thoughtfully. "But real life is far more complex, with countless factors and unknown possibilities. In a real conflict, it's not just about winning or losing a game—your life and the lives of your friends and supporters are at stake. Now, it's your move."

Mordecai hesitated, carefully considering his options before making his next move.

"The key to success," Shimei said, leaning forward, "is getting inside your opponent's mind and unsettling their balance. Pressure them to act on your terms. Like this..." He moved his queen toward Mordecai's king. "Check!"

"Oh no! Let me take that move back," Mordecai pleaded.

"No problem," Shimei chuckled. "You can go back two moves. This is a lesson, not a contest of pride, and my king doesn't complain."

"Thank you," Mordecai said, sighing with relief.

"In real life," Shimei continued, "defending is often easier because defenders can choose and fortify their position. But attackers have the advantage of surprise. The best strategy combines both—predicting or even forcing your opponent's next move."

"Can you give me an example?" Mordecai asked eagerly.

Shimei smiled. "Here's a famous one: The Canaanite General Sisera commanded 900 chariots, and Israel couldn't defeat him on the open plains. Deborah, the prophetess, instructed General Barak to move his troops into the narrow valley of the Kishon River after the spring rains had passed. Sisera was irritated at the thought of fighting a woman and worried Barak might capture the hills on either side, cutting off his army. So, he attacked. But his chariots became trapped in the muddy riverbank, and without mobility, his forces were easily defeated. Barak had perfectly timed the battle, predicted Sisera's actions, and turned the predator into the prey."

"Sisera should've been suspicious," Mordecai remarked, his brow furrowed in thought. "Barak moved his army in broad daylight instead of sneaking in at night."

"Yes, but Sisera was under immense pressure to act, whether it was day or night," Shimei responded, nodding thoughtfully.

Shimei became Mordecai's constant tutor, guiding him through languages, law, mathematics, and history, constantly pushing him to master even the smallest details. Mordecai absorbed everything eagerly, like a sponge, turning learning into a game. Before long, he could speak seventy languages and dialects, his mind sharp and ready for the day he might converse with royal hostages from distant nations in the heart of Babylon.

CHAPTER 2

My daughter invited me to my grandson's twelfth birthday, soon to be his Bar Mitzvah, and I felt a wave of excitement. As we sat together, he eagerly shared his progress—how he excelled in school, karate, and violin lessons.

"Do you have friends?" I asked gently.

"Not really," he replied, his voice soft. But then, his eyes sparkled with sudden excitement, and he asked, "Can you tell me what happened to Mordecai?"

With a knowing smile, I leaned in and whispered, "Today, Mordecai will find a friend—a best friend for life."

———— ❧ ————

From his upper window, Mordecai watched a boy his age wandering nearby, hands in his pockets, kicking rocks along the road. The boy wore a purple ribbon. *Just like me,* Mordecai thought. *He has no one to play with.*

Mordecai's heart ached for a companion—a friend who would listen, understand, and care. He had been silently watching the boy for hours, peeking through the curtains, wondering if they could be friends.

Suddenly, a stern voice interrupted his thoughts. "Stop it. We know what you're thinking," a finger jabbed between Mordecai's eyes. "You are our prince. Your life is precious. You have responsibilities. Stay away from those murderous Babylonians! You don't know how to be friendly, and your awkwardness could bring disaster upon us. God's mercy!"

Mordecai shrugged almost imperceptibly and raised his chin. *I don't want to be alone anymore. That boy doesn't seem dangerous. So what if he wears a royal purple ribbon? He's not going to kill me. Why would he?*

When the adults weren't paying attention, Mordecai slipped out the back door, quietly trailing behind the boy. He kept his distance, matching the boy's every step. When the boy stopped, so did Mordecai. When the boy stepped once, Mordecai Mordecai kept behind. Finally, the boy spun around, locking eyes with him.

"My name is Harvona," the boy declared confidently. "I will be your commander."

"Yes," Mordecai replied, startled, mimicking Harvona's Babylonian accent despite his nerves. *Now I'm stuck,* he thought.

Despite Harvona's muscular build, Mordecai realized he was actually younger. They played together until the sun dipped below the horizon, the day slipping away in laughter and adventure.

The next morning, a loud, commanding knock rattled the front door. Startled, Mordecai's family rushed around in a flurry, whispers of worry filling the air. A servant hurried to the door, muttering a prayer under his breath. He opened it to find a boy standing tall, hands on his hips, feet planted firmly.

"Bring Mordecai, now," the boy demanded, his voice steady with authority. The servant bowed low.

Hearing his friend's voice, Mordecai rushed past the servant, ignoring the outstretched hand trying to stop him. As Mordecai sped to join Harvona, he noticed his family huddled in fear, their eyes filled with concern. But Mordecai smiled to himself. *I have a friend. He cares about me. He's powerful. I'm rising above them all now. No one can make me do what I don't want to. I don't have to study all day anymore.*

As he moved toward the door, Mordecai caught his grandfather's gaze—heavy with sadness and disappointment. His chest tightened. *I'm not abandoning you,* he thought, willing his grandfather to understand. *I'm just making a friend. Please don't be sad. You know I love you most.*

Mordecai slowed his steps, torn for a moment. But then, with a deep breath, he quickened his pace again and rushed out, the thrill of newfound freedom pulling him forward.

He slipped outside, a grin spreading across his face, ready for another day of adventure.

From that day on, Mordecai and Harvona became inseparable. They whispered secrets, heads close together, and raced hand-in-hand through the bustling city streets.

Thanks to Harvona's father, the chief commander of the royal army, the boys roamed the city freely. Commoners would step aside in fear, bowing and murmuring blessings as the two passed by. In the marketplace, vendors eagerly offered free samples, wary of the consequences of displeasing Harvona. Though Harvona often left a silver coin behind, he never haggled.

The boys climbed the city's defensive walls, explored the guard towers, and even marched behind soldiers—no one dared stop or question them. But despite all the freedom, Mordecai couldn't shake the feeling that he was always a step behind Harvona. Without his friend, his lowly status was painfully clear.

Harvona's father often took his son to the military headquarters, where Harvona observed strategic discussions, just as his own father had done before him. The officers respected Harvona, knowing he might command them or their sons one day.

Together, Harvona and Mordecai reenacted these strategies, building sand mountains and cities along the Euphrates River. Harvona, the general, and Mordecai, his strategist, spent hours plotting victories, and tackling challenges as a team. Mordecai would declare an obstacle—rain, a forest fire, a collapsed bridge, enemy forces—and the two boys would solve the problem, laughing and negotiating as they went. Sometimes, Harvona objected to the difficulties, but they always worked it out, and their bond grew stronger. Mordecai felt important, loved, and elated.

One day, after hours of play, Harvona picked up a fist-sized pebble and hurled it at their carefully crafted sandcastle. "Smash!" he yelled, but the stone missed its mark. "Ugh!" he grumbled in frustration.

"That reminds me of something," Mordecai said thoughtfully.

"Yeah? What's that?" Harvona asked, his mood lifting.

"Next time, we should practice using slings," Mordecai suggested. "It's a safer way to fight."

Harvona, still annoyed at his missed throw, brightened. "Great idea. Let's do it now."

They fashioned makeshift slings from their belts and began launching pebbles into the river, practicing their aim until they felt proud of their progress.

Imitating his father's commanding stance, Harvona raised his chin and asked, "How can we defeat our enemy?"

Mordecai hesitated, caught between his new friendship and the deeper loyalty to his people. *Should I help the nation that has traumatized mine?* He wondered. *But I need friends, and my mission is to save the Jews, not to seek revenge.*

Drawing on his grandfather's wisdom, Mordecai replied, "First, we must analyze the strengths and weaknesses of both sides. That's the key to victory."

Harvona leaned in closer, his voice lowered. "We have more soldiers, but they're lightly armed. The Greeks, with their heavy bronze armor, are much stronger. My father says each Greek soldier could take on twenty of ours and win. But luckily for us, they're too busy fighting each other to bother attacking us."

Mordecai furrowed his brow, deep in thought. "We need to turn their strength into a weakness."

"What do you mean?" Harvona asked, his eyes fixed on Mordecai's lips, eager for an answer.

Mordecai remembered a story his grandfather had told him about the prophetess Deborah. "The Canaanites had chariots with blades, but Deborah instructed General Barak to lure them into muddy ground. The chariots got stuck, and without their armor's advantage, the Canaanites were defeated. Your honored father could use a similar strategy. Draw the Greeks into difficult terrain—mud, swamps, something that would slow them down. Even if they don't chase, your father won't suffer any losses."

Harvona's eyes widened with excitement. "That's brilliant! My father *must* hear this!"

A few weeks later, Mordecai saw Harvona sprinting toward him, waving his arms wildly and shouting with unrestrained excitement. Breathless, Harvona bent over, hands on his knees, trying to catch his breath. "Mordecai! My father won the war!" he exclaimed, his voice trembling joyfully. "He followed your plan exactly! He had his soldiers wear wide, straw sandals and lured the Greeks onto muddy ground. Our men moved easily, but the Greeks got stuck in the muck with their heavy armor. We took their armor and drove them out of Anatolia! Total victory!"

When Harvona's father returned to Babylon, Harvona rushed to find Mordecai, beaming with pride. He pointed to the golden stripes on his uniform. "Look, Mordecai! I've been promoted to an officer in my father's elite regiment! The king himself is hosting a grand victory parade for my father. You *must* come with us!"

Mordecai shook his head, his shoulders slumping as he gazed at the ground. "No, this is your moment. You've earned it," he said softly.

"Please, Mordecai," Harvona pleaded, his voice almost desperate. "My father wants to honor you. You'll even meet the king! He might let you kiss his ring!"

Mordecai shook his head again and bowed deeply. "Thank your esteemed father—may he live long and prosper—for his kindness toward his humble servant. Just remember me when you rise to greatness. I'll always be cheering for you from afar."

"I'll never forget you," Harvona promised, before turning and sprinting back to join the parade.

Mordecai watched his friend disappear into the crowd, a deep sadness weighing heavily on his heart. His advice had brought victory to Harvona and his father, but now Harvona was a celebrated commander, basking in glory. Mordecai, on the other hand, felt the sting of losing not only his closest friend but also his protector.

As the victorious army marched through the city's main street, cheers erupted from the crowd. People tossed flowers in the soldiers' path, celebrating their triumph over the Greeks. Mordecai clapped as Harvona and his father passed by, but his heart felt leaden. Behind the general, several dozen Greek soldiers were being dragged in chains, their faces hollow with defeat. Mordecai overheard whispers in the crowd—they would be forced to fight lions in the royal arena.

While his face remained composed, inside, Mordecai was deeply unsettled by the cruelty he witnessed. *What have I done?* he thought, his mind swirling with guilt. *Did I help bring this about?* The thrill of strategic triumph was now overshadowed by the brutal reality of the Babylonians' victory.

His thoughts turned inward, and in the privacy of his mind, he prayed: *Please, God, this is too painful to bear.* But a deeper question gnawed at him. *Is this an excuse to abandon my mission?*

CHAPTER 3

On the way to school, I continued, "Finding a mentor is essential. Not only will you serve, but you'll learn every step of the way. A mentor guides you, helps you grow, and shows you how to become your best self."

———◈———

Years passed, and when Mordecai turned sixteen, Shimei decided the time had come to introduce him to Gdaliahu Ha-Nasi, the most prominent Jewish leader in the Babylonian Empire and a descendant of King David. As they prepared for the meeting, Shimei leaned in close to Mordecai and said, "I promised to teach you how to win."

"Yes," Mordecai replied eagerly, his eyes lighting up with anticipation. "I've been waiting so patiently for this."

Shimei smiled knowingly. "The conditions weren't right before. Timing is everything when it comes to success. There are many lessons still to come, but for now, here's one of the most important: lure your target into a trap. Set up something irresistible, bait they can't refuse, and when they take it, you strike. You'll have predictability on your side and the advantage."

Mordecai's brow furrowed with curiosity. "Can you give me an example?"

Shimei nodded, his eyes gleaming with the satisfaction of a mentor sharing wisdom. "Of course. When Esau approached Yakov with his army of four hundred men, Yakov split his camp into two."

"I know this!" Mordecai interrupted, eager to prove his knowledge. "Esau thought Yakov was offering him half of their mother Rebekah's dowry—the portion Lavan gave to Yakov."

Shimei smiled, pleased with his grandson's insight. "That's an excellent explanation. But let me give you another layer. Yakov sent five separate flocks of livestock to Esau, each led by ten shepherds. Esau accepted these gifts without realizing he was also accepting fifty loyal shepherds—like soldiers—each armed with a long-range sling, positioning themselves behind him. Esau was now surrounded— two armies in front, one behind. Yakov had complete control of the battlefield while still preparing to welcome his brother with peace and honor, as if nothing had ever happened. Only Yakov and Esau knew the full truth of that encounter. Now, so do you."

Mordecai's eyes flickered with newfound understanding. "But why did Esau accept the gifts? He could've refused."

"Greed, respect, carelessness," Shimei replied thoughtfully. "Who knows for sure? But even if Esau hadn't accepted the gifts, the shepherds would have been strategically placed at his rear. Always be wary when accepting gifts from an adversary, a stranger, or lady luck, Mordecai. What seems like luck offering you an opportunity might be nothing more than bait."

Mordecai pondered for a moment, then countered, "But Esau could have killed the shepherds, one group at a time."

Shimei chuckled softly. "Yes, he could have. But think of this: if Esau had slaughtered the first group, the remaining four would have stayed back, positioned on the hills, watching from a distance, flanking him. He couldn't have chased them all down. Instead, curiosity and courtesy prevailed over violence, and in doing so, he unknowingly gave Yakov the upper hand."

My grandson's eyes brighten as he comments, "This sounds like the Trojan Horse! Did Yakov invent it?"

"Possibly," I say with a smile. "We believe Yakov lived hundreds of years before the Trojan War."

"So, the Trojan Horse should really be called 'Yakov's Gifts,'" he declares with a grin.

———❧———

"Later, when Esau realized Yakov's battle formation—two armies in front, one behind—it was too late. His display of force crumbled. War was avoided," Shimei explained.

Mordecai furrowed his brow. "Yakov avoided war. Is that always the goal?" His thoughts flashed to the Greek soldiers, cruelly thrown to the lions.

Shimei nodded gravely. "Leaders must make difficult choices. The goal is always to win, but winning does not mean abandoning morality or beneficial compromise."

Mordecai hesitated, then asked, "And what is your plan today?"

Shimei paused, his gaze steady and thoughtful. "We are the heirs of King Saul. Throughout history, our family has always served King David's descendants as trusted allies and advisors, just as David and Jonathan were bound in friendship. You, Mordecai, were destined to serve as the companion to Gdaliahu Ha-Nasi's crown prince. But you were too young then."

Mordecai took this in, feeling the weight of his lineage and the expectations placed on him. "And now?" he asked quietly.

Shimei's smile was faint, almost sad. "Now, we continue to serve, as we always have. But soon, it will be your time to choose your own path. A new opportunity has arrived."

Mordecai's heart raced as Shimei's words hung in the air.

"Some of our leader's sons have died in childhood—a bad omen," Shimei continued, his voice low and solemn. "The only surviving son shows no interest in what it takes to be a great leader. Gdaliahu is heartbroken. He knows it may mark the end of King David's dynasty. I waited for years, hoping the boy would change. But now it's clear—he is unfit."

"And...?" Mordecai urged, his heart pounding with excitement.

Shimei nodded, a mischievous smile creeping across his face as he mimed rolling dice in the air. "While the prince failed, I succeeded. I'm offering Gdaliahu a bait—a lamb, destined to become a magnificent ram: you, Mordecai, heir of King Saul. And in doing so, I get what I've long desired: to advance our mission. Even if I don't live to see it fully realized."

He paused, locking eyes with Mordecai. "I am giving you to Gdaliahu Ha-Nasi. You will be his loyal servant. Your life will belong to him. Every moment, you must give him your unwavering devotion."

Mordecai, unable to contain himself, let out a loud laugh. "Baa!" he bleated, hiding his face with his hands. Yet inside, the thought of power and love stirred deeply. *I do want to be powerful. I do want to be loved.*

Shimei's stern expression softened as he chuckled. "Good you reminded me, my beautiful lamb. It's time to shear that handsome mane of yours. What are you, Shimshon? Abshalom? God forbid! At least you don't let your nails grow wild."

Mordecai grinned but remained silent, feeling the weight of Shimei's words pressing on him.

Shimei's tone shifted, growing serious again. "You're stepping into adulthood now and must present yourself as a serious courtier. You'll offer wisdom, not beauty. After your haircut—short, like a soldier's— we'll visit Gdaliahu. You must look like a man destined for greatness."

Mordecai and Shimei entered the palace, Mordecai's eyes wide with awe at the grandeur surrounding them. Smooth white marble columns stretched upward, holding a ceiling that seemed to touch the sky. Beneath their feet lay a vibrant mosaic, depicting the twelve months of the year and the seasons and holidays of Judea. Mordecai marveled at the intricate details, his gaze tracing the familiar images.

At the center of the room sat an elderly man on a golden chair, his posture slightly stooped with age. A thin circlet of gold rested upon his head, nestled in wisps of white hair, while a fiery red beard, streaked with silver, flowed down his chest. His sharp, piercing eyes locked onto Mordecai's, and a subtle, knowing smile tugged at the corners of his lips.

Behind him, inscribed in large Hebrew letters on the wall, were the words: *"Love your fellow man as yourself."* Mordecai's gaze lingered on the inscription, and when his eyes met the elder's once more, an unspoken connection passed between them. They exchanged a brief smile, each acknowledging the other's understanding.

I know that he knows that I know to read Hebrew, Mordecai thought, a quiet satisfaction welling up inside him.

Shimei stepped forward, bowing deeply, his voice reverent. "Blessings to you, Great Leader Gdaliahu Ha-Nasi, to whom God has granted wisdom and power."

Gdaliahu's face warmed with a smile. "Welcome, Shimei, heir of Prince Jonathan," he said, his tone filled with respect. He gestured for Shimei to rise.

"I humbly offer the services of my grandson, Mordecai," Shimei said, his voice steady and deliberate. "If it pleases you, would you be so kind as to take him under your wing?"

Gdaliahu's gaze shifted sadly to his own son, seated nearby. Partially bald at the front, the man absentmindedly twirled his beard, utterly oblivious to the conversation. Mordecai caught the brief glance and quickly assessed the situation. *The son sees me as no threat,* he thought. *He's a prince, but unworthy of his crown.*

Gdaliahu sighed, his disappointment palpable, but he turned back to Shimei with a forced smile. "We are surprised you didn't bring him sooner. It is our honor to have him."

He fixed his gaze on Mordecai, his tone both welcoming and stern. "But remember this—hard work and honor are your guiding stars."

Mordecai's chest swelled with pride, but a pang of guilt rippled through him. *I'm taking the first step in displacing his son. Yet, Gdaliahu, the father, is welcoming me with open arms.*

Out loud, Mordecai spoke with confidence. "I will do my best!"

Gdaliahu's expression hardened, his disappointment evident. "When you fail, shall we take comfort in knowing it was your best?"

The words hit Mordecai like a cold wind. He recoiled slightly, his cheeks flushing. After a moment of reflection, he responded with more caution. "I will learn and plan. With your advice and guidance, I will not fail."

Gdaliahu's features softened again, a flicker of satisfaction passing through his eyes as he briefly closed them. The meeting was over.

As they left the palace, Shimei placed a proud hand on Mordecai's shoulder. "Success," he said, his voice brimming with satisfaction.

"Amazing," Mordecai replied, still buzzing from the encounter. "Wasn't it easy?"

Shimei smiled knowingly. "When you spend years planning, learning, and waiting for the perfect moment to strike, everything seems easy in the end."

Mordecai nodded, absorbing the wisdom.

"I saw you noticed the writing on the wall," Shimei remarked, his tone reflective. "'Love your fellow man as yourself.' It's how it's written in our Torah. But I prefer to think of it as, 'Help your fellow man.' Love is an emotion, but help—that's action. Be helpful—always. Even when no one sees. Cast your bread upon the waters. The reward will come."

"Thank you," Mordecai whispered, his respect for his grandfather deepening. He extended his hand, and Shimei grasped it firmly. The bond of trust between them grew stronger, as Mordecai felt the weight of his future settling on his shoulders.

CHAPTER 4

As the warmth from the fire filled the room, my grandson nestled closer to me on the sofa, his eyes reflecting the soft glow of the flames. I could feel the weight of his curiosity, heavy and expectant, as I spoke, sharing the wisdom passed down through generations.

"Successful people," I began, "often find their purpose early. They identify a mission, something that gives their life direction. It's that sense of purpose that helps them focus their energy, narrow their path, and dig deeper into their efforts. It's how they move forward, no matter the obstacles."

He nodded, his attention fixed on my words. The fire crackled, filling the brief silence between us, and I smiled, knowing that these quiet moments were just as important as the lessons. "Patience, perseverance, and understanding that challenges are just steps toward a greater goal," I added. "These are the foundations of true success."

Years passed, and under Gdaliahu's guidance, Mordecai grew into a capable and trusted administrator. His goal was always to meet and exceed Gdaliahu's expectations, secure his place in the court, and earn his mentor's trust. Yet despite his success, Mordecai found no peace. His grandfather Shimei's teachings haunted him, and the weight of those lessons loomed ever larger.

The day finally came when Shimei lay on his deathbed. His body had weakened, but his mind remained sharp, as clear as ever.

Mordecai stood by his grandfather's side, watching helplessly as Shimei's strength faded. He knew the well of wisdom was running dry, that these would be their last moments together. Shimei gestured weakly for Mordecai to come closer.

"I won't be here much longer," Shimei whispered, his voice a mere rasp. "The priest gave me a sweetened poppy cake to dull the pain, but even that can't quiet the thoughts that weigh on me." His eyes, though tired, were filled with urgency.

"I've accomplished some of my goals—educating you, my beloved lamb—but one thing troubles me deeply." Shimei paused, gathering the last of his strength. "A hundred years before we were exiled from Judea, the Assyrians scattered the ten tribes of Israel. They were lost—assimilated, stripped of their language, stories, and culture. And now it's happening to us—the last two tribes, Judah and Benjamin. Our people are scattered across this empire, and if nothing is done, our culture will disappear just like theirs."

Mordecai tried to reassure him. "God will save us, as He did in Egypt," he said, his voice filled with conviction.

Shimei shook his head, frustration cutting through his weakened state. "Did He save our temple? Did He save the ten tribes?" he spat bitterly. "God told Moses, 'Stop crying and move forward.' That's my motto. Don't sit and wait for miracles, Mordecai. We must plan, fight, and win our own battles."

His strength failing, Shimei slumped back onto the bed, his breath shallow. "Closer," he wheezed. Mordecai leaned in, his heart pounding.

"Swear to me," Shimei gasped, his voice barely a whisper. "Swear now, in the name of our fathers and mothers—I.S.R.A.E.L—Isaac, Yakov, Sarah, Rebekah, Rachel, Abraham, Leah, and Lavan. Swear you will work to save the children of Israel. They are your children now. Use our ancient stories as your guide. Be wise like Joseph, strong like Judah, brave and cunning like Shimon and Levi. Learn from Moses." He paused, struggling for air. "God will bless you."

Mordecai's mind raced. *How can I do this? Why me? I'm not Moses.* But as the weight of his grandfather's words settled on him, he knew he could not refuse. He gripped Shimei's frail hand tightly, pressing it to his forehead. "I promise, Grandfather," Mordecai whispered, his voice shaking. "It is my mission."

Shimei winced slightly. "Not so tight... you're hurting my hand."

"I'm sorry, I'm sorry," Mordecai sobbed, loosening his grip. "Please, don't go. I still need you."

With a soft smile, Shimei rested his trembling hand on Mordecai's head. "I've given you all I have. Title. Time. Thoughts. Now soar, my lamb. Fly. Thank you for being my grandson. I love you."

Mordecai watched, his heart breaking, as Shimei's breaths became labored, each one seeming more strained than the last. With his mouth slightly open and his eyes closed, Shimei's body fought for air—until finally, it stilled. His tongue moved once, then stopped. He was calm. Quiet. Gone.

Mordecai collapsed to the floor, overwhelmed by grief. "I promise," he whispered through his tears. "One small step at a time."

In his mind, he heard Shimei's voice, faint but unmistakable. *I heard you. Just keep moving forward.*

CHAPTER 5

We played basketball, but I mostly just watched and chased after the loose balls.

"You're too short to dunk," I said with a grin. "But that's no problem. Focus on being a three-point sharpshooter. Success often comes from thinking outside the box—finding your unique edge. When you see an opportunity, don't hesitate. Think, consult, discuss, and then go for it."

After a tiring game, we sat down together. "It's not about being the best at everything," I continued. "It's about using your strengths to turn challenges into opportunities."

When Mordecai was eighteen, Babylon was under siege. Harvona brought grim news—King Cyrus of Persia had used his mounted cavalry to crush the Babylonians on the open plains. Harvona's father and most of his troops had been killed, and the Babylonian army, abandoned by its mercenaries, fell into disarray. Panic and chaos gripped the city as people fled in droves.

The nations of the Empire refused to come to Babylon's aid, seeking revenge for the years of heavy taxation and brutal treatment under Babylonian rule. The Babylonian king, cut off from reinforcements, was left to face the Persian onslaught alone.

To shore up the city's defenses, royal hostages were conscripted to work for the army. Young, able-bodied men were sent to dig ditches and fortify the walls. Because of his position at Gdaliahu Ha-Nasi's court, Mordecai was initially exempt.

"Please, let me join my brothers," Mordecai requested of Gdaliahu.

"You are more valuable to us here," Gdaliahu replied.

"Thank you," Mordecai insisted, "but it's my duty to stand with our people, to share in their suffering."

Reluctantly, Gdaliahu allowed Mordecai to go. Mordecai joined the other hostages in the scorching heat, digging ditches around the city walls and flooding them with water. The labor was grueling, the workers drenched in sweat, their hands raw from the sand-covered shovel handles. Progress was slow and exhausting.

One day, Mordecai noticed a high-ranking Persian officer observing from across the river. The officer sat under an elaborate canopy, fanned by servants and shielded from insects by clouds of smoke. He leaned forward, talking strategy with his aides and gesturing toward the city. Mordecai had a gnawing suspicion that the officer was plotting something.

While working in the ditch, Mordecai spotted a book and some measurement tools left near the edge. Fearing they would be buried in the sand, he climbed out of the trench and carefully placed the items on a nearby table. An officer saw him and, angered at what he thought was Mordecai abandoning his post, strode toward him, smacking his baton against his boots.

But upon seeing Mordecai's care for the tools, the officer's expression softened. Impressed by his thoughtfulness, he promoted Mordecai to assistant manager. Mordecai took on new responsibilities, organizing resources like water, straw hats, and gloves for the workers. He also adjusted the shifts to avoid the worst day heat, boosting productivity. The officer praised the workers' newfound efficiency.

Yet despite the compliment, Mordecai muttered bitterly, "We know how to be good slaves."

At one point, one of the workers needed to relieve himself. To minimize disruption, Mordecai organized his team of twenty to line up at the river's edge and urinate simultaneously, facing the Persian army. This unexpected display provoked an uproar from the Persian side, a mixture of surprise and laughter. The Persian officer under the canopy, startled at first, jumped to his feet and ordered his men into battle positions.

Some of Mordecai's workers panicked and began to flee, but Mordecai barked at them to hold the line. Soon, thousands of Persian soldiers appeared from behind the dunes, lining up along the other riverbank. On command, they all urinated toward the city in a symbolic retaliation. The river's edge turned into a yellow stream as both sides roared with laughter.

Mordecai then ordered his men to bow to the Persian army. The Persian officer, amused, waved back in acknowledgment, diffusing the tension.

Later, Harvona, having heard about the incident, summoned Mordecai away from the ditches, concerned for his safety.

"Our city will never fall," Harvona declared confidently as they watched the enemy's futile attempts to cross the river and breach the walls. "Building in the middle of the Euphrates was genius. We have unlimited fresh water, and ships are still delivering food."

Mordecai responded thoughtfully, "True, but every strength can become a weakness."

The Babylonians fought valiantly, repelling wave after wave of Persian assaults. But one day, the attacks mysteriously ceased. King Cyrus sent messengers to the city, offering safe passage to anyone who wished to leave.

Harvona, optimistic, exclaimed, "They're retreating! We've withstood their attacks, and now they think they can talk us into submission."

Mordecai was unconvinced. "Armies don't retreat without a plan."

"Nonsense," Harvona dismissed, waving him off. "They couldn't handle it anymore."

But days later, the arrival of supply ships came to a halt. Harvona's confidence began to waver. "They're tampering with our water," he muttered, growing pale.

Weeks passed, and the mighty Euphrates River, once the city's lifeblood, began to dwindle, until it became little more than a dry riverbed. Mordecai and Harvona stood by, watching in horror as the exposed riverbed stretched before them.

"Ingenious," Mordecai murmured, a mix of awe and dread in his voice. "They diverted the river."

Harvona shot him a look of anger and despair, his face drained of color.

Fish flopped helplessly in the mud, desperate to survive as their water disappeared. Mordecai watched solemnly. "This is the full spectrum of decisions and consequences," he reflected. "Survival and death."

"We're the fish!" Harvona cried, his voice breaking as he noticed the defeated posture of the Babylonians and the advancing Persian forces, now moving unopposed toward the exposed, unprotected city gates. "Our king must have decided to surrender."

Shaken, Harvona knew that the Babylonian king had gathered the ruling class and generals at the palace for a drinking party. He ordered the army not to resist, hoping to avoid a massacre.

Harvona drew his sword, his face hardening. "We may face death."

"No!" Mordecai shouted, fear in his voice, pushing Harvona's sword back into its sheath. He ripped off Harvona's purple ribbon. "There's a time to stand, and a time to bend!"

Mordecai grabbed Harvona by the arm and led him toward the Jewish quarter. "Get inside!" he ordered, shoving Harvona through the door of his house before he could argue. Kneeling by the door, Mordecai pressed his face to the cold marble floor, catching his breath, hiding the sweat and fear that gripped him from the dash to safety.

A Persian officer approached, and Mordecai raised his head to greet him, his voice calm and fluent in Persian. "Peace upon you, brave commander."

The officer smiled slightly, intrigued. "Who are you? Are you hiding anyone here?"

Mordecai lied without hesitation, his face betraying no fear. "I am a Babylonian hostage. I welcome you. There is no royalty here."

The officer studied him for a moment before nodding. "Very well. Stay put, and you'll live. Don't get involved." He marked the house and left.

Harvona, still catching his breath, looked at Mordecai, half-relieved, half-irritated. "You weren't entirely truthful."

Mordecai raised an eyebrow, offended. "Not truthful? I answered a different question entirely. Are *you* of royal blood?"

Harvona chuckled despite himself. "Very funny. Still, sometimes a good lie saves us from greater problems."

In a single decisive blow, the Persians captured the capital and the royal hostages of the conquered nations. The entirety of the Babylonian Empire fell into the hands of King Cyrus. To their surprise, the subordinate nations welcomed the Persian army with gifts and food. It was no secret that the Persians were far kinder rulers, limiting collective punishment and even paying wages to slaves based on their skills and productivity.

Although the Persians had a superior army, Mordecai noticed something about them. The nomadic Persians were simple people—plain food, modest clothing, and little knowledge about art. In stark contrast, the Babylonians had achieved the heights of sophistication, from fashion to elegance, from art to architecture. Observing this cultural disparity, Mordecai devised a plan: he would introduce Babylonian culture to the Persian court, elevating both King Cyrus's reign and his own fortunes.

King Cyrus decreed that the Babylonian king arrange a grand victory celebration in his honor, to be held in the opulent Babylonian royal hall. Cyrus, now victor, claimed the Babylonian throne, sitting confidently on the king's royal chair with legs wide apart, a sign of his conquest. He announced a pardon to all Babylonians who had fought against him, provided they swore loyalty to his rule.

Mordecai was taken aback by the humane treatment the Persian king offered to the defeated enemies.

To the celebration, the former Babylonian king and his family, along with the ruling class, were summoned as honored guests. Their names were meticulously recorded upon arrival. One by one, the deposed king, his generals, priests, and the Babylonian elite knelt before Cyrus, kissed his ring, and swore loyalty to him in the name of their gods, Ishtar and Marduk. They each presented gifts as tribute. The festivities lasted several days until all dignitaries had paid their respects.

Harvona, too, attended the celebration. He had chosen to cooperate with the Persians, hoping to rebuild his father's army and perhaps earn the general title. Inviting his father's former officers to the palace, he strategized his path forward.

The next day, Harvona excitedly sought out Mordecai to share astonishing news. "King Cyrus has requested the hand of the beautiful Princess Vashti—granddaughter of King Nebuchadnezzar the Great— to marry his grandson, Crown Prince Ahasuerus. The marriage will unite the two empires and secure royal prestige for Cyrus's dynasty."

"A forced marriage," Mordecai mused. "And how did the Babylonian king react?"

"He didn't have much choice," Harvona replied. "He ordered Princess Vashti to present herself. The generals made it clear— disobedience was not optional. It's being hailed as a great honor for the Babylonians. The children of their princess will one day rule the united empire," Harvona added with excitement. "I saw Princess Vashti myself—she's incredibly proud and quite beautiful. She wore an ivory crown adorned with rubies and sapphires when she was introduced to Prince Ahasuerus. She's well-educated too, but Prince Ahasuerus… he's younger than her and looks rather innocent. I wouldn't be surprised if she ends up eating him alive."

King Cyrus is playing the same cunning game my grandfather once spoke of, Mordecai thought to himself. *Still, this reminds me of another marriage—the union of young David to Michal, King Saul's daughter. That marriage brought David into royalty but led to the ruin of Michal. Will history repeat itself? It often does.*

———⋙———

A few days later, Harvona burst into Mordecai's quarters, his face twisted in panic. "Look what's just been published!" he cried, thrusting a decree into Mordecai's hands.

The decree read:

**The conquered city of Babylon
shall provide
five hundred young men each year
to serve as slaves in the Persian court.**

**For the first lottery selection,
only the upper class of Babylon shall participate.**

The city erupted in cries of despair. Some families frantically attempted to flee, while others hid their sons. But the Persian soldiers were relentless in their search. Servants, lured by the promise of reward and hate, eagerly betrayed those concealed young men. Families who refused to surrender their sons were arrested and tortured. Before long, the soldiers swept through the city, rounding up the young men and herding them into a makeshift corral—like cattle destined for slaughter.

Harvona, trembling beside Mordecai, looked stricken. "I have to go," he whispered hoarsely. "They took my name at the victory party. They are searching for me." He squared his shoulders, a mixture of defiance and resignation etched on his face. "I promised my father I would protect our family. I can't let them suffer because of me."

"You might not be selected," Mordecai said softly, trying to reassure him. "The lottery is in God's hands."

Harvona shook his head, forcing a weak smile. "We'll soon find out. If I'm chosen…, please, promise me one thing: write to me, and look after my family when you can."

"I will," Mordecai vowed, his throat tightening. "You have my word."

Harvona's eyes welled with unshed tears. "I'm so afraid," he confessed, his voice breaking. "Mordecai, pray for me—to Marduk, the god you're named after. Maybe he'll show mercy."

"I will," Mordecai whispered, embracing him tightly. "God's plans are mysterious, Harvona. Good and bad often seem reversed. We won't know the outcome until the end."

They held each other for a moment longer, then Harvona took a deep breath and stepped away, his gaze steely with resolve. He disappeared into the chaos of the city streets.

Due to his formidable size and confident demeanor, Harvona was quickly pulled from the lottery line and singled out for interrogation. He spoke of his father's military achievements and his own contributions to the victory over the Greeks, offering to reassemble his father's forces to serve King Cyrus. The interrogator, impressed by his bearing and boldness, assigned Harvona as a bodyguard for the royal family—a great honor.

When Mordecai heard the news, his grandfather's voice echoed in his mind: *"An important opportunity to harness. Support the fallen."*

Mordecai pondered his next move, recalling his grandfather's teasing remark from years before: *"Do you need a written invitation? You befriended Harvona against my advice. It seems God has outsmarted me. You planted a seed. Now go—harvest!"*

Determined, Mordecai headed to the corral where the captured young men were held. Disguised as a servant, he arrived with a wheelbarrow filled with dark honey-filled carobs—a small comfort and a valuable energy source. Many of the young men were weeping, their faces pale with fear. Mordecai stood by the fence, discreetly accepting letters to their families and offering the sweet carobs as a small token of comfort. He noted the names and addresses of those who courageously approached him, promising to stay in touch.

Suddenly, a young man broke from the group, eyes wild with rage, clutching a jagged stone. "This is your fault!" he screamed, charging toward Mordecai.

Mordecai stepped back, wary, as the boy hurled the rock. It struck Mordecai square in the chest, knocking him to the ground. Gasping for breath, Mordecai looked up, clutching his ribs, while others subdued the boy.

Rising, he dusted himself off, and to everyone's astonishment, he extended his hand, offering him a handful of carobs.

The young man stared, bewildered and seething with anger, tears streaming down his cheeks. "Why would you—"

"Take it," Mordecai interrupted gently. "Eat. May you grow stronger."

The boy, still shaking, snatched the carobs and turned away, sobbing. Mordecai, his voice steady, blessed and forgave him aloud. "You're not alone," he called out softly, gathering the attention of the others. "None of you are alone. Be brave."

Gradually, more young men gathered around him, their eyes wide with desperation and hope. Mordecai instructed them to stand in line, each one receiving a handful of carobs. The guards, puzzled but indifferent, did not intervene.

As the Persian soldiers led the young men away, Mordecai stood by the fence, calling out to those he knew, offering words of encouragement and pledges not to forget them. Some turned back and gave him sad, fleeting smiles of recognition, while others bowed their heads, their faces resigned to their fate.

Tears burned in Mordecai's eyes as he watched them disappear over the hill, each step taking them further into the unknown. "I will not forget," he whispered, the vow filling his heart. "I will not forget any of you."

The Persians transported the Babylonian treasury—gold, jewelry, weapons, and invaluable historical texts—to their capital, Shushan. Among the spoils were the royal chair of the Babylonian king and the Jewish treasures looted from Jerusalem during its fall.

In a surprising show of diplomacy, the Persians freed the former Babylonian hostages, allowing them to return to their homelands and govern their people. Instead of returning home, many of these former captives chose to relocate to Shushan as ambassadors for their nations. Gdaliahu, the leader of the Jewish people in the Persian Empire, advised King Cyrus to appoint Ezra as the leader of the Jews returning to Judea. King Cyrus issued a proclamation, authorizing Ezra to rebuild Jerusalem's walls and restore the Temple.

Kaffir-Ariot, Gdaliahu's right-hand man and a descendant of King David, declined to leave Babylon. Gdaliahu appointed him as the Jewish leader in Babylon and promoted Mordecai to Kaffir-Ariot's former position. Mordecai accompanied Gdaliahu to Shushan.

Despite the upheaval, Babylon remained a vital economic and cultural hub, with a thriving Jewish population. Kaffir-Ariot, renowned for his extensive scholarship, greatly influenced the Jewish community, becoming a spiritual and intellectual leader in the region.

Mordecai, ever observant, recognized that King Cyrus would likely seek to elevate the Persian court's sophistication after witnessing the grandeur of Babylon. Before departing Babylon, Mordecai met with wealthy Jewish merchants, arranging for them to supply the new Persian rulers with luxury goods and skilled artisans. The merchants, eager for opportunity, welcomed Mordecai as a partner.

In Shushan, Mordecai quietly began reaching out to the enslaved Babylonian young men, gaining their trust by delivering messages between them and their families. He shared news of King Cyrus's desire to elevate the royal court's elegance and prestige. Mordecai provided designs for royal garments, recipes for extravagant meals and wines, and plans for opulent gardens and palaces. Those who followed his advice were soon praised and promoted within the court.

Mordecai also maintained contact with Harvona, who had risen to prominence as a bodyguard for Prince Ahasuerus. He regularly updated Harvona's family in Babylon on his success and growing influence.

As Mordecai's reputation grew in Shushan, he became one of the most sought-after bachelors in the Jewish community. Many families hoped he would marry their daughters, eager to align themselves with such a promising figure. Yet, Mordecai declined every offer. He feared marriage could entangle him in family politics or expose him to manipulation and blackmail. Worse still, he didn't want to risk the reputations of those he rejected or create enemies.

I don't need enemies, Mordecai thought. *Do they think this is a beauty contest? I cannot afford to be burdened with a family—one mistake or even a perceived mistake, mine or theirs, could endanger us.*

As he pondered Harvona's sacrifices, Mordecai's thoughts turned to his only living blood relative, his cousin Hadassah. *By the way, where is she now?* He wondered, feeling a pang of guilt for losing touch.

CHAPTER 6

After dinner, my grandson went to practice his violin. "Come with me," he invited, and I followed him to his room. I settled on the carpet, leaning against his bed, watching as he began to play. The music filled the room, its soft notes stirring memories of my own days with the violin.

Since my stroke, I've lost the ability to move my left hand, which ended my own violin playing. When taking a short break, I said, "You're doing well," I encouraged him. "Keep practicing. Success comes with patience and persistence."

He nodded, still focused on the music, his bow moving smoothly across the strings. As he played, I added, "Did I ever tell you about Hadassah? Loyalty is crucial. It fosters trust, and trust is the foundation of success. Remember that."

Though his attention was on the violin, I hoped my words about loyalty and its role in success would resonate with him.

Abihail, the elder brother of Mordecai's father, had only one daughter, Hadassah. He had always longed for a son to inherit King Saul's royal title, but fate had not granted him one. Thus, Mordecai, by family right, was in line for the title.

Abihail and his wife decided to make a pilgrimage to the new Temple in Jerusalem, built with the permission of King Cyrus. They intended to pray for a son to carry on the family line. Mordecai, however, opposed the dangerous journey, fearing Amalekite attacks along the way. Yet, he didn't prevent them from going, not wanting to be accused of sabotaging the trip to secure his hold on the family title. Though

Mordecai wasn't particularly interested in the title, he understood the weight of public perception and how easily it could shift.

Mordecai's position as Gdaliahu's right hand far outweighed any personal claim to King Saul's legacy, but still, he insisted that Hadassah stay behind. Her mother supported his recommendation, seeing it as a way to keep her daughter safe.

Hadassah was only ten when her parents departed for Jerusalem. Abihail entrusted his brother-in-law, Shimon, his business partner, with the care of Hadassah and the management of his estate. Abihail avoided leaving Hadassah in Mordecai's care, fearing that people might suspect Mordecai had plans to marry her—a concern that could damage her prospects for other potential suitors. He believed Mordecai's interest in Hadassah, though purely familial, might be misunderstood.

As feared, tragedy struck. On the road to Jerusalem, Abihail and his wife were ambushed and killed. Their heads were severed, their bodies left exposed, and their valuables stolen. Arrows found near the scene pointed to Amalekite raiders as the culprits.

When Mordecai received the devastating news, he acted swiftly. He sent a party to retrieve the bodies and ensure they received a proper Jewish burial. He arranged for professional mourners to chant laments, and traditional food was served to those attending the funeral. Clad in black and covered in ashes, Mordecai held Hadassah close, offering her comfort in her grief.

At the gravesite, Mordecai delivered a heart-wrenching tribute, vowing to protect Hadassah for as long as he lived. After the burial, he distributed silver coins to the beggars and poor at the cemetery gates, ensuring that the final act of the day would be one of charity and kindness.

"I saved her life. Is she mine?" Mordecai wondered to himself, the thought lingering in his mind.

A few months later, a servant arrived at Mordecai's home, his face half-hidden beneath a scarf. Without explanation, he demanded a private meeting with Mordecai. His harsh, pleading tone grated on

Mordecai's nerves, prompting him to slam his pen down in frustration. Rolling up his parchments, Mordecai motioned for the visitor to approach, his heart pounding with a mixture of curiosity and unease.

Mordecai sat upright at his desk, signaling his personal servant to stay close. Mordecai watched the trembling visitor, who was twisting his hat nervously.

"Your honor, I am a servant of your uncle, Ssimon," the man whispered urgently, covering his mouth with his hand as if to guard the secret.

Mordecai narrowed his eyes, offering a faint smile. *My Efraim tribesman,* he thought, amused by the man's pronouncing 'Ss' instead of 'Sh.' "Go ahead," Mordecai urged.

"Since her parents' death, Hadassah has been treated like a servant," the visitor continued in a hushed tone. "Sse's been working with Ssimon's wife, sse's lost weight, her eyes are red with dark circles... and—sse has an unpleasant smell."

"What?" Mordecai shot to his feet, his chair rattling behind him. "Never repeat that last statement!" he warned sternly, his finger pointed sharply at the servant. "True or not, you are *severely* warned."

The servant dropped to his knees, his face pale with fear. "Forgive me! I didn't smell her myself! A young master told me to say it. I swear, I'll keep quiet. Please, have mercy!"

Mordecai exhaled, the tension in his shoulders easing slightly. "Anything else?" he asked, his voice still firm but calmer.

"Yes... Ssimon took away her books."

Mordecai's hand instinctively went to his desk, where he retrieved a silver coin. He placed it on the table in front of the servant, who hesitated before retreating, wary of being caught and forced to reveal the source of the expensive coin.

As the servant left, Mordecai paced the room, his mind racing. The loss of education troubled him deeply. *I had promised my grandfather to care for the Jewish people, and here I'm failing Hadassah.*

CHAPTER 7

Seeking advice, Mordecai approached Gdaliahu. "I've heard rumors that Shimon isn't treating Hadassah well," he said cautiously.

Gdaliahu frowned. "What do you mean? Is she being abused?"

"No," Mordecai replied, "but she's not receiving the education her father valued."

"Education for women?" Gdaliahu scoffed. "That's not our way. Educating women is considered unnecessary."

"Unnecessary?" Mordecai retorted. "The Israelites respected Judge Deborah, a prophetess, and Barak fought alongside her."

Gdaliahu's eyes narrowed. "You may harm her marriage prospects by educating her, Mordecai. Think carefully."

"Her father valued her education, and she deserves to be treated like a princess," Mordecai pressed. "Even Queen Vashti is educated."

"True, but it hasn't exactly helped Vashti's situation, has it?" Gdaliahu countered.

Mordecai stood firm. "I want to take Hadassah away from Shimon and adopt her as my daughter. It's essential."

Gdaliahu paused, considering the request. "That's a serious step. Shimon won't be pleased, especially since her inheritance might attract his sons. I suggest you arrange a meeting at his house. Propose a business deal."

"What kind of deal?" Mordecai asked.

"Ask him to ship ten camels loaded with his finest silk to my nephew Zechariah in Egypt," Gdaliahu replied, a mysterious smile crossing his lips. He nodded toward his head-guard. "Take three of my bodyguards with you."

Mordecai raised an eyebrow. "Why would I need bodyguards for a business deal?"

"Overwhelming force brings tranquility and decorum," Gdaliahu said calmly.

Mordecai mouthed to himself, *"To win, do not go feebly into the lion's den."*

———≈———

Mordecai frequented the public bathhouse, where his status as Gdaliahu's confidant made him a key figure in local discussions and intrigue. The steamy baths were a place where people sought his guidance, shared gossip, or even made discreet requests. He often used these moments to subtly assign tasks or spread carefully crafted rumors.

He knew Shimon was a regular at the bathhouse, especially on Tuesdays. Mordecai decided today would be the day to confront him. As he scanned the steamy room, his eyes fell on Shimon, reclining on a marble bench with two friends. Not wanting to miss the opportunity, Mordecai moved swiftly toward him, drawing the attention of others in the room.

Shimon, noticing Mordecai's approach, straightened with a mix of pride and anticipation. His friends quickly made space for Mordecai, their eyes flickering with curiosity.

Mordecai leaned in close, keeping his voice low but direct. "I have a lucrative job for you."

The air in the bathhouse grew tense, with everyone subtly tuning into the exchange. Shimon, basking in the attention of having Mordecai—a man of such influence—approach him, smiled broadly. He raised his voice so it would carry through the steam-filled room. "Mordecai! It would be an honor if you joined me for dinner at my house this Saturday night."

The bathhouse patrons exchanged glances, intrigued by the invitation.

Mordecai nodded quietly, his expression controlled. "Thank you," he replied, acknowledging the invitation.

After exchanging a few pleasantries and shaking hands with those nearby, Mordecai took his seat and patiently listened as a line of petitioners approached him. Each voiced their concerns, and he responded briefly. He invited some to his office for more in-depth discussions.

But even as he spoke with others, his mind was already turning over the plan for Saturday. He had made his move—and the game was just beginning.

Three hours later, his body refreshed and his mind saturated, Mordecai left the bathhouse, his role as a central figure in the community more firmly established than ever.

As planned, Mordecai arrived at Shimon's house that Saturday evening in a stately chariot, flanked by three imposing guards. Their uniforms gleamed in the evening light, weapons at the ready. Two guards rode ahead of the chariot, while one trailed behind, watchful and alert.

Upon arrival, the guards dismounted and placed sacks of grain over the horses' heads, allowing the animals to feed, shaking their heads, scattering grain into their mouths.

Shimon greeted Mordecai at the door with a broad smile, his arms open in a gesture of warmth and familiarity. He embraced Mordecai, shaking his hand firmly and nodding with approval at the impressive guards. "You've brought quite the company," he remarked, gesturing them inside. A servant took Mordecai's cloak and hung it up, while Shimon led him toward the dining room. Mordecai subtly signaled for the guards to remain stationed in the central hall.

In the dining room, an elegantly arranged table awaited. The silverware sparkled under the glow of oil lamps, and shimmering plates reflected the flicker of the flames. Platters of roasted meats, fresh bread, crashed salt, and olives were artfully displayed, with bottles of fine wine at the center of the feast.

Mordecai surveyed the room. Shimon's sons, Michael and Netanel, stood expectantly, waiting for him to take his place. By the kitchen door, dressed in black and an apron, with her hair covered by a simple scarf, stood Hadassah. Her face was blank, her eyes shadowed with sadness. Mordecai gave her a subtle nod, maintaining a neutral expression. Hadassah did not acknowledge him.

With a slight raise of Shimon's chin, Hadassah approached the table, carrying the ritual washing cup for the men to cleanse their hands. As she neared, Mordecai inhaled, catching a clean, pleasant scent. His heart softened, but he kept his composure. *She's been prepared for this evening,* he thought, relieved that she at least appeared well-cared for.

After Shimon blessed the wine and food, Mordecai took in the aroma of the dishes. The familiar scents of roasted lamb, spiced vegetables, and freshly baked bread stirred memories of his mother's cooking—something he had not experienced in years. The absence of a mother, a wife, or someone to care for him, gnawed at him more than he expected.

Once dinner had concluded, Mordecai followed Shimon into the library for their business discussion. Despite his youth, Mordecai's status as Gdaliahu's right hand commanded respect, and Shimon treated him accordingly. Fresh fruit and wine were laid before them, but Mordecai ignored them, focusing on the task at hand.

Shimon leaned back in his chair, waiting for Mordecai to speak.

Mordecai's hands trembled slightly as he pushed the fruit plate aside. "I didn't come here just for business," he began, his tone serious. "I came to investigate."

Shimon raised an eyebrow, caught off guard. "Investigate?"

Mordecai's gaze was unflinching. "King Gdaliahu Ha-Nasi wants to know how Hadassah is being treated."

Shimon shot to his feet, his face twisted in anger. "A woman's place is—" he began, but Mordecai's sharp gaze and raised palm cut him off mid-sentence. Insulted, Shimon considered calling his bodyguard.

Hearing the raised voices, two of Mordecai's escort guards appeared at the door. Shimon's face faltered.

"Sit down," Mordecai quietly commanded, his voice leaving no room for argument. One guard made another step forth, inclined forward, ready to pounce.

"You wouldn't…," Shimon's eyes said, his body shaking with terror and fury. "In my house? In front of my family?"

Mordecai was alert. He closed his eyes briefly, tightened his lips, lowered his chin, and held a sad face. *Don't push me! Submit!*

Shimon hesitated, visibly wrestling with his pride. The room fell into a heavy silence as Shimon glanced nervously at the guard, his presence looming over him. Slowly, his anger gave way to fear and resignation. He lowered himself back into his chair, defeated.

"Hadassah," Mordecai continued, his voice cold but controlled, "is the daughter of Abihail, and her father ensured she was educated and treated with dignity. I expect no less."

Shimon's hands clenched into fists at his sides, but Mordecai remained calm, letting the silence hang heavy between them.

Mordecai relaxed slightly, clearing his throat before addressing Shimon with calm authority. "Hadassah is of royal descent, from the lineage of King Saul. From this moment on, she is my daughter."

Shimon's face went pale. His objections crumbled beneath the weight of the moment, stifled by the guards' silent watch. He let out a long sigh, accepting the inevitable.

Seeing Shimon's compliance, Mordecai's gaze softened. He pulled the fruit plate closer, plucked a grape, and ate it—an unspoken gesture of truce. "The Jewish leader requests that you send ten camels, loaded with your finest silk, to his nephew Zechariah in Egypt." He placed a hefty bag of coins on the table, the clink of gold unmistakable. The sum was clearly more than the silk was worth.

Shimon weighed the bag in his hand, recognizing the sound of a generous offer. A shy smile crept across his face. "Thank the Jewish leader. It will be done," he said, his tone subdued.

He didn't object to the triple payment. *I bought Hadassah too,* Mordecai thought, though he kept the words to himself.

Mordecai nodded. "Thank you for caring for Hadassah. She has learned valuable lessons in your home, lessons that will serve her well."

Shimon returned a sad smile, nodding in silent agreement.

"Please have Hadassah's belongings delivered to my home by tomorrow," Mordecai continued. "And each year, on Passover, provide me with an annual report of her estate. Pay yourself well for your efforts, and accumulate her share in the estate, available for her wedding."

"As you wish," Shimon agreed.

At that moment, Shimon's sons entered, carrying Hadassah between them, legs in the air. They unceremoniously lowered her in front of Mordecai. Her head was bowed, shoulders hunched, avoiding his gaze. Michael, Shimon's elder son, held her hand tightly, a single tear glistening in his eye as it trembled on the verge of falling.

"Come here, my daughter," Mordecai said gently, beckoning Hadassah forward. Michael refused to let go, his grip firm, until Hadassah shot him a warning glance. Reluctantly, he released her hand.

Mordecai draped his robe around her shoulders, pulling her into a protective embrace. Her eyes, filled with tears, flickered between Shimon and Mordecai, but she remained silent.

With a reassuring smile, Mordecai guided her toward the door. As they neared the exit, Hadassah instinctively reached to retrieve Mordecai's coat, but he gently stopped her. "You're no longer a servant, my daughter," he whispered. "You are Princess Hadassah now. Leaders use their heads, not their hands."

Moved by the gesture, Shimon draped his wife's shawl over Hadassah's shoulders and handed Mordecai his coat. Bowing his head, Shimon said, "May God bless you and your family."

"And yours," Mordecai replied with a nod.

A new family now, they all thought.

As they stepped outside, the bond between them was sealed. Hadassah's relief and happiness were palpable, and for the first time in a long while, she felt the warmth of hope as they left Shimon's home behind.

Outside, they climbed into the chariot. As it began to roll forward, Hadassah glanced back. She saw Shimon, arms wrapped tightly around his sons, comforting them as they stood watching the chariot disappear into the distance. The steady thump of the wheels over the cobblestones echoed in sync with Hadassah's racing heartbeat.

Sensing her lingering confusion and uncertainty, Mordecai spoke softly, his voice calm and reassuring. "No, my daughter, this isn't a dream. You will not be forced to return to that house."

Hadassah smiled faintly, a mixture of relief and wonder. "Can you read my mind?"

Mordecai let out his distinctive loud laugh, the sound filling the air with warmth. "No, but when it's written all over your face, it's easy to guess," he teased, gently squeezing her hand. "You will be safe with me. Always."

When they arrived home, Mordecai thanked his guards, rewarding them each with a gold coin for their service, before sending them on their way.

In the following days, Mordecai formally announced to the Jewish court that Hadassah had been officially adopted as his daughter. The announcement was met with joy and celebration, culminating in a grand banquet held at the newly established Jewish Academy of Law and Business Studies. The hall was filled with well-wishers, scholars, and community leaders, all gathered to honor Hadassah's new beginning.

CHAPTER 8

My grandson called me, and as always, hearing his voice made me smile.

"I'm not feeling well," he said softly, sounding sad. "I didn't go to school today."

"You can still learn on your own," I suggested gently.

"I tried," he admitted, but then his tone lightened with a hint of hope. "But I'm bored. Can you tell me more of your stories?"

His words warmed my heart. "Of course," I said, ready to share another lesson from the past.

———❧———

I will ensure she receives an education and find a suitable husband for her, Mordecai resolved. *I don't need to swear an oath to make this promise. She may even assist me in my mission, for there are things a woman can achieve that even the wisest man cannot.*

As his only child, Hadassah became the heart of Mordecai's household. He meticulously planned her education, believing she should be proficient in Hebrew, as well as the primary languages of the empire, if she were to aid him in his work. He explained to her that most communication was either distorted or deliberately misleading. To combat this, he taught her how to read between the lines, discerning the emotions behind the words. "Remember," he would say, "both words and body gestures reveal a person's true intentions."

Mordecai also appointed a young kitchen maid, Sarah, to be Hadassah's companion. After completing her lessons each day, Hadassah would teach Sarah what she had learned, giving them both a chance to practice. Little Sarah was overjoyed to be treated like a princess, and soon, the two girls formed a close bond.

Hadassah proved to be a quick learner. Using Biblical quotes, she soon became skilled in analyzing cryptic messages from multiple angles. Hadassah shared the tales of Joseph and his rise to power in Egypt through his interpretation of Pharaoh's dreams with Sarah. She also recounted the story of Moses, who led the Israelites to freedom, and spoke with admiration of Ruth and Tamar, biblical heroines who shaped their fates through bold choices and received God's favor. Hadassah dreamed of emulating their courage and wisdom.

Though she enjoyed the tales of King David, Hadassah was most drawn to the detailed records of her forefather, King Saul, which Mordecai had inherited from his grandfather. She was saddened by the account of the prophet Samuel cursing Saul for sparing King Agag of the Amalekites, learning the harsh lesson that God's commands must be obeyed. The story of Michal, Saul's daughter, who insulted King David during his celebration before the Ark of God, left Hadassah frustrated. Michal's punishment—confined to isolation and having her children executed—shocked Hadassah. Yet, she remained grateful to David and his heirs for preserving the lineage of Prince Jonathan, Saul's firstborn and her ancestor.

As Hadassah matured, both her inner strength and outer beauty captivated those around her. She transformed from a quiet servant into a confident young woman. One bright spring day, Mordecai made a significant announcement: "Hadassah is now thirteen years old, and she will oversee this year's Passover celebration as the mistress of the house."

Hadassah rose to the occasion. She gathered the household servants and maids, standing tall before them, her voice clear and commanding. "We are going to prepare a beautiful Passover. We will work hard, as if we were slaves, and then we will celebrate like masters."

Under Hadassah's leadership, the house was thoroughly scrubbed. Windows were washed, drapes cleaned, carpets beaten, and floors polished until they gleamed. A second table was set in the kitchen for the servants to join in the celebration. The dining room glowed with the shimmer of polished silver plates and goblets reflecting the warm light of oil lamps. Round matzos were neatly arranged on the table, and special wine from Jerusalem was brought out for the occasion.

Hadassah herself prepared a particularly bitter herb mixture to remind the guests of the bitterness of slavery in Egypt. Her attention to every detail, both grand and small, reflected the wisdom and grace she had cultivated under Mordecai's watchful care.

Hadassah playfully instructed Mordecai to have his hair and beard neatly groomed for the occasion. Though he initially waved it off as unnecessary, she reminded him, with a smile, that she was now the master of the house. Relenting with a chuckle, Mordecai agreed. She then carefully selected his attire, choosing garments that would honor the guests soon arriving. Hadassah and Sarah also spent the afternoon preparing small gifts for both the guests and the servants, adding a personal touch to the celebration.

Just before the festivities began, Mordecai approached Hadassah with a hand hidden behind his back, his face lit with a warm smile. "For you," he said, revealing a golden tiara adorned with sparkling red rubies.

Hadassah's eyes brimmed with tears as memories of her mother wearing that same tiara flooded her heart. Mordecai gently kissed the top of her head before placing the tiara on her hair. She removed it for a moment, gazing at it with a mixture of nostalgia and pride, then set it back on her head, her posture straightening as she embraced the moment.

Soon, the first guests arrived—Shimon and his family. As they removed their fur hats, gloves, and heavy cloaks, Hadassah hurried to greet them, lifting her dress with one hand and holding the tiara with the other. They bowed to her, but she embraced both of them together, her affection breaking the formality. Michael, Shimon's eldest son, gently took Hadassah's hand and kissed it, a tender smile on his face.

Hadassah, glowing with happiness, looped her arms through those of her two cousins, guiding them toward the dining table. Her face beamed with a wide smile. "So much light and warmth," Netanel remarked, taking in the scene.

"We've lit hundreds of oil lamps," Hadassah explained, her eyes sparkling with the reflection of the shimmering flames.

"It's wonderful how the light glistens from the glass cups and silver," Michael added, squeezing Hadassah's hand lightly.

The air was filled with the rich aroma of roasting lamb mingling with the sharp scent of bitter herbs, a reminder of the ancient traditions they were celebrating.

"Help me bring in the flowers," Hadassah said, turning to her cousins.

"Flowers?" Netanel asked, puzzled. "There were no flowers in Egypt or on Mount Sinai."

Michael teased him with a playful smile, "Already questioning?"

Hadassah grinned. "It's springtime. A time of renewal. Flowers bring beauty and joy—they're festive and feminine."

"Beauty and love," Michael added with a knowing look, as they carried the flowers into the room.

They carefully arranged vases of vibrant spring flowers down the center of the table, their red, yellow, white, and blue colors complementing the glowing wooden, silver, and glass already on the table. The sweet fragrances of the blossoms blended with the scent of roasted lamb and fresh bread, creating a sensory tapestry that heightened the festive atmosphere.

As the guests settled into their seats, Mordecai's eyes fell on the beautiful narcissus flowers in his proximity. Their delicate scent reminded him of something cherished, and he smiled warmly at Hadassah. "Your attention to detail is remarkable," he said softly, expressing his gratitude.

Hadassah nodded, then signaled a servant to bring the ritual washing cup and towels. Mordecai led the blessing, and the guests washed their hands in reverence. Then, they filled their cups with sweet wine. Mordecai offered another blessing, and they all drank in unison, the warmth of the wine spreading through their bodies.

The celebration was attended by two dozen men, with Mordecai seated at the head of the table. Hadassah, the only female present, sat with her younger cousins at the other end. Though unusual for a woman to be present, she engaged confidently—singing, speaking, and conversing with the men. Her status as Mordecai's only child commanded respect, and no one dared object.

As the evening unfolded, Hadassah's thoughts wandered. *Next year,* she mused, *I'll ask Mordecai to let Sarah and all the wives and daughters join us at the table. We were all slaves in Egypt; we should all celebrate together. Similarly, I, traveled—from Shimon's house to studying Torah with Mordecai.*

"Hadassah," Mordecai's voice broke her reverie, "please, tell us about Passover."

Hadassah hesitated, feeling the weight of the request. "Please, no," she murmured softly, but Mordecai persisted.

"You must," he encouraged gently.

"Earn your seat!" her cousin Netanel teased with a playful grin.

At that moment, Hadassah caught a sarcastic glint in Shimon's eyes, but she quickly dismissed it. Michael, seated beside her, leaned in and placed a reassuring hand over hers. "You can do it," he whispered. "I'll help if you forget anything."

Hadassah smiled shyly at Michael's support, then, with a deep breath, she leaned on the table to steady herself as she stood. "I will... ah... tell you the story of Joseph in Egypt," she began, her voice tentative. A few of the older men pursed their lips, unaccustomed to being addressed by a young woman, but Shimon leaned back in his chair, curiosity piqued.

Mordecai watched Hadassah closely, a swell of pride rising within him as she spoke. Her education, her growth—everything he had worked to instill in her—was now on full display.

"Pharaoh dreamt of seven healthy cows grazing in the field," Hadassah continued, her voice growing more confident. "Then seven sickly cows came and devoured the healthy ones." She paused, scanning the room. "The ministers were afraid to interpret the dream. But a wise servant suggested they consult Joseph."

The guests leaned in, fully engaged by her storytelling. Though they all knew the tale, Hadassah's interpretation brought fresh insight. Her growing confidence captured their attention.

Hadassah quickened her pace, her voice lively. "Joseph immediately understood that Pharaoh was worried about his wealth. What else would concern a king? Hah," she laughed lightly, and the men chuckled along with her, momentarily forgetting that she was a girl. Mordecai smiled to himself, pleased with her poise.

"The seven cows reminded Joseph of the seven years his father worked to marry Rachel," Hadassah went on, "only to be given Leah—who was fertile—and then working another seven years for Rachel, who was barren." She paused, her eyes glinting. "Joseph explained that seven prosperous years were coming, followed by seven years of famine."

Netanel, her cousin, raised an eyebrow and asked, "Is that really how it's written in the Torah?"

"Ssh," Michael whispered with a grin. "It's her interpretation, but it's excellent."

"I've never heard it quite like that before," Mordecai admitted with a smile, glancing at the guests as if apologizing for his own surprise.

Hadassah grinned. "To prepare for the famine, Joseph suggested storing food. Pharaoh made Joseph his second-in-command, placing him above everyone in Egypt except himself and whoever sat on the royal chair. And... Joseph was given a royal ring—the signet seal—, a golden chariot, and a golden necklace. And *everyone* knelt before him."

"How could they store wheat for seven years?" Shimon asked, his brow furrowing.

"Egypt is hot and dry—perfect conditions for preserving grain," Hadassah explained confidently. "Joseph taxed the people and used Pharaoh's resources to build silos and store the grain. Remember, Joseph had already managed Potiphar's estate, so he knew how to run large operations. He also built new canals, dams, lakes, roads, and bridges. He even used boats to transport fertile soil from the Nile Delta to the sand dunes, creating irrigated fields. Egypt became united, prosperous, and secure. The fields produced three times more than before, and Joseph bought all the surplus to prevent the wheat market from collapsing."

"Then came the draught," Michael interjected, eager to contribute.

"How could there be a draught in Egypt?" his brother asked, puzzled. "It's already a desert."

"Not lack of rain. The story mentions a hot wind from the eastern desert," Hadassah responded, her voice calm and measured. "It doesn't say there was no water in the Nile. But a few days of scorching winds could easily destroy crops. The famine was in Canaan too, but surprisingly—only God knows how—livestock survived."

"Nice explanation," Mordecai said, nodding. "The part about the famine always confused me."

"People often have mistaken assumptions that cloud their thinking," Shimon added thoughtfully. Hadassah cast a sideways glance at Shimon. *Look at you,* she thought. *What about your own bias against women's education?*

Hadassah continued. "Once the silos were full, Joseph stopped construction and laid off workers, which caused an economic recession."

Netanel's face scrunched in confusion. "Why would he do that? I don't get it."

"It was all part of Joseph's plan to fulfill his prophecy," Hadassah explained. "By laying off workers and halting planting, he deliberately caused unemployment and hunger. Joseph understood that the famine wasn't just a disaster—it was God's way to bring his family to the Nile Delta—Goshen. There, they would live separated from the Egyptians and their idols culture, prosper, supplying wool, milk, and meat to Egypt, grow in number, eventually become enslaved, and then, in God's time, they would escape Egypt. On their journey back to the Promised Land, God would give them the Torah at Mount Sinai, fulfilling the divine plan."

"Wow. That's a new way of looking at it," Michael said, clearly impressed.

"Not entirely," Hadassah continued. "God used a similar pattern with Abraham. Abraham went to Egypt during a famine, received gifts from Pharaoh, and after God struck Pharaoh with disease, Abraham was sent back to Canaan."

"Easy for you to say," Netanel remarked. "How do we know Joseph understood all this?"

Hadassah smiled, a spark of confidence in her eyes. "I'm sure Joseph was smarter than me. And, as you know, everything he predicted came true."

Netanel opened his mouth, ready to argue, but Michael discreetly kicked his leg under the table, silencing him before he could speak.

Hadassah glanced around the table, surprised to see all the men listening intently, their eyes fixed on her. "In the first year of the famine, those who hadn't saved enough food had to pay for it with gold," she continued. "By the second year, their money was gone, so they offered their animals in exchange. In the third year, they surrendered their land. And when they had nothing left, they agreed to work Pharaoh's land, paying a fifth of their crops as tax."

She paused, her eyes gleaming with satisfaction. "Joseph not only saved the Egyptians' lives, but he enriched Pharaoh and brought the Israelites to Egypt... so that one day Moses could lead them out."

A triumphant smile spread across her face, and just as she finished, Shimon stood up and began clapping, prompting the rest of the guests to join in with cheers and applause. Hadassah blushed, bowing her head slightly, her smile softening with embarrassment as she thanked them.

"To complete the story," Mordecai added, rising from his seat, "since Joseph married into the priesthood exempted from taxes, the Israelites also remained tax-exempt for generations. This changed only when a new Pharaoh, who did not know Joseph, came to power. Even today, taxes are mostly imposed on goods from fields, forests, flocks, and mines. We Jews, being professionals and merchants, remain largely untaxed. But remember—one day, this might draw the authorities' wrath upon us."

The room fell into a contemplative hush, and the festive mood temporarily dimmed.

"Let's bring back the celebration," Shimon interjected with a smile, steering the conversation away from its somber turn.

Hadassah gave a discreet signal, and the traditional dishes were brought out. The elders offered their blessings as the warm, fragrant plates of food filled the table. Hadassah, eager to partake, took a bite of matzah with bitter white horseradish. The pungent taste hit her hard, almost choking her, and the sharp scent burned her nostrils. She coughed and waved a hand to fan in cooler air.

Michael quickly rose and handed her a glass of water. She drank gratefully, her eyes sparkling with appreciation as she smiled up at him.

Once the main dishes were served, Mordecai addressed the guests, his voice warm with tradition. "As is customary during Passover, it's time for the young ones to ask questions."

Shimon's younger son leaned forward. "Mordecai, why do you keep moving around the table, sitting with different guests instead of staying at the head?"

Mordecai chuckled, his eyes twinkling. "I want to be close to everyone I've invited. In this house, the head of the table is wherever I sit. It's not the place that brings honor; it's you who bring honor to the place."

Hadassah, smiling, added playfully, "Still, no one dares sit in your chair."

The guests erupted in laughter.

"Even if you did sit in my chair," Mordecai responded with a grin, "you wouldn't become me. You'd still be you."

Laughter filled the room again, the warmth and camaraderie of the gathering wrapping around them like a comforting embrace.

Shimon nodded thoughtfully. "Pharaoh told Joseph that his chair would always remain above Joseph's. He warned him not to attempt to take the throne from his weak son. He who rises to power by luck or trickery must learn quickly or risk being overthrown."

Hadassah, barely audible, muttered, "He or she."

The room fell silent, all eyes shifting toward Mordecai. He felt anger bubbling inside but kept it in check. "Very true, Shimon," he replied carefully. "And thank you for the reminder." He raised his cup of wine, and the guests followed his lead, returning to the celebration with a clink of cups and renewed chatter.

Hadassah stood up, her voice firm and clear. "Many years after Joseph's death, the Israelites grew numerous and prosperous. Then, a new Pharaoh, who did not remember Joseph, imposed hard labor and heavy taxes upon us. And... God sent Moses to ask him to free our people. When Pharaoh refused, God brought ten plagues upon Egypt and its gods. But after the fifth plague, it is written that God *hardened* Pharaoh's heart, making him stubborn and unwilling to let us go. Does that mean that, had God not intervened, Pharaoh might have released us earlier and spared Egypt the additional plagues?"

A storm of voices erupted around the table as the guests eagerly debated.

"It was to punish Pharaoh for the suffering he caused," one man argued.

"Moses wanted him to suffer for forcing us to flee," another voice chimed in.

"You don't question God," one of Hadassah's cousins said firmly.

"Pharaoh deserved every plague," his brother retorted.

Mordecai sat back, listening as the room filled with passionate arguments and clashing opinions. He watched Hadassah, who stood patiently, waiting for the room to settle.

When the noise finally subsided, Hadassah spoke again, her voice calm but resolute. "I found the answer in our book. God tormented Egypt so that we...we would learn—and teach our sons, and our daughters—about the Lord's awesome power."

Mordecai smiled at her, pride evident in his eyes. "Well done, Hadassah. You've raised an important moral point. Pharaoh's heart was hardened from the start. Remember, he asked Moses with arrogance, 'Who is your God? I've never heard of Him.' He disrespected our God. The ten plagues were meant to humiliate the Egyptian gods and demonstrate the Lord's power. In the end, even Pharaoh told Moses, 'Go. And ask your God to bless me too.' Pharaoh played a key role in shaping our nation's destiny. I doubt Moses ever blessed him, but perhaps we should offer him a blessing now."

Laughter rippled through the room, lightening the mood.

"Sometimes," Shimon added, "even terrible actions lead to unexpectedly good outcomes. Pharaoh pursued us because he wanted to reclaim us as slaves. We feared he would kill us, so we hurried across the Sea of Reeds. Once we were on the other side, trapped in the desert, there was no turning back. Pharaoh was a *tool* in God's hands, a necessary instrument for our deliverance."

The guests nodded in agreement, reflecting on Shimon's words.

"I have another question," Netanel said, his eyes sharp with curiosity. "Why did Pharaoh rush to Moses in the middle of the night after the death of his firstborn son? The punishment was over. Why didn't he wait until morning?"

Mordecai observed his young relative closely, recognizing the significance of the question. *As the second son of Shimon,* Mordecai thought *the concept of birthright is close to his hear*t.

After a brief pause, Shimon answered, "We don't know for sure. Perhaps you tell us?"

Netanel's face lit with satisfaction. "Yes. It's said that whoever sits in his father's chair will die. It wasn't just the firstborns at risk. After the firstborn son's death, the second son would become the next in line, and then the others would follow, one by one. Pharaoh rushed to Moses because he feared losing all his sons."

The room fell into an awed silence as the weight of Netanel's insight sank in. Mordecai watched the boy with newfound respect, nodding approvingly.

"I have a question... Actually, never mind, it might be complicated," Michael hesitated, his voice trailing off.

"Go ahead, ask. There's no wrong question," his brother encouraged. "We always learn from questions, even conflicting ones."

Shimon nodded in agreement. "Exactly. Questions lead to understanding. Ask away."

Michael, his expression tinged with pride, gestured with his hands. "It's said we must remember to erase the memory of Amalek. Should we remember or forget?"

"The Amalekites were cruel, yes," Shimon began, "but cruelty reappears in every generation. We must remember their evil deeds and learn from them, but we must also punish and erase the names of the wrongdoers."

Mordecai waited, choosing his words carefully. "True. But there's a deeper lesson here. The command to erase Amalek is for leaders, to remind them that force should only be used when absolutely necessary. It's better to wield overwhelming, threatening power to achieve your goals without resorting to violence. And bad memories can be erased with lasting peace."

Hadassah noticed Mordecai's subtle glance toward Shimon, his palms slightly raised, as if silently asking, *What could I have done differently? Can we forgive and forget?* Shimon nodded, lowering his gaze. *They're talking about me,* Hadassah thought, her chest tightening.

Mordecai continued, his voice louder now. "In the original story, God and Moses led the Israelites through the desert, but some people refused to follow. Moses didn't send soldiers to force or protect the rebels, and God didn't intervene either. The Amalekites took advantage of this—they attacked, robbed, and enslaved those rebellious. After a few attacks, everyone promptly obeyed Moses. The Amalekites became a *tool*, a harsh *motivator*. So why punish them, you might ask? Go ahead, ask."

Hadassah smiled supportively, eager to respond. "Why should they be punished?"

Mordecai grinned. "Thank you, Hadassah. The Amalekites volunteered for that cruel job. They didn't just attack; they took pleasure in it. For that, we are commanded to destroy all evildoers and erase their culture. We must smite them and their descendants with the same finality as the firstborn plague."

"Why us?" a guest asked.

Mordecai's eyes flickered. "Because, as strangers in foreign lands, we're the first targets of emerging evildoers. If not us, then who? We must act early, outsmart them, and eliminate the threat before it grows."

He paused, his expression shifting, as if a realization struck him. *We are all tools in God's hands,* he thought, his mind racing. He coiled a long curl of hair around his finger, a habit when he was deep in thought. *I vowed to protect the Jews from assimilation. Am I becoming a tool—no, a sledgehammer?* His thoughts swirled. *Is this justice? Can I do this with kindness? Should I flee like Jonah? Were my grandfather's words truly from God?*

Mordecai wiped a tear from his eye, overwhelmed. Hadassah, watching closely, noticed his distress. *What is he thinking?* she wondered, her mouth twitching with concern. *He's in pain. Confused.*

Sensing Hadassah's worried gaze, Mordecai pulled himself from his thoughts. He smiled, stood up, and clapped his hands. Bowing to Hadassah, Michael, and Netanel, he said warmly, "Well done, all of you. You've taught me valuable lessons tonight."

The youngsters beamed with pride and returned his bow.

But Mordecai's thoughts remained unsettled. *Is God speaking to me? There are two ways to accomplish my mission: Prosperity and Pain—both together. Prosperity, and sweet honey came from the punishing, strong lion. Could that be the path?*

The evening continued as the guests prayed for the success of their Persian king and the well-being of their Israelite nation. They sang, talked, and debated late into the night.

The younger guests moved to play *Pur*, a Persian board game involving dice. Netanel's attention was on Sarah, Sarah's on Michael, Michael's on Hadassah, and Hadassah focused on the game.

Finally, they blessed Mordecai and Hadassah for the wonderful celebration, the hospitality, and the delicious food. After escorting the departing guests to their chariots, Mordecai turned to Hadassah as the quiet of the night settled around them. "Thank you, Hadassah, for organizing such a wonderful celebration."

Hadassah smiled, her lips tightly pressed together. "Thank you."

Mordecai hesitated before asking, "I noticed you talking with Michael."

"Yes," she replied, her tone calm.

"… And…?"

"He told me he admired my education and said he would love me forever."

"… And…?"

"He asked me to marry him when I'm older."

"… And…?"

Hadassah laughed softly. "I thanked him. He said I would be his queen."

"… And…?"

"I told him it's too soon."

"… And…?"

"I asked him if he plans to become a king."

"… And…?"

"We both laughed. That's all."

CHAPTER 9

Sitting at the kitchen table, struggling with homework, my grandson sighed and exclaimed, "Math is hard!"

"Not really," I replied with a smile. "It's just a process. The answers are always there, waiting to be found. You'll face a lot of problems, but the solutions are out there—if you keep going and don't give up."

He looked up, curiosity flickering in his eyes. "Can you give me an example?"

"Absolutely! Let me tell you about Mordecai and Hadassah. They faced a problem much bigger than math, but they found a solution. Come on, let's sit on the swing."

We moved out to the front porch, the warm breeze carrying the scent of the garden. Settling into the cushions, I began the story, his attention fully drawn in as we gently swayed back and forth.

King Cyrus died four years after conquering Babylon. His grandson, Prince Ahasuerus, inherited a troubled empire after the brief reign of his weak and sickly father, who had ruled for only a year. Former Babylonian hostages, released by Cyrus to govern their own nations, revolted, refusing to pay their annual tributes. Facing this unrest, King Ahasuerus delayed his inauguration celebration while the royal Persian army focused on quelling the rebellion.

Revolting? Mordecai thought with disdain. *They see the young king as weak. They've likely used the tax money and labor to strengthen their own power. But they're in for a rude awakening. These rebels lacked the time or resources to fully fortify their cities, train a formidable army, or build alliances. Old rivalries have resurfaced, and they're already at each other's throats.*

One afternoon, Gdaliahu and Mordecai met for herbal tea, discussing the latest developments of the revolt.

"I've been hearing reports," Mordecai began, setting down his cup. "Over the last couple of years, the royal Persian army has been systematically defeating rebel leaders, one by one. They've also been constructing a network of paved roads and bridges across the empire to rapidly deploy troops and supplies. It seems most nations now see the benefits of a united empire and have welcomed the king's forces."

"Yes, the new roads are a boon for commerce," Gdaliahu acknowledged. "But what about those who still refuse to surrender?"

"They're being brutally crushed," Mordecai said, slamming his right fist into his left palm. "Like blood-sucking ticks. In many cities, the citizens have thrown their leaders' heads over the city walls. Persisting rebels are being enslaved."

Gdaliahu frowned. "I've heard Ezra the Priest returned to Judah with many Jews. He's rebuilding Jerusalem's walls but facing resistance from neighboring tribes. Have you heard from him? It's a difficult balance—paying tribute to the Persian king and tithing tax for the priests. Many Jews are hesitant to leave the diaspora for Judea. Could Ezra be tempted to rebel?"

Mordecai shook his head. "Fortunately, no. Ezra remains loyal to the king."

"That's a relief," Gdaliahu sighed. "Too many of our people still believe that God will always save us from our mistakes."

Mordecai chose not to comment on that, steering the conversation in a new direction. "The roads the Persian army is building will make travel to Jerusalem much easier."

"Or anywhere else," Gdaliahu observed thoughtfully. "The victorious army displayed a trove of looted goods and materials before the king."

Mordecai nodded. "Yes, Harvona told me the king was particularly impressed with the variety of new offerings."

———≈———

A few days later, a royal decree was published:

Royal World Fair

**In the third year of His Majesty, King Ahasuerus' reign,
all governors, dignitaries, and wealthy merchants
are hereby summoned to attend the
Royal World Fair, to be held from Shevat to Elul.**

**Each governor is required to host a grand banquet in honor of
His Majesty, the Royal King of Kings, and his esteemed guests.
These festivities will include entertainment, tributes, and the
presentation of gifts.**

**This grand event celebrates unity and prosperity across the
empire, and all participants are expected to engage
with the utmost respect and dedication.**

Gdaliahu summoned Mordecai to his palace with a sense of urgency. "Mordecai, the king has decreed a Royal World Fair," Gdaliahu said, his voice heavy with the significance of the occasion.

Mordecai, unfazed, responded calmly, "Yes, Harvona recommended it."

Gdaliahu's sharp gaze locked onto Mordecai, his tone shifting. "Does Harvona act on your every suggestion? What exactly is your true intent behind this?"

A flicker of concern crossed Mordecai's face. *Was Gdaliahu doubting his motives or questioning his loyalty?* He paused, taking a deep breath.

"You mentioned the influx of goods to the king and the prosperity from the new roads. I thought a World Fair would be the perfect tribute to honor King Cyrus, who allowed us to rebuild the temple in Jerusalem, and to acknowledge our current king for ignoring the denunciation letters from our enemies in Judea. By suggesting this, we gain favor with the king, even if he's unaware of our influence."

Gdaliahu studied Mordecai for a moment, then shifted the conversation. "In my name, send a decree to all Jewish communities across the empire, instructing them to attend the fair. I'll inform my nephew Zechariah in Egypt to join as well."

"Considered it done" Mordecai said.

Gdaliahu continued, "And, in the spirit of this unity, the king has commissioned two new royal crowns—one for himself and one for the queen. They will be called 'Unity Crowns,' crafted from reddish gold in the shape of a rose. Each nation must contribute two unique stones for these crowns, with an explanation of their significance."

His expression darkened. "We have only seven days to fulfill this. Mordecai, it's your responsibility to ensure our stones are selected and delivered. If you can't manage this, I will have to seek help elsewhere."

The thought of losing his role or failing his mission alarmed Mordecai. He nodded, concern etching into his features. "Do you have any suggestions for which stones we should send?"

Gdaliahu leaned back, his voice firm. "You are our adviser. Advise!"

Mordecai's mind raced. *It has to be something special, something the Jews cherish and the king would value.* A thought flickered. *Perhaps a saltstone from the Dead Sea?* But he quickly dismissed the idea. *No, it would dissolve in water. A terrible omen for our people.*

Disturbed by the weight of the decision, Mordecai returned home, sharing his dilemma with Hadassah. "I'm in a difficult position," he confessed, pacing. "I have only a week to select stones worthy of the Unity Crowns, but our true home is known as the 'land of milk and honey,' not precious gems. The copper mines of King Solomon are scarcely productive these days. I'm at a loss."

Hadassah watched him with concern, sensing his inner turmoil. She felt a deep empathy for him and grew determined to help. *There must be a solution,* she thought. *There's a riddle to solve, and I will find it.*

That evening, Mordecai's mood was somber. He pushed away the meal Hadassah had lovingly prepared, barely speaking as he continued pacing, the tension evident in his every movement. His hand absentmindedly coiled a lock of hair around his finger, a familiar sign of his frustration. His mind, burdened by the weight of his mission, raced with thoughts he could not quiet.

Hadassah, sensing his growing anxiety, whispered softly, "We'll find the answer, Mordecai. Together."

———≈———

Hadassah paced her room, her thoughts racing through a whirlwind of ideas. "Mother-of-pearl from the Red Sea? No, not meaningful enough. The pebble David used to defeat Goliath? Too large and insignificant for the king's Unity Crowns. Stones from the altars built by Abraham, Isaac, and Jacob? They're just ordinary stones."

She halted suddenly, her eyes widening in realization. "There are no special stones in the land of Judea," she muttered to herself. *That a relief, at least no need to continue the search there.* Then, with a sudden spark of inspiration, she shouted, "Wait! I know! I know!"

With renewed energy, she ran to find Mordecai. Breathless and unable to contain her excitement, she stood before him, her hands trembling, a grin spreading across her face.

Mordecai looked at her with curiosity, his face brightening at her enthusiasm. "What's gotten into you, my dear?" he asked, intrigued.

Hadassah laughed joyfully. "Ha! I've been thinking… What is 'predator became prey, sweet emerged from the strong? Wait, that's another riddle!" She giggled, then composed herself, her eyes alight with revelation. "Who created the Earth and gifted the sweet manna?"

Mordecai furrowed his brow in confusion, unsure of where she was going with this.

Hadassah's eyes sparkled. "It is said, 'Out of Zion shall come the Torah, and the word of the Lord from Jerusalem.'"

Mordecai's expression turned inquisitive, still unsure of her point.

Hadassah rocked on her heels, her excitement barely contained. "The answer has been in front of us the whole time," she declared triumphantly.

Mordecai leaned forward. "What answer?"

"The special stone—the most precious stone of the Jews!" she exclaimed. "We are blessed by the Torah. Why not create a small depiction of the Ten Commandments tablets? Imagine it—the king would carry the words of God over his head. Isn't that perfect?" She giggled again, her joy spilling over as she covered her mouth with her hands.

Mordecai's initial surprise turned into a broad, proud smile. He hugged Hadassah tightly, kissing the top of her head. "Our King, our God... perfect!" he whispered.

Hadassah, still caught in the moment, sang softly, "Our King, our God..."

Mordecai, beaming, added, "It's more perfect than you know! God has truly blessed you, Hadassah. Who knows? One day, you may carry a royal crown yourself."

Hadassah's eyes widened in awe as she whispered, "A queen? I... could be a queen?"

Two small, pea-sized white marble stones were meticulously crafted into flat tablets. Using delicate magnifying glasses from Greece, skilled artisans inscribed the Ten Commandments in tiny, precise script on both sides of each tablet, ensuring that the words of God would always be visible, no matter which side was facing outward.

Gdaliahu presented the tablets to the king, explaining their deep significance and reciting a brief account of God's glory in Egypt and at Mount Sinai.

King Ahasuerus, deeply impressed, admired the intricate craftsmanship and the spiritual weight of the stones. He added them to the Unity Crowns and even kept the magnifying glass as a treasured memento of the divine words he now carried above his head.

CHAPTER 10

"I'm thinking about buying an apartment building," I said to my grandson, glancing his way. "How about coming with me? We can evaluate the property together."

He raised an eyebrow, curiosity sparking in his eyes. "Do you think it's a good investment?"

"We won't know for sure until we check it out," I replied with a smile. "But no matter the outcome, we'll gain valuable experience. It's important to develop the skill of recognizing a good opportunity when it comes—and knowing when to seize it."

His face brightened with enthusiasm. "Sounds good! Let's go, and you can continue your story on the way."

———❧———

The city of Shushan buzzed with anticipation as preparations for the Royal World Fair reached a fever pitch. King Ahasuerus expected hundreds of thousands of visitors from across the empire. The king's army oversaw the massive effort, directing thousands of slaves, each dressed in distinct colors to signify their roles. In accordance with Persian law, slaves were treated fairly, compensated for their labor, and given the opportunity to buy their freedom eventually.

Wagons streamed in, laden with goods—timber, textiles, exotic wares, and precious stones. New roads crisscrossed the campground, with each section assigned to a different province. Flags flapped in the breeze, marking territories, while hastily constructed hostels provided accommodations for the endless influx of guests. Sewer and freshwater canals were swiftly installed, ensuring sanitation and convenience. Vendors worked tirelessly, stockpiling provisions to feed both people and animals throughout the event. Open spaces were cleared for the grand display of merchandise, showcasing the diversity of the empire's wealth and talent.

Caravans from all 127 provinces, spanning from the distant frontiers of India to the far-flung lands of Ethiopia, converged upon Shushan. Provincial leaders, mindful that their absence could lead to rivals speaking ill of them before the king, felt compelled to attend. The Royal World Fair presented a crucial opportunity to win favor with King Ahasuerus by showcasing their wealth, influence, and wisdom, all while offering lavish gifts to secure his goodwill.

Princes arrived in grandeur, accompanied by legions of soldiers and merchants, their processions reminiscent of the Queen of Sheba's legendary visit to King Solomon. At the appointed time, King Ahasuerus himself made a regal entrance on his magnificent white Cilician horse, wearing his Unity Crown. He paused, standing in the stirrups, scanning the vast sea of spectators. With a subtle smile, he nodded left, center, and right, raising his golden scepter and waving to the roaring crowd. The sight of their king, the royal King of Kings, sent waves of excitement through the people.

A priest stepped forward and offered a blessing in the names of Marduk and Ishtar. On a small hill, behind the king, a towering bonfire was ignited, with logs added to create colorful flames and dazzling sparks—a symbol of sacrifice and power.

The fair unfolded as a vibrant spectacle. Camps stretched across the valley, and the air was thick with the hum of commerce and the exchange of knowledge. People marveled at new technologies, sampled exotic goods, and traded valuable materials and knowledge.

King Ahasuerus allowed the visiting leaders to approach him, where they knelt with their heads to the ground in a display of submission. Through translators, he conversed with them, receiving their assurances that the fair was a monumental commercial and political success.

———≈———

"Mordecai, go attend the World Fair," Gdaliahu instructed, his tone firm but playful.

Mordecai frowned. "Thank you, but I don't need the honor. Too many people, too much noise and smell. I really don't see the point."

"Honor?" Gdaliahu laughed, clapping him on the back. "This isn't about honoring you—it's punishment for organizing this whole thing!"

Hadassah dressed Mordecai in fine garments, the fabric woven with colorful stripes, and tied a light blue ribbon adorned with a golden star around his arm. As he left the house, Mordecai discreetly untied the ribbon and slipped it into his pocket, feeling far too conspicuous.

Reluctantly, Mordecai trudged toward the fair, his steps slow and hesitant. He felt out of place, unsure of where to go or what to say. As he wandered aimlessly, two merchants approached him.

"Shalom!" one called out cheerfully.

Mordecai looked around, assuming they must be addressing someone else. When he realized no one else was nearby, he smiled shyly.

"We recognize you," one of the merchants said with a grin. "You're Mordecai, our lord's assistant."

"Me? No, no!" Mordecai protested, waving his hands in denial.

The merchants ignored his protest and insisted with enthusiasm, "We're thrilled to meet you! Please, come visit our camp. You'll be our guest of honor! We'll introduce you to everyone."

They took hold of his hands and pulled him along before he could refuse, their grip firm and friendly. Mordecai's heart sank as he hoped they hadn't brought along their daughters—his discomfort with the idea gnawed at him. Still, he allowed himself to be led, unsure of what the day would bring.

Mordecai joined the merchants and politely inquired about their businesses. The merchants eagerly took the lead in conversation, guiding him from camp to camp, and introducing him to other Jewish traders. Everywhere he went, he was welcomed with warmth and treated like family. As the day wore on, Mordecai's initial shyness began to fade.

Strange, he mused. *Why hasn't anyone offered me a daughter? Not one. Very odd.* Despite the relief he felt, a small part of him remained puzzled and insulted.

As Mordecai made his way through the fair, something remarkable caught his attention: while the Jewish delegation from Judea—his ancestral homeland—was modest, nearly every province included a significant contingent of Jewish merchants. Their economic influence was unmistakable, and Mordecai was particularly struck by how Hebrew had evolved into a common, international language that united Jews across the vast empire and beyond.

Ever the strategist, Mordecai pulled out his notebook and began meticulously recording details. He jotted down the merchants' names, their residences, and the types of goods they traded. Tearing a page from his notebook, he cut it into small squares, marked each with his signet, and distributed these to the merchants as tokens of goodwill and future collaboration.

"The fair is an overwhelming success," the merchants told him. "You should make this an annual tradition."

Mordecai nodded in agreement. "It truly is a triumph. No more revolts, no unrest. The world's leaders are dazzled by the empire's wealth and strength. We've established a lasting global marketplace."

As he neared home that evening, Mordecai discreetly tied the blue ribbon back around his arm, ready to present himself as expected.

Each day, Mordecai continued his rounds at the camps, gathering more information and building connections. In the evenings, the visiting dignitaries attended extravagant banquets at the king's palace. Every night, a different leader hosted a celebration, showcasing their nation's pride with elaborate displays of food, wine, music, and dance. The entertainment ranged from belly dancers to acrobats, clowns, snake charmers, and magicians, delighting the king and his guests.

Leaders competed fiercely, offering lavish gifts in a bid to win King Ahasuerus' favor. The race to present the most extravagant tribute, while done with grace, was an unspoken and often humorous contest—a grand parade of bribes disguised as gifts, each leader striving to outdo the next.

———————≈———————

Mordecai was summoned to Gdaliahu's palace to meet Zechariah, Gdaliahu's nephew and a wealthy merchant from Egypt. Mordecai, curious and slightly apprehensive, was pleased to meet the esteemed guest. As he entered the room, his eyes were drawn to a young woman standing beside Zechariah. They exchanged respectful bows, but Mordecai deliberately avoided looking at her directly.

"Why did you insist on those ten camels of silk?" Zechariah asked, scrutinizing Mordecai's expression.

Mordecai smiled, trying to ease the tension. "I had to. Didn't you make a good sale? You still owe me for the silk," he teased lightly.

Zechariah's face softened as he placed a gentle hand on the young woman's back, nudging her slightly forward. "Yes, I did. And here is…" he paused for effect. "This is Rebekah, my daughter."

Gdaliahu smiled, a gleam of satisfaction in his eyes that Mordecai couldn't ignore. The pit of Mordecai's stomach tightened.

Mordecai's neck hair prickled as he tilted his head and looked at Rebekah, his gaze lingering a little too long. Her bright eyes studied him intently, her lips parted in a slight twitch as if she was holding back words. Taller than most women, her dark hair and olive skin contrasted with her father's lighter complexion, and her white teeth seemed to glow. She blushed, lowering her gaze and covering her mouth with delicate fingers.

She's a pretty girl, Mordecai mused, noting she seemed around the same age as Hadassah. A shiver ran up his spine. *Gdaliahu Ha-Nasi has played me.* The realization hit him like a stone. *He tricked me into sending ten camels—just like Abraham's servant bought Rebekah for Isaac! And like a fool, I fell for it.* His thoughts spiraled. *This is what I've been set up to 'purchase,' and she knows it!*

Mordecai's mind raced. *That's why no one offered me a daughter at the World Fair. It's a conspiracy! Gdaliahu is matchmaking, hoping to unite King David's dynasty with King Saul's. How do I refuse without offending everyone?*

Sweat began to form on Mordecai's forehead. *I need to escape. Now.*

Mordecai moved toward Gdaliahu's desk, his eyes scanning for a distraction. He spotted a page inscribed with Moses's 'Song of the Sea.' Picking it up, he smiled tightly to himself and presented it to Rebekah with a formal gesture, holding it horizontally with both hands. She took the page with both hands; the text was upside down for her, but her face lit up with pride.

Mordecai observed her reaction closely—she didn't turn the page around. *She can't read,* he realized. *Uneducated.*

Zechariah reached out instinctively, then stopped midway, his face flushing with embarrassment before offering a weak smile. Rebekah glanced at her father, a mix of surprise and sadness in her eyes, before mirroring his confused smile.

Does she think I just gave her a marriage contract? Mordecai's heart sank. *Another mistake! I'm completely trapped, and through the page, I touched her!* He almost laughed at the absurdity of the situation.

"I'm… I'm sorry," Mordecai stammered, his voice trembling as he backed away. "I must leave."

He fled the room in haste, leaving Rebekah standing, clutching the paper to her chest. Her face contorted with a mixture of terror and desperation, her eyes filling with tears. She stretched her right hand toward Mordecai's retreating figure, her fingers trembling as if grasping at the air. She watched him until the door closed behind him, then slowly let her hand drop, her knees buckling slightly as despair overtook her.

After Mordecai's abrupt exit, Gdaliahu approached Rebekah and gently tried to take the page from her hands, but she resisted.

"This isn't a marriage agreement, my dear," he said softly, allowing her to keep the paper. He placed a comforting arm around her shoulders, squeezing her gently. "But it's a good sign. He understands. The seed has been planted."

Rebekah looked up at him, her tear-filled eyes pleading. "How can you be sure?"

Gdaliahu smiled confidently. "Did he ask for the money for his silk?"

Rebekah's face brightened, a hopeful glimmer returning to her eyes. She held up the paper. "May I keep this? It's something of value, isn't it? He gave me something of value!"

Gdaliahu nodded, his voice soft. "Yes, you may. And yes, he did."

Meanwhile, Mordecai hurried home, his thoughts racing. *I forgive Gdaliahu Ha-Nasi for his meddling. He means well. I should have seen through his plan sooner. A refusal now would devastate her, especially when everyone was aware.*

When he arrived home, Mordecai chose not to tell Hadassah about Rebekah.

CHAPTER 11

"I'm really upset," my grandson said, his voice heavy with frustration. "Two of my best friends fought, and now they're both mad at me because I didn't take sides. I was just trying to break it up."

I nodded, understanding the weight of his situation. "That's tough," I said gently. "But sometimes these shakeups can turn into opportunities. It might be a chance to rebuild those friendships in a better way—or even form new ones. Challenges like this can bring unexpected benefits."

I paused, then added with a smile, "This reminds me of something from the story I've been telling you. Let me share what happened next..."

———❦———

Throughout the Royal World Fair, princes from the smaller provinces each hosted the king for an evening-show, food, drink, and gifts, while the larger states hosted him twice or more. After 180 days, all the princes hosted him and the king thought it was time to conclude the event.

Uncertain of guest numbers and food preferences, the princes had brought ample supplies of food and wine. Not wanting to transport the excess back to their lands, they left the surplus with the king. As a result, the king found himself with a staggering amount of leftover provisions—far more than he could ever use or even enjoy.

To prevent waste and as a gesture of appreciation for those who had contributed to the fair's success, the king decided to host a grand banquet in the palace's paridaiza garden for all the people of Shushan.

At the same time, he instructed Queen Vashti to host a separate, formal royal gathering for the dignitaries' wives in the royal hall. In a remarkable honor, he granted her the privilege of sitting on the chair—the very royal chair of her grandfather, King Nebuchadnezzar the Great, which had been looted from Babylon.

Mordecai attended the king's banquet with the Jewish leader, while Hadassah joined the queen's celebration.

"Why does he need more parties?" Mordecai asked, watching the preparations unfold.

"The king wants to honor everyone who helped make the World Fair such a success," came the response.

"And…?" Mordecai probed.

"Well, there's another reason. We believe he simply didn't want to throw the leftovers. Every night they prepared more food and wines than was needed, and now we get to enjoy it."

"Or endure it," Mordecai quipped with a smile.

At Queen Vashti's party, Hadassah couldn't help but be struck by the grandeur of the royal hall. As she wandered through the opulent surroundings, her eyes caught on a few items bearing Hebrew inscriptions. Her mind raced—these were relics looted from the Temple in Jerusalem by the Babylonians. A pang of recognition stirred within her, but she remained silent, carefully navigating the crowd, torn between connecting with her ancestral roots and concealing her true identity.

On the seventh day of the banquet, Mordecai heard the king, slightly drunk, still, his voice unusually clear, instructing his bodyguards, "Bring Queen Vashti, wearing her royal unity crown, so she may display her beauty to my honored guests."

The atmosphere in the banquet hall shifted as the crowd parted, awaiting the queen's arrival. A song praising her beauty began to rise, anticipation rippling through the guests.

"Trouble," Gdaliahu remarked, his voice low with concern.

"Opportunity," Mordecai whispered, eyes glinting. "This will be my first time seeing the queen."

The Jewish leader tilted his head, lips tight with disapproval. "We doubt it. This is not a good situation. The queen is proud, very private." He leaned closer to Mordecai, his voice barely audible. "It's clear the king wants to flaunt her before his guests, but she will likely feel insulted."

"Why?" Mordecai asked, genuinely puzzled. "There are women at Persian parties."

Gdaliahu wagged a finger in warning. "Yes, but the king isn't just asking her to attend. He's treating her like a trophy. It's disrespectful, humiliating."

As the song ended, all eyes turned to the entrance of the royal hall, but the grand doors remained stubbornly shut. Whispers rippled through the crowd like a gathering storm.

"The guards were instructed to bring her wearing the unity crown," Mordecai noted, his brow furrowing. "But the king didn't issue a direct order to her. He expects the guards to persuade her to appear—to show off her beauty and elevate his prestige."

"She doesn't care about his Unity Crown," Gdaliahu muttered. "To her, it's a collection of worthless pebbles. Especially our contribution. Will she honor him, though?"

Mordecai's expression hardened. "The king wants her to symbolize unity—the union of nations and the empire under his reign by wearing that crown."

"It's hard to know the king's true intent," Gdaliahu countered. "He clearly wants to display her beauty. But the way he phrased his command... he didn't mention her attire. Should she show her beauty with or without clothes? Is he testing her, pushing her to see if she views him as a womanizer?"

Mordecai's eyes widened in disbelief. "You can't seriously believe he would order her to come naked?"

"It's not about what the king thinks," Gdaliahu said, frowning deeply. "It's about how she interprets it. She knows she's being tested."

Mordecai shook his head. "I still believe the king is more focused on displaying the power of his empire, not her physical appearance."

"Perhaps," Gdaliahu conceded. "But does she share that vision? After eight years of marriage, she has yet to give him an heir. That's what truly weighs on him."

A short silence fell between them before Gdaliahu spoke again, his tone more thoughtful. "We've never seen her wield any real influence over the Babylonian Empire. She couldn't command the revolting nations to stop their rebellion. She seems more a liability than an asset to him."

Time dragged on, and still, the queen did not appear. The guests, growing restless, began chanting, "Long live the king! Long live the queen!" Their voices conveyed encouragement and desperation, hoping to soothe the king's bruised pride.

"It's taking too long," Gdaliahu said, a note of anxiety creeping into his voice. "She's fortunate the king hasn't sent more guards to force her here."

Mordecai narrowed his eyes. "There's a law prohibiting anyone from approaching the royal chair or the king, uninvited. She's seated on her grandfather's royal chair, and might refuse to acknowledge the uninvited guards. She might consider their intrusion as an insult, especially since the king himself instructed her to host the royal party in that very hall, and the new command contradicts his prior command." Gadaliahu codded grimly.

"Interesting thought," Gdaliahu said, drumming his fingers on the table. "This raises a difficult question: who holds more power—the king or whoever sits on his royal chair? There's no precedent for this situation." He paused, eyes narrowing. "But isn't she just a guest in his royal hall?"

"Harvona and the other bodyguards are from ruling Babylonian families," Mordecai countered. "They were sent to escort her to the king. She knows these men, but she might see their arrival as an attempt to parade her, the Babylonian princess, like a defeated relic—publicly humiliating rather than honoring her."

"Possible," Gdaliahu conceded. "But there's another factor. The king gave his command in Persian. Does she even understand Persian? Would she grasp his exact meaning?"

Mordecai shrugged. "As far as I know, she only speaks Aramaic. The fact that the king sent all his bodyguards—leaving himself unguarded—might have alarmed her. She could suspect something's wrong, maybe even that the king's been killed, and this is a trap to lure her out."

Gdaliahu shook his head. "You're overcomplicating it. The king likely assumed she brought the crown with her. He expected her to host the women's party while showcasing the crown, symbolizing the unity of the empire. But what if she didn't bring it to the party with her, and was caught disrespecting the king?"

Mordecai nodded thoughtfully. "That makes sense."

The crowd continued to wait, whispers intensifying as time passed, but Queen Vashti did not appear.

"She's proud—like Michal, daughter of King Saul," Gdaliahu observed, his tone sharp. "She knows how to deliver a royal insult."

Mordecai stiffened at the comparison to his ancestral aunt. But Gdaliahu's point hit home. "We should move to a safer spot," he suggested.

The king's bodyguards returned without the queen, and a hush fell over the crowd. The tension was palpable. The king made a circular motion with his hand, signaling for the festivities to continue. He sat motionless, his gaze intense, lips pressed tight, and jaw clenched, as the party resumed around him.

"Maybe she asked for more time to explain, change her clothes, or retrieve her crown and will come later," Mordecai suggested.

"From the look on his face, We doubt it," Gdaliahu replied gravely. "How can she admit she didn't have the crown?"

"Do you think he's drunk?" Mordecai asked, eyeing the king.

"No," Gdaliahu said firmly. "He's completely in control of his senses."

More entertainment was provided, but the king remained unmoved—no laughter, no wine, no enjoyment. He sat unblinking, his anger simmering beneath the surface. After some time, he quietly exited the gathering, without the usual formalities or farewells.

"The king's leaving," Gdaliahu whispered. "He's furious. She's finished."

"Yes," Mordecai agreed. "The only question is, how?"

As they left the palace, nervous guards stopped Gdaliahu and Mordecai at the gate. They were searched and forced to identify themselves. The guards scribbled their names onto the guest list with shaking hands.

Hadassah came home late and immediately looked for Mordecai to share what had transpired at the queen's party. She had heard the back-and-forth between the king's and queen's guards, translating from Persian to Aramaic.

"Did you see your stone in the queen's crown?" Mordecai asked, trying to piece things together.

"For seven days, I waited," Hadassah said, her disappointment evident. "But the queen never wore the Unity Crown with my stone. Instead, she wore an ivory crown adorned with large rubies and sapphires."

Mordecai nodded, understanding the implications. *She didn't bring the Unity Crown,* he mused. Gdaliahu had been right—the queen had been caught "naked" symbolically. A smile flickered across his face at the thought—*the naked truth.*

The next afternoon, Harvona arrived using a hidden tunnel connecting the palace to Mordecai's residence. After climbing a rope ladder concealed within a hollowed marble column, he joined Mordecai in a small room atop the palace tower. Mordecai ordered herbal tea and slices of sweet bread, and for a while, they ate in silence.

Harvona was the first to speak. "We went to the queen's royal hall. Mehuman carried the king's flag. When we arrived, the queen's personal bodyguards blocked us. Mehuman, our leader, knelt before her with the flag raised high and repeated the king's order in Persian."

"Big mistake," Mordecai commented, his mind working through the scenario. "He lacked initiative. His task was to bring the queen, not intimidate her by making the king's command seem rigid. Now, he's turned his own failure into the king's. Mehuman will probably be dismissed—or worse."

Harvona sighed and continued, "The queen was furious. She didn't acknowledge the command and instead had her bodyguard warn us that we had entered uninvited and could face the death penalty. I wasn't sure if we had the right to defend ourselves."

"You did," Mordecai affirmed. "The law protects anyone executing the king's orders. You could have fought or killed anyone obstructing you."

Harvona nodded. "Mehuman hesitated but repeated the king's order again. The queen just turned her shoulder to us, chin raised. So we withdrew."

"When the king left the party, he ordered Bizzetha, Mehuman's lieutenant, to secure the palace and arrest any Babylonian general attempting to flee. The king was trembling with nervous energy and ordered the identification of all the women at the queen's party."

Mordecai pieced it together: *The king fears rebellion—that some Babylonian general might try to escape the city dressed as a woman, in an attempt to return and rescue Queen Vashti.*

Harvona's voice softened. "The king promoted me to first lieutenant of his bodyguards, and ordered me to stay with him. Mehuman is gone."

Mordecai smiled slightly at Harvona's promotion. "He's terrified of rebellion," Mordecai murmured.

"The next day," Harvona continued, "the king convened his ministers. They debated the queen's refusal. She wasn't there, nor did she come at night to explain herself."

Mordecai raised an eyebrow. "So she didn't even attempt to justify her refusal?"

"No. And then Memucan—the lowest-ranking junior minister— was the first to speak as is the custom in life and death cases. He suggested that the queen's behavior insulted all husbands and that a 'better' queen replace her from among her friends."

Mordecai's mind raced. *A better queen? Can that even be possible?* He kept his face neutral, though inside, he weighed new ideas. "What else was discussed?"

"The higher-ranked ministers debated whether Vashti had the right to refuse the guards since they entered uninvited and whether sitting in the royal chair gave her more authority than the king himself. They argued whether her lack of speaking Persian was a valid excuse."

Mordecai leaned forward, intrigued. "And what was the final decision?"

Harvona's eyes darkened. "The king agreed with Memucan's punishment but didn't order an immediate search for a new queen. The decree that came out was more subtle: 'Man rules in his own house and speaks according to his people's language.'"

Mordecai exhaled. *They made it seem as if Vashti had violated a known law.*

"Yes," Mordecai nodded, "the decree clarified that the king is stronger than a person siting on his chair. But most people will misinterpret it. They'll think the king has permitted men to humiliate their wives publicly, even parade them naked."

Harvona's face paled. "Naked? You think people believe that?"

Mordecai raised an eyebrow. "It's what people are whispering. They think the king demanded Vashti appear wearing nothing but her crown to flaunt her naked beauty."

Harvona shook his head, disgusted. "I can't believe this about our king."

Mordecai sighed.

Harvona quietly took his leave.

Mordecai sat twirling a lock of hair around his finger. He contemplated a shocking idea of how to get a *'better queen' for the king. Will anyone else come with a candidate before me?*

Soon, Mordecai thought, *I'll speak with Gdaliahu Ha-Nasi.*

———≈———

Queen Vashti was quietly stripped of her crown and placed under house arrest in a modest residence on the palace grounds, heavily guarded. Her name was erased from public discourse, and no one dared speak in her defense. Even the most influential ministers remained silent.

Though the king's anger was palpable, he stopped short of ordering her execution. Mordecai speculated that, despite everything, the king still harbored feelings for Vashti. Deep down, perhaps Ahasuerus hoped she might one day beg for forgiveness, allowing him to regain his wounded pride.

Under the new decree, Aramaic was stripped of its status as the empire's official language. Each nation within the kingdom was now permitted to speak its own language. The former Babylonian hostages, now serving as leaders of their respective countries, were reassigned to act as translators and represent their people at the king's gate.

The decree, translated into every language across the empire, was swiftly delivered to all the provinces by the king's riders.

Meanwhile, as a joke, Harvona, with a hint of mischief, confided with a friend that the queen had refused to appear before the king, wearing only her crown. What began as a lighthearted comment soon exploded into rampant gossip, spreading like wildfire across the empire.

An exciting time lies ahead, Mordecai mused. *The king needs a new queen—and quickly. He needs an heir.* A sudden unease settled over him. *Why am I even thinking about this?* The image of Rebekah flashed in his mind. *Rebekah?* He paused, his heart beating faster, unsettled by the unexpected thought.

CHAPTER 12

"**I** need to complete a project for my Bar Mitzvah," my grandson announced unexpectedly, his voice carrying a mix of excitement and uncertainty.

"Oh? What do you have in mind?" I asked, curious to hear more.

"Something environmental, I think," he replied thoughtfully, as if still piecing the idea together.

I smiled, feeling proud of his initiative. "That sounds like a great idea," I said encouragingly. "You could really make a difference—something that helps the world, even in a small way, can have a lasting impact."

———≈———

Ever since the king decreed that each community within his empire could speak its own language, all royal orders had been translated into these languages and stamped with the king's official signet. Gdaliahu appointed Mordecai as the official Hebrew translator for the Jewish people. This position gave Mordecai immense power, as neither the king nor his officials could read or verify the Hebrew translations themselves. Conveying the king's orders required careful precision—any failure on the part of the Jewish community to comply could result in severe punishment. Mordecai took this responsibility seriously and earned great respect for his diligence and attention to detail.

With Jewish communities scattered across the empire, Mordecai produced handwritten copies of the king's decrees for every region. His office at the king's gate became the busiest of all, producing nearly half of the empire's official documents. Along with each decree, Mordecai included personal letters addressed to Jewish leaders and merchants he had met during the World Fair. These correspondences became priceless to him, as they often contained crucial reports about local weather, crop conditions, snowpack, disease outbreaks, famines, food shortages, celebrations, unrest, inventions, and more. Mordecai realized that seemingly minor events, like rainfall and snowpack in distant mountains, could predict future floods in the river valleys. He also tracked the spread of seasonal diseases as they moved westward from the east.

Mordecai used this information to predict economic trends, requesting details about new products, regional events, and trade disruptions. What seemed like ordinary news to others, he analyzed to anticipate shortages and identify opportunities to buy surplus goods cheaply and sell them for profit. *His vision was an efficient system with prearranged contracts and firm prices, where fully loaded wagons transported goods between regions, creating a mutually beneficial trade network.*

Mordecai, valuing education, urged Jewish communities to send their brightest young men to his academy in Shushan. Admission was based on merit and need, regardless of bloodline or status. The academy grew to a thousand students, with older students mentoring younger ones, as Hadassah had done with Sarah.

Mordecai's students assisted him in managing the empire's trade through his newly established Information Bureau of Commercial Enterprise (IBCE), gathering intelligence and analyzing trends. Mordecai treated them as his own children, and nurtured them as future leaders, viewing this as key to fulfilling the mission he had promised his late grandfather. These students also served as runners, personal guards, and, if needed, a private army.

Senior students collected ideas, which Mordecai reviewed. After blessing the Sabbath wine, he read the best seven aloud, naming contributors. Solid business concepts were implemented through the IBCE. Mordecai encouraged further discussion on proposals he didn't fully grasp, recognizing that even flawed ideas pointed to underlying issues.

One standout student, Yavin, frequently offered insightful suggestions demonstrating a deep understanding of commerce. Quiet and unassuming, Yavin caught Mordecai's attention, earning a promotion to manage the IBCE and oversee the students. Mordecai discreetly set Yavin up with a merchant's shop, connecting it to nearby homes through secret tunnels for added security.

One evening, Mordecai sat with Yavin in a hidden underground room beneath the shop. The space, secure with multiple entrances and sturdy locks, was cool and well-ventilated. A narcissus flower in a vase filled the air with a sweet scent, while musicians practiced nearby, masking any sound that might escape. The setting was perfect for a private conversation, free from spies or eavesdroppers. Mordecai emphasized, "We follow Gdaliahu Ha-Nasi's 'double D' motto—Delegation and Devotion. We delegate freedom of choice, but expect complete *devotion* to our culture. No mercy, no second chances. Do you understand?"

Yavin nodded, fully aware that this was about much more than commerce—preserving their people and ensuring their future.

"Good," Mordecai said, his eyes sharp with intensity. "Now, explain it to your team. Ensure they know—our success depends on their understanding of this principle."

With another nod from Yavin, Mordecai continued. "After observing the World Fair, I envisioned a trade network connecting the empire." He sketched a map, marking major cities and the new roads. "Caravans will travel fully loaded between India, Anatolia, and Egypt. Jews will run this system. Instead of carrying money payments, we'll use sworn promissory notes that we guarantee. Pre-arranged Contracts with firm prices will be honored, risks minimized, and huggling and abuse avoided. This is our 'Sweet Route'—a path to preserve the Jewish people."

"Sweet?" Yavin asked, puzzled.

"Yes, sweet," Mordecai replied. "I want to bring sweet success — like honey—to our people, strengthening their ties to our religion and heritage."

He handed Yavin a parchment scroll tied with yarn. "This is my book, listing merchants I met at the World Fair. Meet them, build your shipping teams, and bring this plan to life. Have them sign your book of credit and seal each deal with a handshake. Our survival depends on personal connections. Every associate must honor our traditions, be literate in Hebrew, and understand this isn't just commerce—it's about our future. This must be a united Jewish effort across the empire."

"I understand," Yavin replied. "It's like the pilgrimage caravans to Jerusalem, but now for all the major cities of the empire."

"Exactly," Mordecai said. "Improve the plan where needed. Encourage your team to contribute ideas and experiment. Don't fear mistakes. We'll learn and grow."

"I'll return," Yavin promised.

Mordecai grinned. "Is that a threat or a promise?"

———≈———

Gdaliahu called Yavin for a private consultation. Yavin first traveled to Egypt, accompanied by a married teacher and his young son. Upon arrival, a speeding rider delivered him a fresh apple from Persia.

While visiting Zechariah's palace, suddenly, Rebekah burst into the room, exclaiming, "I heard an emissary of Mordecai has arrived!"

"Not exactly..., an emissary," Yavin replied, handing her the beautiful apple.

Rebekah calmed down, admiring the fruit, its vibrant colors reminding her of Garden of Eden—*Gift of knowledge, good and bad.* She took a bite, savoring its sweet and sour taste. But then, she noticed a half-worm wriggling inside. Trying not to show her discomfort, she forced a smile. *Can't insult Mordecai. A little worm won't spoil my happiness,* she thought, and continued eating around.

Yavin smiled at Rebekah and then addressed Zechariah, "Mordecai won't marry an uneducated woman."

"Uneducated?" Rebekah's eyes flashed with insult, then, fuming, she turned to her father. "Why didn't you educate me!"

"I've brought a teacher for Rebekah," Yavin cut in before the explosion. "She can study with the teacher's son—if she wishes," Yavin added, raising a calming hand. "Let's not argue."

Zechariah, flustered, began to speak, but Rebekah interrupted, "I *want* to be educated!" Her voice trembled.

Zechariah bowed his head. "I was only trying to..."

"Mordecai gave me something of value, and I accepted it," Rebekah said firmly. "I've dedicated myself to him. It's your duty to deliver me to him."

Yavin held back his frustration. *Why hadn't you started her education already? Didn't you realize that Mordecai had tested her and found her wanting?* He looked at Rebekah and said, "When you're ready, write a letter to Mordecai by yourself." Then, with a subtle smile, he added, "He's sensitive to unfamiliar smells—he uses narcissus as a defense."

Rebekah nodded and left in a huff.

Yavin then explained the IBCE to Zechariah, using charts and diagrams to outline schedules and profits. Despite the external and internal heat, Yavin remained composed, speaking slowly and maintaining eye contact. Thrilled by the prospects, Zechariah eagerly offered to sign Yavin's book as the first merchant.

Yavin, relieved and pleased, shook Zechariah's hand. The presentation had been a success, and with Zechariah on board, Yavin knew other merchants would soon follow. He felt a surge of pride, confident that Mordecai would be pleased with the progress.

———≈———

Afterward, Yavin traveled extensively, from Egypt to Anatolia to India, visiting Jewish communities and learning about their commercial practices. When he returned to Mordecai's palace, he was brimming with excitement and gifts.

"Look at the treasures I've brought back!" Yavin exclaimed, his enthusiasm palpable. "Different varieties of rice—white, brown, black, short, long, and thick—and just smell these herbs!" He was visibly delighted. "The experience was amazing. I felt your authority guiding me, like God Himself was with me. The Jews welcomed me warmly, treating me as a brother and honoring me in your name. I showcased my goods, shared samples, and they eagerly offered their own products to impress you. They're ready to join our transport system and follow the rules. I've compiled a list of traders and had them sign our book of credit."

"Excellent news," Mordecai said, clearly pleased. "This will help prevent the assimilation and extinction of the Jews. I'm thrilled with your success!"

"As you wish," Yavin replied, satisfied that the gift was well-received.

———————

Mordecai's system of prearranged shipments using letters of credit became a model of efficiency and profitability, bringing immense prosperity to the Jewish communities. Jews controlled the entire supply chain—wholesale merchants, haulers, shopkeepers, innkeepers, stable owners—allowing them to ensure loyalty and maintain internal cohesion. The success of these businesses reinforced their national identity, language, and customs.

Their strict hygiene and food preparation standards prevented the spread of diseases as Jewish merchants traveled vast trade routes through India, China, Egypt, and Anatolia. Moving from one Jewish community to another along the new royal roads, they enjoyed hospitality and support that gave them a competitive edge. Non-Jewish merchants, in contrast, often fell ill or struggled with communication, making them less effective rivals. Over time, Jewish commerce became dominant.

As the Jewish network thrived, more merchants joined the IBCE, purchasing charters for specific commodities and agreeing to its rules.

Many merchants sent their children to study at Mordecai's academy, ensuring that education and connections kept their families within the community.

The Jewish prosperity also enriched the empire's cities, prompting princes and governors to issue decrees protecting Jews, with the penalty of death for those who harmed them. While this was a positive development, enforcement remained difficult in rural areas where evidence was harder to gather, and highway robberies occurred.

Reflecting on the success of his system, Mordecai thought, *This would sustain Jewish culture and finance as a nation. But have I truly achieved my mission? Am I free?*

———❦———

Mordecai received news of a plague in the east, threatening to spread across the empire. While Jewish hygiene practices might protect his people, the plague posed a grave threat to the stability and prosperity they had built. Concerned for both his community and his leadership, Mordecai acted swiftly. He ordered merchants to suspend all trade and instructed Jewish communities to avoid contact with the sick, the dead, and anyone exposed to the disease. He mandated strict hygiene measures: covering faces, frequent handwashing, and isolating the ill for seven days until a priest declared them healthy.

Soon after, reports came that hungry people from plague-stricken cities were fleeing, spreading the disease. Despite the danger, Mordecai instructed his people to take the risk and provide food to those in need in infected areas. To his amazement, most of the Jewish community remained healthy. Grateful, Mordecai thanked God for what seemed to be a divine miracle.[1]

Meanwhile, Jewish merchants faced another persistent threat— robbers and kidnappers, particularly from the Amalekites. These age-old enemies were notorious for ambushing travelers, enslaving them,

---

[1]   Today we know that contact with animals immuned them.

and sending ransom demands, often accompanied by body parts, to their families. A custom developed within Jewish communities to visit slave markets, identifying and freeing fellow Jews. Yavin employed a clever method, asking slaves to recite passages from the Bible or prayer book, to verify their Jewish identity.

"Nasty business," Mordecai told Yavin. "If we pay, we encourage them to kidnap, but they would have enslaved them anyway, at least, because we pay a premium, they have the incentive to bring them to us and sell."

"Yes," Yavin said. "For risk and guards, we will just raise prices."

One freed slave recounted his harrowing experience to Mordecai. "My father and I paid Amalekite guides for safe passage, but another group of Amalekites attacked us, killing my old father and enslaving me. Later, I found out the guides were in league with the thieves. I learned that their chieftains pass down secret knowledge about trade routes, hidden water sources, and corrupt officials only to their children. If all the Amalekite leaders and their sons were eliminated in a single day, their criminal society would collapse."

Yavin suggested, "What if we inflict a plague of the firstborn on them?"

Mordecai replied thoughtfully, "It's a good idea, but not something we can achieve now. They are a society obsessed with death, proud to die in battle. We are merchants, and they are robbers."

Yavin continued, "I've begun recording the names of the Amalekite leaders. Should we approach the chief law enforcer for help?"

Mordecai grimaced. "The Agagite? The descendant of King Agag, whom my ancestor Saul defeated? He's no ally. He profits from the loot his people steal from us and bribes the king's ministers to keep his position. The king believes the 'gifts' he receives are unclaimed goods, but they're stolen bribes. When I once reported a thief to him, he pretended to care but simply demanded a bigger cut from the thief. Since then, that thief has attacked us even more."

Yavin added, "His palace in Shushan is almost as grand as the king's. He's robbing our caravans and growing richer by the day."

Mordecai's expression darkened. "I wouldn't be surprised if he was involved in the deaths of Hadassah's parents on their journey to Jerusalem. I wouldn't be shocked to find her parents' jewelry in his possession. But for now, we can't act. The Amalekites know the trade routes better than anyone. Their unjust success will eventually lead to their downfall. Their secrecy will be their undoing."

CHAPTER 13

"You mentioned your friends fought. How did it end?" I asked.

"Well, they didn't talk to me for a few days, but each came to me separately, trying to reconnect. I told them I'd be friends again once they made up. Then, I suggested they settle it with an arm-wrestling match. They agreed—on the condition that I joined in."

"So, how did it go?"

"I didn't win, but now the three of us are best friends again."

———❦———

When Mordecai learned that King Ahasuerus was growing impatient and irritable, he saw an opportunity to advance his plan to protect the Jews. He quickly arranged a secret meeting with Gdaliahu, the Jewish leader, at his palace.

"Peace upon you, Gdaliahu Ha-Nasi," Mordecai greeted.

"Upon you peace," Gdaliahu replied, smiling warmly from his chair.

They shared dinner and discussed the new temple in Jerusalem and the fate of the Jewish people—whether to return to Judea or remain scattered across the empire. Gdaliahu reflected, "Our homeland preserves our identity, but remaining dispersed offers safety. Perhaps both strategies together are best."

Mordecai's eyes lit up. "May we speak privately?"

With a subtle gesture, Gdaliahu dismissed the servants. Mordecai leaned in. "I have a risky plan to crown a new queen. I need your counsel and support."

"Go… on," Gdaliahu urged.

"At Queen Vashti's hearing, it was suggested the king find 'a better queen.' He hasn't acted because he's reluctant to risk losing prestige again. It is impossible to find a 'better queen' in beauty, education, prestige, and pedigree of Babylonian King Nebuchadnezzar who will unite the empire.

"The king desires a son, and soon. A child-king with a regent would lead to instability; for that, he needs a wife," Mordecai explained. "I believe we can find someone beyond the king's wildest dreams, one who will bring even more honor than Vashti did, someone who will fulfill his desires and also protect the Jews. But we must act quickly, before the position of queen is filled."

Intrigued, Gdaliahu asked, "How?"

Mordecai said, "Vashti wounded his pride; now many women will heal it by giving him what Vashti refused. The king will love the idea—he can show Vashti what she lost. Revenge and pride are powerful motivators.

"We'll open a beauty contest to everyone—nobles and commoners alike—from every corner of the empire. The only requirements will be that the women must be young, unmarried, beautiful, and willing to participate, and the king will choose the best in his eyes," Mordecai said confidently.

Gdaliahu nodded thoughtfully.

"We already have several allies in the king's court. If you agree, they'll organize the entire event. They'll eagerly participate because it will bring them power and fame, serving their own interests," Mordecai added.

"Fascinating," Gdaliahu replied. "But how does this protect the Jews?"

Mordecai's smile broadened. "That's the best part. I believe we can choose the winner before the contest even begins—she'll help protect our people."

Gdaliahu raised an eyebrow. "And how do you plan to ensure that?"

Mordecai leaned closer and outlined the details of his plan.

Gdaliahu listened carefully, then shook his head slightly, though a smile crept across his face. "It has real potential. We take it you already have someone in mind?"

"I do. My daughter, Hadassah," Mordecai said firmly.

Gdaliahu's surprise was visible.

"She's the perfect choice," Mordecai continued. "She already speaks Persian, among other languages. She knows our history and loves learning. Plus, she's our princess in every sense. She meets all the requirements—charm, beauty, and intelligence."

When Gdaliahu remained silent, Mordecai pressed on, sensing the importance of his words. "Even if our plan to crown her fails, I can ensure her safety. Michael, Shimon's son, wants to marry her. And if that doesn't work, I'll revert her status back to that of my cousin and marry her myself."

A flicker of doubt crossed Mordecai's mind. *Hadassah? Rebekah?* His emotions warred within him. As he glanced at Gdaliahu, he noticed the older man's face had darkened with tension. *He knows what I'm thinking,* Mordecai realized. *He's stressed.*

Gdaliahu stroked his beard, clearly weighing the risks. "Hadassah would have to break our laws to marry a non-Jew. We would hate to ask her to go against the Torah. This is painful."

Mordecai opened his mouth to protest, but Gdaliahu spoke quickly. "She would be marrying a pagan…"

"Joseph married the daughter of an Egyptian priest," Mordecai countered. "Tamar, Ruth the Moabite, Naamah the Ammonite, and even Bath-Sheba—each used their 'feminine power' to fulfill a greater purpose."

Gdaliahu raised his eyebrows slightly at the boldness of Mordecai's examples, alluding to his own lineage. He sighed, softening his tone. "But we may not need Hadassah for years. Would she remain loyal?"

"If anyone can, she can," Mordecai responded confidently. "Hadassah understands the gravity of this mission. Her efforts will strengthen ours."

Gdaliahu leaned back, deep in thought. "But is this risk justified?"

Mordecai's voice was firm. "I'll explain everything to her—the dangers, the reasons. Remember, Joseph was sold into slavery, and Moses floated down the Nile among crocodiles. This is about preventing the assimilation or extinction of our people. The Jews—and Hadassah—will have to take this risk. I believe it's part of God's plan, just as it was in Egypt. It will be painful, and people may call me harsh. But the wise will understand, just as they did with Moses."

Gdaliahu's expression darkened further. "Are you certain the Jews are in immediate danger?"

Mordecai's face grew serious, the weight of history pressing on him. "No one can ever be completely sure. But look at our history. The ten tribes have all but disappeared, assimilated into the Assyrian empire. We can't let that happen to us."

Gdaliahu considered Mordecai's proposal in silence, his fingers drumming lightly on the armrest of his chair. After a long pause, he nodded slowly. "You've convinced us. Your plan has a real chance of success. Hadassah could play a role as crucial as Joseph and Moses did in Egypt. She will be our Queen of Persia, she will save our people."

Mordecai's heart quickened at Gdaliahu's agreement, but the older man raised a hand, his expression grave. "But before we proceed, we must speak with her. She needs to understand the mission fully—the dangers, the responsibilities. We cannot move forward unless we know she's willing and able."

Mordecai paced the dimly lit room atop his palace tower, his mind a whirlwind of calculations and contingencies. The plan was complex, and every detail had to be perfect before bringing Hadassah into the fold. The stakes were too high to leave anything to chance.

Harvona, seated across from him, listened intently, his eyes wide with enthusiasm. He leaned forward eagerly as Mordecai laid out the intricacies of the plan. "This is brilliant, Mordecai," Harvona said, his voice low but charged with excitement. "I'll speak with Hegai, the headmaster of the king's house of women. He controls everything there—if we get him on our side, we're as good as set."

Mordecai nodded. Harvona's deep ties within the royal court were crucial, but Hegai's support would be even more critical. The headmaster held the keys to the women's quarters and could shape the queen's contest to their advantage.

Without wasting time, Harvona sought out Hegai. As soon as they met, it was clear Hegai was eager to align himself with such a plan. The idea of one of his protégées becoming queen thrilled him. He knew that if Hadassah were crowned, his own status within the palace would skyrocket. Not only would Hadassah owe him her loyalty, but the king himself would be in his debt.

Hegai's eyes gleamed as Harvona shared the plan. "Not knowing her, but trusting your selection, I'll make sure she's ready in every way," he promised, his voice brimming with confidence. "The best tutors, the finest clothes, the most exquisite beauty treatments. She'll outshine everyone."

With Hegai on board, the final piece of the puzzle clicked into place. Mordecai's plan was now set in motion, and the anticipation gnawed at him. The risks were staggering, but the rewards—for the Jews, for their survival—were beyond measure.

The only thing left now was to tell Hadassah.

CHAPTER 14

"Plan your future as if it's already done," I told my grandson, noticing the spark of curiosity in his eyes. "Build a vision so vivid that others can see it too. When people can picture it clearly, they'll want to be part of it."

He nodded, deep in thought. "So, it's like giving them something real to believe in?"

"Exactly," I replied with a smile. "That's how ideas come to life."

As they dined together that evening, Mordecai observed Hadassah with a heavy heart, burdened by the decisions he would soon have to make. At sixteen, she had grown into a graceful young woman—tall and slender, with dark, sparkling eyes that held an inquisitive gleam, and long, soft brown hair that flowed down her back. She was full of life, always moving, talking, laughing, and peppering him with questions. The home she managed for him was warm and vibrant, a reflection of her presence. The thought of losing her, of sending her into the uncertainties ahead, filled him with a deep, unshakable ache.

I wish it could be different, Mordecai thought, his heart heavy with the weight of his decision. *I want her to stay as my daughter forever. But I have no choice—our people need her. No one else has her poise, intelligence, or grace.*

His eyes filled with tears, and he quickly brushed one away. *This is harder than I imagined. Now I understand how Abraham must have felt when he was prepared to sacrifice Isaac.* The thought cut deep. *I am sending her into a life of uncertainty, much like Joseph when he was sold into slavery. Yes, she'll live in a palace, but it will be a gilded cage.*

He wiped away another tear and forced a weak smile, a pit of loneliness already forming in his chest. *And who will take care of me? Who will manage my needs—my food, clothes, and all the little chaos of daily life?* The thought of losing Hadassah, not just as his daughter but as the heart of his household, left a hollow ache in its place.

Hadassah noticed the pain in his expression and furrowed her brow. "Why are you looking at me like that? Did I do something wrong?"

Mordecai shook his head. "No, you've done everything just right. That's why I'm so proud of you."

She blushed and looked away. "You only say that because you're my father. You molded me."

Mordecai gently took her hands in his. "No, I say it because it's true. Have I ever lied to you?"

She hesitated, then raised an eyebrow, her lips curving into a teasing smile. "Hmm. Does manipulating count?"

He laughed softly, despite the tightness in his chest. "I have something very important to discuss with you. As you know, the king is searching for a new queen. Memucan, the junior ministers, suggested finding a 'better queen'—someone who could surpass Queen Vashti."

Hadassah laughed, pulling her hands back. "That might be hard to do. Queen Vashti was incredibly beautiful, and her lineage was impeccable. Do you know what I heard?" Her cheeks flushed with excitement as she leaned in, lowering her voice. "The king supposedly ordered her to show her beauty—wearing only her crown!"

Her cheeks turned crimson, and she quickly looked down, clearly embarrassed. "I would have died of shame if he'd asked me to do something like that."

Mordecai chuckled softly. "That's just gossip, Hadassah. I was there when he made the request, and it wasn't as scandalous as people think. You have to read between the lines. I believe the king wanted to showcase his empire's unity, wealth, and power. By refusing, Vashti insulted him and disrespected the entire empire. During the women's party, she didn't wear the Unity Crown—as you told me. She deliberately disrespected him for seven days, and to cover her offense, she refused to obey his order, trying legal excuses. But that wasn't her real offense."

Hadassah's eyes sparkled, intrigued by the idea of a hidden message. "How did you figure that out?" she asked, her voice full of admiration.

"At first, I wasn't sure," Mordecai admitted, leaning back thoughtfully. "But I started looking at it from different angles. And when the new decree was issued, it all clicked. This wasn't just about beauty. If you think carefully, you'll see it too."

Hadassah's eyes widened with curiosity. "Give me a hint?" she asked eagerly, leaning forward.

"Yes," Mordecai nodded. "At the women's party, Queen Vashti was sitting on the royal chair, the very one King Cyrus took from Babylon."

Hadassah's eyes lit up as she pieced it together. "'The king rules in his house,' but ... sitting on that chair, she felt she had equal authority. And, just as you said, the honor lies with the person, not the chair. So she refused to acknowledge the uninvited guards or even understand their Persian. She could have sent the guards to get clarifications, giving her time to fetch her crown and save face, but she didn't."

She paused, shaking her head in amazement. "I would never have guessed it in a hundred years."

Mordecai shook his head. "You're selling yourself short. You're brilliant—maybe even as smart as Joseph." He smiled warmly. "I have no doubt you would've figured it out. That's why we have an important task for you."

"Me?" Hadassah blinked, her surprise evident.

Mordecai gently took her hands again. "Yes, you. You are of royal blood.... It's time for you to step into your full power." He paused, watching her reaction. "The Jewish leader, Gdaliahu, wants to meet you. If he approves, we have a plan to crown you the next queen of Persia."

Mordecai continued, "With God's help, you will protect the Jews, just as Joseph and Moses did in Egypt. You will work from within to aid us."

Hadassah shook her head. "But how? I wouldn't know what to do."

"We will guide you. Queen Vashti's downfall came because of her empty pedigree, lack of real power, poor social skills, and lack of supportive friends. You are the opposite. Everyone loves you."

"How? You still didn't answer."

"We're organizing a beauty contest. Hegai, the headmaster of the House of Women, will guide you. Follow his instructions closely. Stay alert and learn. I'll be in regular contact with him."

Hadassah said solemnly, "So, as if implementing Memucan's advice to look for a 'better queen' among her royal friends, you are opening the competition to all women, including me."

"Yes. The 'beauty contest' is a way to get the king's attention and make sure you stand out. We'll ensure you'll be the best-prepared candidate. We don't know what the other contestants will do and how the king will view them. And with God's help, you'll be selected as the next queen. The unity crown with your Judea stone awaits you. Think on this tonight. Tomorrow, we'll discuss further."

Hadassah woke with a start, her heart racing and her body drenched in sweat. The dream had been so vivid—she had been sold into slavery, managing her master's house. One day, her master approached her, gripping the edge of her nightgown. He waited patiently while she slipped out of the garment. Naked, she ran, ran, and ran.

The parallel to Joseph's story was clear. His trials led to power and salvation for his family. Perhaps this was a sign, a confirmation that her own path, though daunting, was a part of a greater plan.

As sleep reclaimed her, a sense of calm and purpose settled over her. *Wow, I was Joseph in Egypt. Yes. He will be my guide.* She slept peacefully the rest of the night.

My grandson yawned. "That's enough for today," I said softly. "Time to sleep. We'll pick it up on the way to school tomorrow."

"No, just one more section," he murmured, eyes heavy. Before I could reply, he was already asleep, lost in his dreams.

CHAPTER 15

The following morning, after dismissing the servants at breakfast, Mordecai turned to Hadassah with a serious tone. "It's time for you to take on a new name. Do you know that Hadassah means 'myrtle' in Hebrew?"

Hadassah nodded. "Yes, I love those flowers. Brides often carry them—they have such a lovely scent…"

Mordecai chuckled. "So does the goddess Ishtar, the Babylonian and Persian deity of Love, Fertility, and War," he added, his voice carrying a hint of irony. "From now on, you will be known as Esther, in honor of Ishtar. When the king grew angry with Queen Vashti, he claimed that Ishtar had abandoned his home. You will bring the goddess back into the king's palace—and into his heart."

Hadassah's eyes widened, a wave of panic rushing over her. "How can I worship Ishtar?"

Mordecai gently shook his head. "Who said anything about worship? It's just a game. You don't need to believe in her," he reassured her with a smile. " Look at me—my name is Mordecai, named after the god Marduk. I've played this part for years, and it's served me well." He loudly laughed, quickly covering his mouth.

"But how will I even do that? I hardly know anything about Ishtar," Hadassah said, raising her hands in confusion.

Mordecai leaned in. "The Love Hymn of Ishtar will guide you," he explained. "It tells the story of how Ishtar descended to the underworld to plead with Satan to ease the suffering of her people. As she passed through each of the seven gates of hell, she shed one layer of clothing at each one. By the last gate, she stood completely bare, and Satan captured her. With Ishtar imprisoned, love vanished from Earth. But the god Marduk declaring that love is stronger than death, ordered her release, restoring love to the world. The king, his ministers, priests, and generals are all familiar with this story."

Hadassah nodded slowly, absorbing his words, her expression thoughtful. "So Esther is Ishtar, you are Marduk, and together we'll confront Satan. But first," she paused, her voice quiet yet steady, "I need to be crowned."

Mordecai smiled. "Exactly. And you should know that traditionally, the king's wife and mother manage the king's life, like you are mine. Right now, no one is guiding our king. With God's help, you'll wield the influence of both, and have the power to raise your children as you see fit."

Hadassah listened intently, her eyes betraying her anxiety as Mordecai continued to lay out his plan.

"Remember how I outmaneuvered Shimon when I was invited to his house? I walked into the lion's den with force, and he was too stunned, unable to resist my demands. We'll do the same with the king. We'll trap him with an honor he cannot decline. Your appearance will secure the crown, but it is your wisdom that will truly reign."

Hadassah sighed deeply. "Do you really think I can pull this off?"

"Yes!" Mordecai exclaimed, pounding his fist into his palm for emphasis. "Look at all you've already achieved. The golden Unity Crown—with your Ten-Commendments stone—will be yours. God has chosen you for this."

"The Unity Crown…?" Hadassah asked softly, her voice barely a whisper. "My God…"

"The beauty contest is merely a way for you to present yourself to the king, amidst a crowd of other beautiful women," Mordecai explained. "Everyone believes it's about looks, but the king doesn't want just another pretty look. He's seeking someone who enhances his power and prestige. You, and only you, will offer him that. Are you willing?"

A heavy silence followed. Mordecai waited patiently, silently counting to ten before starting to count back.

Hadassah's expression was blank, but her mind raced. *What should I do? Can I really do this? This plan is so intricate, but it has a chance of success and could be crucial for our people. But if I go, who will care for Mordecai? He relies on me. And Michael—will he hate me? Will he find another love? And Sara...*

Hadassah squeezed her forehead, deep lines creasing between her brows. *If I refuse, will Mordecai select someone else? Oh my God—Sara! He'll pick Sara! I'll be discarded, and sent back to Shimon's kitchen. Oh my God...*

Taking a deep breath, and exhaling slowly, calming her thoughts. *Mordecai has trained me well, and now is's time for me to serve our people.*

She looked up, her voice steady. "You're asking me to make a sacrifice, like Abraham with Isaac. But at least I have a choice—and my chances are far better than Isaac's." Hadassah paused, closed her eyes, took a deep breath, opened them with determination, and said, "I will go!"

Mordecai smiled, feeling a wave of relief. *I am surrounded by Rebekahs,* he thought, feeling confident in Hadassah's strength.

Relaxing, Mordecai added, "It is arranged. Later today, Gdaliahu Ha-Nasi, will evaluate your qualifications."

Hadassah's eyes widened in surprise. *How did he know I would agree?* she wondered, but soon enough, she accepted her path.

CHAPTER 16

Hadassah whispered her new name over and over: "Esther, Esther." It still felt foreign on her tongue and in her ears, but she trusted her father and his plan.

Everything was happening so quickly. Soon, she was in a chariot, on her way to Gdaliahu's palace. As the wheels rattled down the narrow, dusty streets, Esther clasped and unclasped her hands. Trying to recall all the lessons Mordecai had taught her. *I hope I succeed,* she thought. The shouts of street merchants echoed in her ears, heightening her anxiety.

Mordecai, noticing her tense expression, chuckled. "Don't worry, Gdaliahu Ha-Nasi won't bite. We'll soon find out if he approves of you."

Esther offered a weak smile. "When I leave, please let Sarah take care of you."

"Good idea. You are my best daughter," Mordecai responded warmly.

"Also, can you assign Sara a new teacher to continue her education?" Esther requested.

"Yes," Mordecai smiled. "That's an excellent idea."

"Thank you. And one last thing—could you consider opening a class for girls at the Jewish Academy?"

"Bargaining, already?" Mordecai chuckled. "I'll consider it,"

As the chariot passed through the bustling market, Esther observed the lively scene: peddlers shouting their wares, loaded carts squeaking by, and the scent of grilled meats and flowers blending in the air. For everyone else, it was just another ordinary day, but Esther's heart pounded in rhythm with the horse's hooves clattering on the cobblestones.

The palace loomed ahead, its white marble walls gleaming with red feldspar, mother-of-pearl, and blue turquoise. Guards stood stiffly at attention. Esther's stomach fluttered as they passed through the gate. When the stepped from the chariot, servants and guards bowed.

As Esther entered the main hall, she caught her breath. The hall was grander than anything she had imagined, with cotton curtains of blue and white, hanging from colossal marble columns, tied with purple linen cords, tied to gleaming silver rings.

Then she saw him. Gdaliahu, the Jewish leader, sat upon the splendor on a raised platform, his long, white beard, still touched with the fiery hue of his youth, his golden crown gleaming atop his white curly hair.

Mordecai bowed deeply, and Esther followed suit, her legs trembling, and her fists clenched. Her nose itched, but she dared not raise a hand.

"Welcome, welcome," Gdaliahu said, gesturing for them to rise. He dismissed the attendants and motioned for Esther to step forward.

Esther glanced at Mordecai, who nodded reassuringly. Taking a deep breath, she lifted her chin, straightened her back, and walked gracefully toward the leader, bowing low at the base of the platform.

"Esther... Esther ... " Gdaliahu sang out, sending a shiver down her spine. Was it just her imagination, or had he just repeated her name twice, like God called Abraham at Isaac's fiery altar and Moses at the burning bush? *What an honor! He knows my new name. He knows the plan.*

"We have been watching you since the day you were born," Gdaliahu said.

A cheeks flushed, but she willed her gaze steady.

"You are not only beautiful," he continues, "but you are also smart and educated. We need you to be resourceful, patient, and kind to help our people," watching her responses.

Mordecai felt a sense of satisfaction. *Gdaliahu's words were a subtle acknowledgment of the importance of educating women—something Gdaliahu had long resisted.*

Why me? Esther wondered *Aren't there other girls? Actually, there are none. A team—Mordecai and I.*

Gdaliahu smiled knowingly and nodded.

Can he hear my thoughts? Esther puzzled.

Gdaliahu smiled again, this time a bit wider, before resuming his stern expression. "It won't be easy. You will face dangers and abandonment at times. But know this: we will not forget you. We will always be watching. When we communicate, it will be through double meanings, hidden in plain sight, to outwit our enemies' spies. When the time comes, you must act decisively, even if it costs you everything."

Is he trying to discourage me? Esther wondered. *I am not afraid,* she told herself in fear. Her forehead creased with worry, and she exhaled slowly, feeling the heat rise in her ears.

The elderly leader watched her closely, then extended his hand. Esther stepped forward up the platform, and Gdaliahu pointed toward a large candle on a nearby silver stand. "Please light it with the oil lamp."

"Blessed are you, our God, creator of lights," Gdaliahu intoned.

"Amen," Esther whispered, amazed as she had never seen or lit a candle before—a new invention brought from China. She hesitated, but carefully followed his instructions. As the wick caught fire, they watched the flickering flame in silence, the soft light casting a gentle glow on their faces, as if blocking the whole dark world away.

After a few moments, Gdaliahu spoke, his voice steady and solemn. "In the sight of God and man, we entrust you with the fate of our people. You are their mother now. Will you accept this role and give everything to secure our destiny?"

A shiver ran through Esther. She closed her eyes, holding her breath, as tears welled. The weight of responsibility settled on her shoulders.

The words of the Israelites, spoken when Moses asked them to obey the Book of the Covenants, echoed in her mind. She whispered the solemn vow, "I will perform and listen."

Gdaliahu smiled and slowly rose from his chair. With a reverent gesture, he dropped to his knees before her, bowing his head to the ground in a royal salute. Esther, amazed, overwhelmed with emotion, silently prayed in thanks.

Mordecai trembled in awe. The sight before him—a great leader bowing to a young woman, an elder to the young, the powerful to the humble, royalty to his subject, the heir of King David to the heir of King Saul—stirred his soul. Past and future seemed to converge in this moment. *Is this a prophecy?* Mordecai's heart swelled with the belief that Esther would meet her destiny.

Despite the strict prohibition against touching King Gdaliahu without permission, Esther instinctively reached out, gently supporting him by the armpit, as he rose back to his seat.

With reverence, they bowed deeply and walked backward. Then, without a word, they left the palace, their hearts heavy with the significance of what had just transpired.

CHAPTER 17

Shortly after that, Harvona informed Mordecai that the king had officially agreed to the beauty contest and had appointed Hegai to oversee it. With that, a decree outlining the rules of the contest was issued. Hegai, the head of the women's quarters, sent royal officers across the empire to recruit beautiful young women from every town. Mordecai, through his informant, stayed updated on the process.

The Persian officers, traveling with wagons and a contingent of fifty horseback riders carrying the king's lion flag, were greeted with grand celebrations in each city. Soldiers lined the city walls, and crowds gathered to witness the royal arrival. At the city hall, the mayor rose form his seat and offered it to the commanding officer as a mark of respect, while the wealthiest citizens provided food and lodging for the royal soldiers. The king's lion flag was hoisted above the city.

The officer then announced the king's beauty contest, inviting all willing, beautiful young virgins—regardless of their social standing—along with their mothers and two grandmothers, to participate. The excitement was palpable. The officer provided unique, expensive dresses for the contestants. It was clear that any woman who refused to participate could get married or disfigure herself.

Each young woman, accompanied by her mother and grandmothers, paraded before the officer. They displayed their charms, danced, bowed, and answered his questions. They posed, smiled, and even gave stern, commanding looks as requested. The officer also scrutinized the contestants' families to gauge how the contestants might age.

Finally, the officer made his selections. The unchosen contestants wept, while the chosen one and her family celebrated, calling out in joy.

———◆———

The selected women were brought soon under the strict supervision of Hegai to the royal palace. Aware of the king's wariness toward disease, Hegai, isolated the new arrivals from the palace staff and conducted thorough health checks. The women stayed isolated until their menstrual cycle to avoid unknow pregnancy.

For a year, the women bathed in scented oils, practiced music and gymnastics, and prepared elaborate performances. They shared jokes about the infamous story of Queen Vashti being asked to show her beauty, wearing only her crown, to the king and his guests. The contestants assumed that is what the king expected.

Hegai provided anything they asked, but did not tell them the king expected them to speak Persian and to be careful about their food, because their body odor might be repugnant to the sensitive king.

When the time came, each contestant had the opportunity to perform before the king and his guests during an evening dinner. Following the performance, each contestant would spend a single night alone with the king. Those who were not chosen as the new queen were sent to the king's harem as concubines. Once in the harem, they could go to the king only if summoned by name. The concubines were not allowed to provide any insights or advice to the contestants.

———❧———

One day, Michael approached Mordecai, visibly distressed. "Hadassah is beautiful and unmarried," Michael said urgently. "She might be taken to the contest."

Mordecai nodded, his own discomfort apparent. "True," he said reluctantly.

"Please," Michael pleaded, "let me marry her now? I've already asked her."

Mordecai sighed, filled with emotion. "I wish I could say yes. You are tearing my heart. But not right now. Be patient. I will give you a business charter. This will provide you with an opportunity—an opportunity to build your future."

———

As the contest progressed, Harvona and Hegai kept Mordecai informed. Several contestants had already performed for the king, but none had met his expectations. Despite seeing many beautiful candidates, the king still hadn't found a queen who embodied the pride and power that Queen Vashti once commanded.

Mordecai shared this update with Hadassah, and though her heart wavered, a small seed of confidence began to grow.

———

One day, Hadassah was told to remove all her jewelry, cut her hair short, and wear plain clothes. As she and Mordecai walked together, a chariot suddenly approached. A guard leaped out and grabbed Hadassah, dragging her toward the chariot. Though frightened, she glanced at Mordecai, who gave her a reassuring nod. Taking a deep breath, she composed herself and entered the chariot.

As it sped away, Mordecai collapsed, weeping and pleading for mercy. Onlookers gathered around him, offering comfort.

Upon hearing the bad news, Sarah was inconsolable, clutching a lock of Hadassah's hair and weeping bitterly. Mordecai tried to console Sarah, promising that he would continue her education in his household, just in case Hadassah returned.

Michael, devastated, rushed in and bowed deeply to Mordecai. "Please, find a way to save Hadassah. She is not good as a maid. You can declare her my wife and rescue her. I did offer to marry her, remember?" he pleaded, tears streaming down his face and his hands shaking.

Mordecai, looking troubled, hesitated. He stroked his beard, glanced around nervously, and whispered, "It is beyond my power to retrieve her... now. I can't make any promises, but if she ..., I might be able to bring her back ... in a few years."

Michael retreated, overwhelmed. Both Michael and Sarah mourned together, finding solace in shared grief.

Mordecai informed the Jewish community that Hadassah had been kidnapped. The people prayed for her safety. He then asked Sarah to take on Hadassah's role in the household. Overwhelmed with gratitude, Sarah accepted the responsibility, vowing to uphold Hadassah's legacy.

CHAPTER 18

Esther trembled as she asked, "Where are you taking me?"

The guard shot her a sharp look. "Maid—don't talk!" He raised his hand swiftly—Esther flinched, recoiling in fear—and he threw a dark scarf over her head. *I cannot see or be seen*, she thought, a sigh of resignation escaping her lips.

The chariot came to an abrupt halt, and the scarf was roughly yanked away. Just before her stood a maid at a servant's entrance. The guard dragged Esther by the arm, releasing her in front of the maid, and walked away without a word.

The maid looked her over. "I'm Hini," she said, her tone brisk. "You'll be part of my team." She pointed a stern finger in Esther's face and added, "We have roles to play. Don't take it personally. Listen and perform."

Esther noticed a flicker of disappointment in Hini's eyes and lowered her head, on the verge of tears. But to her surprise, Hini approached and gave her a gentle hug, whispering, "Ishtar's blessing on your head, my daughter."

She expected someone better, Esther thought, surprised by the kindness. *Yet she blessed me like Joseph did Benjamin.*

Hini led her to the king's chambers, where Esther was introduced to the other servants. She felt small and out of place. *Back to Shimon's house as a maid*, she thought, *at least, it was only temporary.* Over time, Esther adjusted to her new life. The routine became second nature: spotless cleaning, and perfect precision. Hini's approving nods came more frequently, and slowly, Esther's anxiety eased. The nightmares faded, and she thought, *All is well. Hard, but well. I'm following Joseph's path. Will my trials go further?*

Hini's team of seven women tended to the king's needs, from arranging his robes to assisting with his bath. Esther was strictly forbidden from touching him, especially during the sacred bathing rituals. The first time she saw the king step into the marble tub, she quickly averted her eyes—but not before noticing his muscular frame and graceful movements. In that brief moment, Esther's heart betrayed her. She had fallen in love—deeply, secretly, and painfully in love.

Hini reported the team's progress to Harvona.

Esther couldn't stop noticing the king's dark, thick hair, longing to run her fingers through its silkiness. His deep, commanding voice made her stomach flip, and his calm authority mesmerized her. His very presence radiated power. Every time he was near, Esther's pulse quickened.

In her growing infatuation, Esther asked Hini if she could eat the same food as the king—fruits, vegetables, and herbs. She believed that sharing his diet would subtly affect her scent and perhaps make her more appealing. She had noticed the king's sensitivity to smells and wondered, *Are all men like that?*

Harvona, unaware of her intentions, arranged for the king's personal chef to prepare meals for Hini's team. Esther, worried about gaining weight, requested smaller portions, hoping to remain lean.

Determined to mark herself and leave an impression, Esther experimented with the scent of narcissus, hoping to create an association in the king's mind with joy and pleasure.

One of Esther's duties was to prepare the king's room for a contestant night with the king. One evening, Hini asked her to join her in observing a contestant's private time with the king from a hidden vantage point. Esther's heart sank as she saw the woman—a stunning beauty with seductive grace. The king seemed captivated by her, laughter echoing from the chamber. Esther felt a pang of doubt. *How can I ever compare?*

Tears streamed down Esther's cheeks as she shook with despair. *All for nothing. This must be the new queen. Why am I even here? I wish I'd die right now!*

Noticing her distress, Hini gently poked her in the ribs and whispered, "Stop it. She is not the queen. The king didn't give her the unity crown at dinner. This is just for pleasure. I brought you here to learn."

What? Esther thought, stunned. *Didn't this contestant bring enough prestige to the king?*

Her mind whirled with thoughts as she took in the scene. *Learn and plan.*

Esther watched, covering her mouth as the foreign contestant performed an exotic, seductive display for the king. Shocked, she couldn't tear her eye away. She observed every detail: who, where, when, how strong, how long, how loud. *Wow.*

Esther stayed silent, breathing quietly as she witnessed it all in, watching until the king and the contestant finally fell asleep.

"No one can be more beautiful and pleasing than her," Esther muttered, her voice heavy with doubt and sadness.

Hini, always composed, responded calmly, "I've seen many come and go. Yes, they're excellent, but they're all the same. Our good king is searching for something more—someone special." She paused, her eyes narrowing thoughtfully. "Only Marduk knows what is truly in his mind." Esther's mouth dropped in surprise.

Later, while laying out the royal wardrobe, Esther found herself gazing at the sleeping king. He rested on his back, propped up by a soft down pillow. It was early, and Esther hadn't covered her hair or face yet. Standing at his feet, her eyes traced the lines of his face, lost in daydreams, filled with hope and excitement. The desire to embrace him swelled within her, and before she could stop herself, she puckered her lips and blew a soft kiss toward the sleeping king.

Suddenly, King Ahasuerus opened his eyes and looked directly at her. Sunlight streamed into the room, casting a golden glow over Esther's hair. She froze, her heart pounding as she quickly shifted her gaze to the space behind him, trying to disengage the intimate eye contact. For a moment, the king's face softened in awe, before he closed his eyes. Esther's face went pale as all the blood drained from her cheeks. Without a sound, she tiptoed out of the room, her heart racing with fear.

Hini, who had witnessed the entire scene, approached Esther as she exited the bedchamber. "What do you think you're doing?" she hissed, her voice trembling with anger and fear. "You could ruin everything! No—you *have* ruined everything! I'm dying, dying—oh God!"

Esther stared at the floor, hands covering her face as silent sobs shook her body. She collapsed to the ground, curling into a fetal position, her mind spiraling. *What have I done? Please, God, help me!* She prayed desperately.

Hini, rattled and unsure of what to do, rushed off to find Harvona and report the crisis.

Not long after, Hini returned, her expression a mix of surprise and excitement. "I spoke to Harvona," she said breathlessly. "He was tense and worried before I even told him what happened. But when I explained, he laughed and said, 'Now I understand! Don't worry, I overheard the king saying he saw a beautiful angel in his dream— an angel with white wings and a glowing halo. He closed his eyes to protect himself, and when he opened them, she was gone. His adviser told him this means he will have an angel for a queen.'"

Esther exhaled a deep breath of relief. Her heart flooded with gratitude. "Thank you, God, protector of the fools," she whispered softly. *Truly, Your ways are beyond understanding.*

CHAPTER 19

Mordecai—aware that Esther's image was imprinted in the king's mind, and he might recognize her too early—was deeply concerned for Esther's mission, and decided she must be moved from the king's chamber.

Hegai moved quickly, relocating Esther to the house of the women along with her chambermaids. He gave her the finest room—a space he had reserved for her since the beginning of the contest. When Hegai addressed her as "Your Majesty," the chambermaids exchanged wide-eyed looks of shock and immediately fell to the ground, weeping.

They're trying to remember if they ever mistreated me, Esther thought with a wry smile.

"Please, get up," she said gently, helping the women to their feet. Then, in a warm gesture, she embraced each one. "We have important work ahead of us. Let's hope for good things to come."

Seeing the new royal clothes prepared for Esther, the maids eagerly rushed to dress her, their earlier anxiety replaced with excitement.

Mordecai and Hegai met daily, exchanging updates on the contest and discussing ways to further Esther's education. Hegai often brought her books and instructions from Mordecai. Esther accepted them gratefully, seeing each as a sign of her growing progress. She practiced for hours each day, learning the sacred dances of Persia and India from instructors Hegai had arranged. Her pride in her new skills blossomed, and her confidence grew.

One day, Mordecai sent her a lion cub as a gift, carefully selected for its temperament. Esther fed the cub milk from a waterskin and later chewed its food for it, just as a mother lion would. The cub, growing more obedient and friendly under Esther's firm but loving care, soon became her loyal companion. She even practiced her dances with the lion, who followed her graceful movements with devotion.

Yet despite her growing self-assurance, Esther couldn't help but notice the worry in Hini's eyes. The older woman's face revealed her doubts as she silently prayed.

She still doesn't believe I can win, Esther thought, feeling a pang of sadness. *Oh, my dear Hini...*

"Why are you so sad?" Esther asked.

"How can you win with just this?" Hini replied, gesturing to Esther's body, her tone tinged with worry.

"I'm only meant to do what Queen Vashti refused. Can't I manage that?" Esther asked, a hint of frustration creeping into her voice.

"But she was..." Hini hesitated, her expression clouded with concern.

———◆———

Meanwhile, Mordecai, who appointed himself to the position of chief justice in the High Jewish Court, was burdened with endless responsibilities. Each morning, a sack full of messages awaited his review and response. In addition to his judicial duties, he managed the Jewish Academy and continued his official tasks for Gdaliahu at the king's gate.

Esther, mindful of Mordecai's well-being, often sent up silent prayers. *Please, God, protect Mordecai. With so much to do, how does he still find time to check on me?*

The beauty contest stretched on for four long years. At that time, Esther celebrated her twentieth birthday. The once-trembling girl had grown into a poised and confident young woman.

I'm ready, she told herself with quiet determination. *As ready as I can be.*

CHAPTER 20

Mordecai was troubled by news from his merchants: the Buchara District had deliberately cut its rice supply, creating a shortage and driving up prices.

"Our rice dealers are colluding," Mordecai muttered to Yavin, his trusted manager. "They're gouging the people, and this could lead to unrest and hatred aginst us."

He paced the room, tugging at his beard, unable to sit still. Yavin, ever patient, watched silently.

Finally, Mordecai stopped. "We must act," he declared. "We could purge them... but it may cause backlash. Some merchants might resist."

Yavin dismissed the concern. "We'll purge them too if we must. They're replaceable."

Mordecai nodded but urged caution. "No need to go that far. But we must fight this corruption for the people's sake." He paused, then said, "Yavin, write a letter. I'll dictate."

Yavin readied his quill.

Mordecai began, "We've uncovered illegal practices in Buchara. Caleb's and Chamor's rice charters are terminated, and they are excommunicated. No one is permitted to trade with them. Our success is rooted in honesty and fairness, guided by the Torah. Just as we prosper together, so too will we suffer if even one among us seeks personal gain through dishonesty."

He paused. "Wait—change, 'and they are excommunicated' to 'until further decision.'"

Yavin wrote it again with the correction and handed it to Mordecai for approval.

Mordecai nodded. "This will do."

———◆———

Later, Mordecai presented the declaration to Gdaliahu, explaining the potential backlash. "This could cause a revolt," he warned.

"Possibly," Gdaliahu replied.

"Please, release me from my duties," Mordecai pleaded, lowering his head. "I dream of having a family. I'm tired."

Gdaliahu stood abruptly. "What are you saying? Look at what you've built! The business you formed united the Jews across the empire. This will preserve our nation. Troubles will come, but as you've said, 'Troubles bring opportunity.' You won't cause division—you'll bring unity! You are the leader God chose. Publish the declaration. Let us see our enemies." His tone softened. "And why aren't you married? What are you waiting for?"

Gdaliahu's words hit Mordecai with a mix of relief and renewed purpose. "You're right," Mordecai admitted. "I've been so focused on the challenges that I've neglected my own life. I'll move forward with the declaration—and with my future."

Mordecai's decree sent shockwaves through Jewish communities across the empire, causing concern among merchants. While many supported him, letters and visitors dwindled. In Babylon, Kaffir-Ariot, a prominent leader, publicly challenged Mordecai's authority, excommunicating him. Yavin, Mordecai's confidant, brought the news, reading the proclamation:

"Mordecai, the impostor Jew, is a cursed Benjamin... Down with him! Mordecai is excommunicated!"

Mordecai took a deep breath and said calmly, "It begins. Kaffir-Ariot is driven by pride and revenge. He's envious of my position under Gdaliahu and seeks to divide us for his own gain."

"What will you do?" Yavin asked.

"I'll shake him and the whole Jewish world so that they will never forget it. I'll put him under house arrest and threaten to send his children to the Babylon annual slave lottery, until he revokes his order," Mordecai said.

Horrified, Yavin exclaimed, "What?"

"It's a bluff," Mordecai reassured him. "He must believe the threat is real to understand the seriousness of his actions."

Yavin sighed. "He'll be shocked."

Mordecai smiled. "I can always commute his sentence. My own decrees do not bind me."

Yavin, still uneasy, asked, "Will the people of Israel ever find peace?"

Mordecai chuckled. "I once asked God this exact question ... God answered me: 'Yes, but not in my lifetime.'" They shared a brief laugh amid the tension.

———————

Mordecai explained the situation to Gdaliahu. "I regret this conflict with Kaffir-Ariot, your former right-hand man, but he's challenging my leadership and threatening our unity. I believe he'll back down, and it could unite us."

Gdaliahu, after a thoughtful pause, agreed. "He's attacked both of us. Convene the Jewish court."

In court, Mordecai presented Kaffir-Ariot's excommunication letter, likening it to Korah's rebellion against Moses. "Korah defied Moses, and the earth swallowed him. We must crush this revolt swiftly."

The court ruled: For Kaffir-Ariot rebelious letter, he must accept a house arrest, forbidden to speak or write about Mordecai, whether positively or negatively. If he violated the terms, his family would face the king's annual slave lottery up to the fourth generation.

The news spread quickly. No one came to Kaffir-Ariot's defense, as the people, thriving under Mordecai's leadership, stood by him.

Shortly afterward, Kaffir-Ariot requested a hearing with Gdaliahu. A court was convened, summoning Jewish leaders from across the empire. Kaffir-Ariot appeared with his seven sons. In solemn silence, he knelt and crawled on his elbows to the center of the hall. His beard was unkempt, his cheeks hollow from fasting, and though he wore his finest robe, it was torn and singed. As an offering of submission, he placed his gold headband, chain, ring, and key on the floor before the court. Prostrating himself, his body cast no shadow, while his sons stood behind him, their eyes filled with tears. The eldest held the hands of the two youngest. They all wore long, pale-blue garments, cinched with wide white belts, their clothes shimmering in waves of changing colors.

"Please, great leader, forgive my sins," Kaffir-Ariot begged, his voice trembling. "What I have done is inexcusable. I ask for mercy, not for myself, but for my children, who had no part in this. Please, take them into your care."

Gdaliahu glanced at Mordecai, lifting his chin in a signal for him to respond. A large lighted candle flickered before Gdaliahu.

Mordecai rose, ascended the platform, and stood beside Gdaliahu. Illuminated by the fire, Mordeci's shadow stood like a giant behind him, stretched all the way to the ceiling. His shimmering garments and blazing eyes gave him the appearance of Moses descending from Mount Sinai. The room held its breath.

After a long pause, Mordecai crossed his arms and studied the man before him. "Is this truly what you believe?" he asked, his voice steady.

Kaffir-Ariot's voice quivered. "I should never have written those hurtful words. Please, show mercy."

Mordecai's gaze remained unyielding. "Very well," he said firmly. Pointing at Kaffir-Ariot's children, he thundered, "Your children will join the Jewish Academy in Shushan. Your house arrest is suspended." He paused, wondering, *Am I educating them or taking hostages? Or perhaps, protecting them from their father's folly?*

After counting silently to three, Mordecai continued, "And... in the name of our great leader..., in the communities of Earth and Heaven..., with the approval of this court and all who are present, from this moment forward..., there shall no longer be separate tribes of Israel. We are one tribe, the children of Israel, responsible for one another. We are all Jews. Any attempt to divide our nation will be crushed! We will neither stumble nor falter!"

His words echoed through the hall, leaving the assembly stunned. With a single decree, Mordecai had abolished tribal divisions, dissolving the social hierarchy that had persisted for centuries. No more would records of tribal affiliation or ancestral land ownership be kept for future reclamation.

As Mordecai walked backward while descending the platform, he misstepped, nearly falling. He caught himself by placing a hand on the top step. For a moment, the room was silent—then, laughter erupted, breaking the tension. Mordecai smiled, and Gdaliahu nodded in approval.

"All those who accept the court's ruling, step forward," Gdaliahu said calmly.

The assembly moved forward in unison.

"So recorded!" Gdaliahu declared. "Now, let us sing from the Book of Psalms."[2]

God chose the tribe of Judah and His beloved Mount Zion.

Judah became His sanctuary, Israel His dominion.

Gdaliahu, the venerable leader of the Jews in the Persian Empire, rose slowly from his seat, leaning heavily on his walking stick as he staggered out of the court. Once he had departed, Mordecai approached Kaffir-Ariot, who remained prostrate on the floor. Extending his hand, Mordecai said, "Peace be upon you, Kaffir-Ariot. Retrieve your items

---

[2]   A combination of parts from Psalm 78:68 and Psalm 114:2.

of authority and join us for a discussion with Gdaliahu." Kaffir-Ariot, humbled, accepted the assistance and rose to his feet.

Mordecai then turned to the esteemed Jewish leaders to join him for a celebration in his palace.

As they walked to Gdaliahu's chamber, Yavin leaned in and whispered, "Did you stumble on purpose back there?"

Mordecai shot him a playful glare. "Shame on you! Didn't you see me practicing?" With a smile, he added, "I may have stumbled, but I didn't falter."

Yavin exhaled in relief. "I just needed to know."

Upon reaching Gdaliahu's chamber, they bowed before the elder leader, who lay reclined on a cushioned divan, a wool blanket draped over him as he strained to read a document held at arm's length.

"Thank you for inviting me," Kaffir-Ariot said gratefully.

"Thank you for submitting," Gdaliahu responded.

"I apologize for the harsh treatment," Mordecai said sincerely.

Kaffir-Ariot nodded. "Thank you for pardoning me."

"It's only a suspension," Mordecai reminded him, his tone firm but fair.

"True," Kaffir-Ariot responded, the fear still evident in his voice. The ordeal had clearly left its mark on him.

Mordecai acknowledged the weight of the situation with a knowing nod.

After a brief pause, Kaffir-Ariot spoke again. "Uniting the tribes was a brilliant move. I hope one day the lost ten tribes will join us as well."

"Amen," Mordecai replied, his voice filled with hope.

"This unity was made possible because of you," Gdaliahu said solemnly.

Kaffir-Ariot gave a hollow, brief laugh, though his face betrayed a mixture of lingering sadness and surprise.

Mordecai shifted the conversation. "Now, to the matter at hand. We've heard about your efforts in establishing a research center in Babylon for Torah study. Your interpretations and rulings are becoming foundational to our faith. I've tasked my students with gathering biblical stories from their hometowns, and my merchants are doing the same across the provinces. I will send you copies of these stories. Our business model is thriving, and your educational efforts are vital in preserving our nation from assimilation."

"We need each other," Gdaliahu emphasized, his voice filled with conviction.

"Work with us, and we will all succeed," Mordecai urged, his tone carrying a subtle undercurrent of caution. *Of course, we don't truly need you,* he thought privately, *especially with Governor Ezra's parallel efforts in Jerusalem.*

Kaffir-Ariot, regaining a measure of pride, responded, "Thank you for the honor you've shown me. I will cooperate fully."

Mordecai continued, "Your children will remain in my care. I will assign them the task of gathering and sorting biblical documents. You may oversee and guide their work."

Kaffir-Ariot bowed deeply, a wave of relief washing over him. "Thank you. You have brought great joy to me … and to my wife!"

Mordecai, observing the scene, couldn't help but imagine Kaffir-Ariot's wife's reaction upon hearing Mordecai's earlier decree against her family.

"Go in peace," Gdaliahu said, offering a final blessing.

Mordecai and Kaffir-Ariot bowed once more to Gdaliahu and then left for Mordecai's palace, the air heavy with both resolution and reconciliation.

———≈———

Mordecai hosted a grand banquet at his palace for the Jewish leaders and their sons, who were students at the Jewish Academy. As he and

Kaffir-Ariot entered the hall, the room fell silent. Mordecai took his place by his chair while Kaffir-Ariot stepped forward to address the assembly.

"Honored guests," Kaffir-Ariot began, "I acknowledge that Mordecai and the court were right. I abused my power and was wrong. I ask for your forgiveness."

Mordecai whispered, "You are pardoned," before turning to the crowd. "Caleb and Chamor from Buchara, please step forward." The two merchants approached, heads bowed in shame.

"I have discussed their situation with them," Mordecai continued. "They now understand the goals of the IBCE. They are forgiven and will relocate to—to Darnk to begin in a new city."

He then addressed the assembly, "God has blessed us with good fortune because we have spread prosperity and His name throughout the empire. It is our ... our most sacred obligation—to bring blessing to the nations of the world with all our Might and Mind. Neglecting it will bring us Resentment..., Rage..., and Ruin...."

Caleb and Chamor bowed deeply, and their children embraced them. Mordecai mingled with the guests, shaking hands and blessing the leaders and their children. He instructed the students to explain their studies and training in the IBCE to their fathers, filling the room with pride and praise.

The Jewish leaders reaffirmed their loyalty to Mordecai, who reciprocated with blessings. The sweet route had been established, economic success and religious centers flourished, but Mordecai wondered if his mission was complete.

In his mind, he heard his grandfather's voice: *"No! Your plan must continue until it mirrors God's plan in Egypt."*

Realizing he couldn't manage everything alone, Mordecai announced the senior students who would lead the Jewish Academy, the high court, and the translation office, all reporting directly to him.

CHAPTER 21

I n the seventh year of King Ahasuerus' reign, Hegai finally arranged for Esther's long-awaited meeting with the king. He deliberately selected a long, cool winter night for the occasion.

Recently, the king has grown increasingly restless, still unable to find a suitable queen among the dwindling pool of contestants. Despite enjoying both the public and private displays, no candidate managed to heal his injured pride.

Hegai visited Esther, finding her deep in thought, holding a palm-sized golden statue of Ishtar. The cool metal had warmed to her touch. Without looking up, she said softly, "Ishtar carries a dagger. If Ishtar, then Ishtar!" Her voice was calm but resolute.

Hegai's face tightened, his emotions barely contained. He bowed and left, fists clenched. Some time later, he returned, breathless, with urgency in his voice, "Harvona warned that coming armed before the king is punishable by death. Mordecai reminded us that women are prohibited from carrying weapons. We all agree—it's unnecessary and could lead to imprisonment or worse."

Esther, unflinching, regarded him with calm determination, "Bring me the most beautiful dagger from the king's treasure," she instructed. "This is how you train a lion: with a firm hand from the beginning."

Hegai opened his mouth, then closed it. Wordlessly, he turned and left.

———✦———

At Mordecai's suggestion, Hegai procured a golden dagger, its hilt crowned with a brilliant red ruby. Mordecai had carefully instructed Hegai to tell Esther the dagger's legendary history: it was said to be the very weapon used by the prophet Samuel to slay King Agag the Amalekite at Gilgal. Once preserved in the Jewish temple in Jerusalem until the Babylonians looted it.

Hegai presented the dagger and recounted its significance. Esther's eyes gleamed with delight, admiring its beauty and its symbolic history. "I am ready to meet the king," she declared with newfound confidence.

As she turned the dagger over in her hands, Esther mused, "My father and his stories! Or is this a hidden message? Could our true enemy somehow be connected to Agag's lineage?"

The king's servants had orchestrated an extraordinary dinner party, inviting all the dignitaries of Shushan, including Gdaliahu and Mordecai. Anticipation hummed through the hall as guests eagerly awaited the evening's entertainment of female beauty. Even the king, began to fidget in his chair, casting expectant glances around the room.

Finally, the head servant stepped forward, knocked on the floor three times, and announced, "Honored guests, please direct your attention to the raised platform."

In a swift, practiced motion, workers assembled a raised walkway from the king's royal chair to the grand double doors of the hall, laying out a plush red carpet on top. Moments later, the golden doors swung open, and the crowd collectively gasped.

Standing in the doorway, regal and imposing, was a nearly fully-grown lion. The guests instinctively pulled back, their murmurs of disbelief filling the room. Even the king, startled, leaned back in his chair as his bodyguards moved forward, hands on their swords.

But then Esther appeared, calm and graceful, walking alongside the lion. She reached out and gently stroked its head, and the lion nuzzled her hand affectionately before licking it. The hall fell silent in awe as the king's eyes, wide with astonishment, stayed locked on her.

The head servant, his voice booming with dramatic flair, declared, "Behold, the magnificent goddess of love, fertility, and war graces us tonight. Presenting I-sh-t-a-r!"

A chorus of trumpets blared, and a hush fell over the hall. Though many had visited Ishtar's temple before battles and weddings, the goddess herself had never appeared in such a striking form.

Bathed in a soft, ethereal glow, Esther stood poised in the doorway, every eye in the room fixed on her. Her luxurious hair cascaded over her shoulders, and her eyes sparkled with an otherworldly light. She wore a flowing white gown symbolizing the goddess, layered sevenfold, with a glittering diamond belt cinching her waist. There, nestled just above her navel, gleamed the golden dagger adorned with the large red ruby.

The mood shifted from festivity to reverence as a solemn, almost sacred atmosphere enveloped the hall. Esther's face remained serene, her enigmatic smile unchanging as she stood motionless for several long moments. The crowd held its breath, transfixed by her presence. Finally, with a subtle tilt of her head—first to the left, then to the right—she acknowledged the gathered dignitaries.

Raising her arms gracefully, she began her slow, deliberate walk down the red carpet. The golden bands on her arms glimmered in the flickering lamplight. Beside her, the lion, regal and obedient, padded along before sitting at her signal.

A low hum filled the air as she advanced, her every step drawing the crowd deeper into the spell of her presence. The guests, lining both sides of the walkway, bowed their heads and stretched their hands in prayer toward her, paying homage to the goddess they believed had come to life before their eyes.

As she neared the king's throne, the crowd, unable to contain their awe, erupted into a hymn dedicated to Ishtar, their voices swelling in reverence.[3]

The goddess—with her, there is counsel.
Our fate rests in her hands.
Her gaze brings joy,
Her immense power sustains both body and soul.
She is draped in pleasure and love,
Brimming with vitality, charm, and allure.
In gatherings, her wisdom is sought.
Marduk reveres her,
Overflowing with intelligence, cleverness, and wisdom,
A delight to her lord.
She is draped in pleasure and love,
Brimming with vitality, charm, and allure.

Mordecai stood with Gdaliahu, hidden in the shadows, tears welling in his eyes as he watched Esther, his daughter, a vision of divine beauty. "Praised are You, Lord of the Universe, who has protected Esther," he whispered.

"Amen," Gdaliahu replied softly.

Esther took a deep, calming breath, her chest rising and falling as she steadied herself. The grand hall, with its marble statues and golden fixtures, looked just as magnificent as it had when she had last attended Queen Vashti's banquet. The scent of spiced roasted lamb and sweet wine lingered in the air, mingling with the blare of trumpets that still echoed in her ears. Then, she spotted the king, seated on his throne, flanked by his seven bodyguards.

Her face remained composed, but inside, her heart raced, her nostrils flared, and her ears burned with the heat of anticipation. Her

---

[3]   A modified small part from an Akkadian hymn to Ishtar (1600 B.C.), translated by Ferris J. Stephens. *Old Assyrian Letters and Business Documents.* 1944. http://www.piney.com/HymIsht.html

knees threatened to buckle, but she stood tall, her resolve unwavering. The king was just as she remembered—broad-shouldered, athletic, and undeniably handsome.

The crowd's eagerness to please him was palpable, yet Esther sensed a deeper truth behind the king's regal presence: he was lonely, craving a trustworthy and loyal companion. She willed him to sense the silent message she sent with every graceful step: *I am yours. True love has arrived.*

Carrying a holy myrtle branch braided with golden string, Esther smiled warmly, blessing the guests as she moved with an almost ethereal grace along the raised walkway, appearing to glide through the air.

From his hidden vantage point, Mordecai watched the king's generals. They bowed their heads, whispering prayers to Ishtar. It was customary to seek the goddess's favor for successful campaigns, and none of them could risk disrespecting her image, even in this unexpected form.

The high priests of Ishtar, however, exchanged irritated glances. Mordecai could see them trying to puzzle out who had sanctioned the use of the goddess's name, yet they could not afford to discredit their deity publicly. Trapped by their own beliefs, they joined in the celebration, their hands clasped in prayer, likely hoping Ishtar's "manifestation" would bring prosperity to their temple.

Mordecai's eyes returned to the king, who was no longer restless or distracted. Tears glittered in the king's eyes as he stared at Esther, completely transfixed. Mordecai smirked with satisfaction. *Have you ever seen a performance with such power?*

As Esther neared the king, carrying her golden dagger, Harvona, the second-ranking bodyguard, stepped forward, his face a mixture of anger and alarm. His body tensed as if to block her path. Before he could, the king subtly raised two fingers. Harvona froze.

Esther remained calm, her thoughts focused. *He must play his role,* she reminded herself.

Esther reached the king, bowed deeply, and offered him the decorated myrtle as a sacred tribute. *She's offering him her power,* Mordecai thought, watching closely.

The king's gaze lingered on the radiant figure before him, his arms extending cautiously to accept the gift. Mordecai's mind raced: *He is now obligated to return a gift to Ishtar.*

The king smiled, his eyes drifting toward the queen's unity crown beside him. He picked it up, glanced at Esther, and quietly murmured, "I saw you in my dream, a glorious angel."

Esther's heart raced. *This is a marriage proposal.* But she remained composed, reminding herself, *Ishtar is not bound to accept a mortal crown.* She studied the king's every gesture, holding her role as the goddess with poise.

The king's hopeful smile deepened.

Inside, Esther's heart sang with joy: *Hooray, hooray, hooray. I've won!* Yet her expression remained serene, goddess-like, as she held her emotions in check.

The king straightened, pulling the crown tightly to his chest. *Oh no, is he hesitating?* Esther's breath caught. *Is he displeased?* A wave of fear washed over her, but then, just as her anxiety peaked, the king leaned forward, shifting to the very edge of his throne. With deliberate grace, he extended the crown toward her once more, this time almost brushing it against her forehead.

I can't wait any longer, Esther thought, and she knelt before him. As her eyes caught the glint of the small stone engraved with God's words in the queen's crown, her heart skipped a beat. Bowing her head to both God and the king, she accepted her fate.

With a reverent gesture, the king placed the unity crown on her head. The room fell utterly silent, all eyes fixed on the king, awaiting his next move.

"My queen, would you honor me by repeating your grand entrance?" he asked, his voice filled with awe.

Esther smiled and rose gracefully. She called for the lion to come to her. A bodyguard escorted her to a side door, and moments later, the roar of the lion signaled her readiness. She re-entered the hall, now crowned as queen. The crowd erupted in astonishment and admiration.

Hegai's men led the chant, and soon, the entire assembly joined in: "The queen is Ishtar! Ishtar is the queen! Long live the king, long live the queen!"

Mordecai and all the guests prostrated themselves before her. With regal grace, Esther walked toward the king, her head held high, her crown gleaming. The king, holding his golden scepter in one hand and the holy myrtle in the other, smiled proudly.

"Blessed be our king," the guests chanted, their voices rising. "Blessed be our queen. Blessed be our Ishtar."

Mordecai wore a satisfied smile. Esther had not only fulfilled the king's desires, but had surpassed them. She had given him more than just a queen—she had elevated his status to that of a husband to a goddess. His future children would now be seen as divine offspring, heirs of the goddess Ishtar herself.

Esther approached the king with deliberate grace, ignoring the customary distance, coming so close she could almost touch him. She knelt deeply, balancing the crown on her head.

Is she offering the crown back? Mordecai thought, perplexed. *Who told her to do that?* But then he realized, *The king would never dismiss the goddess from his court. The goddess Ishtar had united the empire under his reign. She would bear him a son, and there could be no greater queen.*

The king's smile broadened, his eyes gleaming with pride. He nodded and motioned for Esther to sit at his left, on the royal chair prepared for her.

As Esther took her seat beside the king during the dinner, the entertainment commenced as Hegai had planned. Four contestants, once hopeful queens, now reduced to the concubines' quarters, performed magnificently. Their beauty and talents still dazzling. Esther observed their reactions—surprise, sadness, confusion, and even anger.

Mordecai chuckled quietly, though a flicker of sympathy crossed his heart. They were indeed beautiful and capable. "Hallelujah. Thank God, Lord of the Universe," he whispered, squeezing Gdaliahu Ha-Nasi's hand. "We made it."

"With God's help," Gdaliahu gently corrected him.

Mordecai nodded. "I always knew my plan would succeed. The king values honor and glory. He wasn't just seeking pleasure, but a queen who could elevate his empire. The contestants misjudged him, offering nothing more than what any other beautiful woman could. But God has a purpose for them, too. Their efforts paved the way for Esther's success."

"Amen," Gdaliahu agreed softly.

This is only the beginning, Mordecai thought. *Esther still has many more challenges ahead. Please, God, help her,* Mordecai prayed.

After dinner, the king retired to his room, and Esther went to prepare herself. *Am I already the queen?* She wondered. *Did I accomplish my mission? No, she reminded herself. There is still much to prove.*

As she entered the room where her seven maids were kneeling, their foreheads touching the floor, Hini crawled forward, bowing at Esther's feet. "Ishtar, please forgive my doubts. I failed to recognize..." Hini began crying, her voice trembling.

Esther gently lifted Hini's face with both hands, raising her head. "You are my guardian angel, my second mother," she said, kissing her on the forehead.

As they made their way to the king's room, Esther asked, "Hini, can you ensure no one peeks? I'm so embarrassed."

"For tonight, Harvona assigned blind and deaf maids," Hini smiled.

"What?" Esther's alarm was evident.

"It's us, my queen," Hini reassured her with a grin. "We're the team whenever you go to the king. No one will peek... for long."

"Ha!" Esther relaxed and smiled.

Upon entering the king's bedchamber, his personal bodyguards exited, leaving them alone. Esther was led to a royal bath filled with hot, fragrant water, scented with narcissus, floating flowers, and aphrodisiac oils. The king reclined, his arms stretched along the tub's edge, waiting.

At last, it is my turn, Esther thought, stepping forward. She paused as her maids formed a half-circle around her, fluttering white and colored peacock feathers like an excited bird. The eyes of the feathers seemed to watch the king.

Her maids circled her, hiding her from view. Behind the feathers, Esther shed one layer of her dress, echoing the myth of Ishtar's descent through the seven gates of the underworld. Soft, loving music played outside the door.

When she reappeared, she wore a light orange dress and carried her golden dagger. Her short curls tumbled down to her shoulders, framing the unity crown still perched on her head.

As the dance continued, the maids shielded her again, and she reemerged in a shorter, brighter red dress.

The king chuckled in approval, his eyes glistening.

Each time Esther approached, her dress grew shorter and more vibrant, revealing her youthful beauty. But as she neared the bath, a wave of trepidation washed over her. *Will I disappoint him?* she wondered, her inexperience weighing on her.

Her cheeks flushed as she cast her eyes to the floor, but it was clear the king was pleased.

Summoning all her courage, Esther shed her final garment, standing before the king in nothing but the unity crown and the dagger. Her posture was strong, her gaze unwavering. *I will protect you and the crown with my life,* her very presence seemed to declare.

Enchanted by her scent, the king was captivated in a way he had never experienced before.

"Come in, Ishtahr," the king called softly, using the true Persian name of Ishtar. *Oh well, no one told him,* Esther mused. *So be it.*

Her maids removed the crown and dagger as Esther slid into the hot water, letting the warmth envelop her. She submerged herself briefly, then swam toward the king.

Their first night together was filled with warmth and tenderness. He treated Esther with reverence. For the first time, he sought to please his mate, honoring the goddess of Love. They slept tight in the long, cool night, and repeated at dawn.

By morning, she was escorted to her new queen's quarters, Hini following closely behind, cradling the unity crown with care.

"Am I the queen?" Esther asked at last, her voice quiet.

"Yes, my queen. Forever!" Hini answered, tears in her eyes as she held the crown close to her chest. "We will always protect you."

CHAPTER 22

The king celebrated his marriage to Esther with a grand feast, inviting ministers and palace officials. Among the honored guests were Gdaliahu and Mordecai.

As they watched Esther, Gdaliahu recalled Lavan's blessing, "Our sister, may you be a mother to thousands, and may God punish your enemies." "Amen," Mordecai replied.

"It's interesting that the king hasn't inquired about her nationality or invited the provincial princes," Mordecai observed.

"He likely wants to keep it secret," Gdaliahu explained. "He doesn't want to stir jealousy and hostility or involve her family, preferring to present her as a goddess within his palace, a uniting force. Are you hoping for her help to become a minister?"

"Becoming a minister isn't my goal," Mordecai responded. "Esther and Harvona already give me enough influence. It's better if I remain in my modest role."

"More plans?" Gdaliahu questioned, gesturing at the opulence around them. "Isn't all this enough?"

Mordecai smiled. "Of course not."

"The king has sent gifts to the nations and granted tax breaks. He wants everyone to join in the celebration of his wedding. None of the other contestants have returned home, and no one but us knows that Queen Esther is Hadassah. He's good and tolerant, and we should respect his wish for her nationality to remain secret. Now she belongs to all the nations," Gadaliahu concluded.

"Have you seen her new bodyguard?" Mordecai asked, his tone serious. "His name is Hatach, one of the king's trusted guards and a friend of Harvona. We need to watch him closely—he might be spying for the king."

———————

A few days after the royal wedding, Mordecai invited his cousin Michael, Shimon's eldest son, to a meeting at Yavin's store. Guided by an armed guard, Michael entered a private, windowless room lit by flickering oil lamps. The room was cold and damp, adding to the tense atmosphere.

Mordecai sat at a table, silently pulling at his beard, while Yavin sat nearby. After a long pause, Mordecai finally spoke. "Thank you for coming."

Michael nodded respectfully. Yavin broke the silence, "Your business seems to be thriving."

"Thank you," Michael replied, trying to ease his tension.

"Good, good," Mordecai muttered, his eyes fixed on the table. He wiped an imaginary spot of dirt from its surface, stood up, leaned on the table with his knuckles, sighed, and met Michael's gaze. "Yes … yes," he said hesitating before continuing, "A queen has been chosen. Still, I cannot free Hadassah. I hope you understand." Mordecai sank back into his chair, signaling the end of the conversation.

Michael collapsed to his knees, tears streaming down his face. "Why not? Please… Hadassah… my Hadassah … please… please."

Mordecai's voice softened, "You love her.… ," he said gently, "One day you will …" He gave Michael a stern look. "Find another wife to love. I will assist you with all my power. The matter is firmly settled."

Michael, shocked, glanced at Yavin, then at the guard. He nodded with resignation. "Thank you. It is God's will."

As Michael left, Mordecai asked Yavin, "Will he stay silent?"

Yavin replied, "He'd better."

CHAPTER 23

Esther couldn't rest, even as queen. The king still had hundreds of beautiful concubines at his disposal, always ready to entertain him. When the king ordered Hegai to bring in fresh virgins, Mordecai smiled knowingly. He had been right—the king had chosen Esther for her wisdom and grace, not just her beauty. Yet, Esther had to remain vigilant, ensuring she stayed close to the king's heart.

Each month, when summoned to the king's chamber, Esther meticulously prepared, bringing small gifts or captivating stories. She never interfered in his affairs, maintaining the air of mystery the king adored. Her status as queen, even as a goddess-like figure, went unquestioned.

Esther's only formal duty was the annual blessing of the troops. Riding a tall white Cilician horse, adorned with peacock feathers and a crown, Esther arrived to bless the elite guards and officers. Wearing her unity crown, she inspected the yearly distinguished soldiers. Then she rode up a wooden ramp in front of the army, the rhythmic pounding of hooves commanding the soldiers' attention. At the top, her horse reared up dramatically for a long minute, then bowed in respect.

In one fluid motion, Esther swung her leg over the horse, revealing a glimpse of her long leg through the slit in her dress. Facing the crowd, she gracefully slid to the platform. A murmur of surprise spread through the troops. She rewarded her horse with a carrot, stroking its neck as it neighed.

Dressed in her Ishtar regalia, Esther raised her arms and blessed the troops with wishes for victory. The soldiers roared in approval, singing her hymn as flags dipped in respect. The procession marched past, presenting their colors in admiration.

In the king's harem, Esther lived in luxury, surrounded by bodyguards and eunuchs. No other men were permitted to enter the women's quarters, ensuring her security and privacy. Hegai provided her with everything she desired, from fine clothes to perfumes. Her chambers boasted rare comforts: a marble bath with hot water, a flowing sink, and a squat toilet.

For good fortune, Esther adopted a sleek black kitten with shining yellow eyes, naming her Lucky. With just a small patch of white fur on her chest, Lucky quickly took charge, communicating with flicks of her tail and headbutts. Esther and Lucky shared a strong bond, comforting each other during quiet moments. One day, Lucky presented a mouse to Esther, who laughed and touched her dagger, saying, "We are both hunters."

Though Esther rarely left the palace, her maids roamed the city, bringing her anything she desired, often from Yavin's exotic goods store. Esther also hosted gatherings with the king's concubines to maintain harmony while carefully concealing her Jewish identity. It was widely known that the court was a place where trust was rare.

CHAPTER 24

Gdaliahu, the aging Jewish leader, was in constant pain and nearing the end of his life. Unable to sit or walk without help, he called for a final meeting. Jewish leaders from across the empire gathered, eager to reconnect and introduce their sons, the next generation. The room buzzed with discussions of politics and commerce, while fine fabrics and jewels reflected in the candlelit hall.

When Gdaliahu entered, supported by a servant, the room fell silent. Slowly, he was eased into his golden chair. With a trembling hand, he summoned Mordecai, who knelt before him.

In a frail voice, Gdaliahu gave his blessing: "May the Lord bless you and guard you."

"Amen," the room responded.

"May the Lord show favor and be gracious to you."

"Amen," came the unified reply.

"May the Lord show you kindness and grant you success."

"Amen, amen, amen," the room echoed in response.

Mordecai noticed the change—'success' not 'peace,' sensing a coming challenge. *Am I to face war?*

It was clear that Gdaliahu had passed the mantle of leadership to him. Mordecai kissed his hand in gratitude, then stood and addressed the assembly, meeting each leader's gaze.

"I am honored to serve you," Mordecai declared. "Together, we will prosper." He announced his first decree: "Every community shall build a Jewish center, serving our people from birth to death. These centers will house courts, schools, and business chambers, ensuring full employment and support for all."

He added, "You may use one year's IBCE fees for construction. For the sake of our people and in God's name, education must be our highest covenant. God blesses those who create life and educate their children, as God proclaimed: 'Guard God, his edicts, laws, books, and tradition.'[4] It is our sacred duty to live honorable lives. Remember the command: 'Love your fellow man as yourself.' In doing so, God will bless us all."

The crowd murmured in approval, "Amen, Selah. So be it," unified by Mordecai's vision for the future.

The men gathered around Mordecai, praising his leadership and vision. Many were inspired to contribute beyond the required amount for their community centers, knowing it would enhance their influence.

Despite his new responsibilities, Mordecai frequently visited Gdaliahu, always removing his official symbols out of respect. Gdaliahu welcomed him warmly, often asking for updates on the empire's affairs. Their lively debates were marked by mutual respect, as both understood that "the beauty of advice is that you don't have to take it." Gdaliahu never questioned whether Mordecai followed his counsel, content with the exchange of ideas.

———◆———

Hegai informed Queen Esther about Mordecai's promotion. She acknowledged it with a slight nod and a tightened expression. After a pause, she gave a directive.

"Deliver a message to Mordecai," she instructed.

At their daily meeting, Hegai relayed the Queen's words: "Queen Esther says, 'May God bless you in your new role. Many Jewish leaders, like you, have no sons to help them in business. Use your influence and the precedent of Zelophehad to establish a class for girls at the Academy. Educating girls will benefit God's nation!'"

Mordecai nodded thoughtfully and replied, "Sarah will be perfect for this."

---

[4] Genesis 26:5

CHAPTER 25

Sometime after the celebrations, Mordecai met Yavin in the backroom of the merchant's shop. They locked the doors, descended to the basement, and entered a hidden room.

"We've restored the king's pride," Mordecai began. "He now has a better queen—Ishtar herself. But we must protect her. Esther is like my daughter, and those Babylonian generals may try to kill her and reinstate Queen Vashti from house arrest."

Yavin, ever practical, said, "I'll investigate her guards."

Mordecai stroked his beard thoughtfully. "That's a start, but not enough," Mordecai replied. "We also need to protect the king. He's been good to us, allowing work on the temple in Jerusalem."

"I'll look for signs of a plot," Yavin suggested.

Mordecai smiled wryly. "Good luck with that."

Yavin leaned in. "What if we start a conspiracy? Draw in the rogue guards, then expose them, and fright others. Saving the king from assassination would earn us a great debt."

Mordecai nodded, intrigued. "How do we stir them up?"

Yavin grinned. "Lately, some guards have been neglecting their appearance. Enforcing stricter grooming could provoke those with resentment. Harvona can issue the order."

Mordecai's eyes gleamed. "Brilliant! Agitate them. The disloyal will reveal themselves, and we'll eliminate the threat. Recruiting them will be easy, since many of them are Babylonians, and they trust me. Don't explain to Harvona—it'll be a good test for him, too."

Yavin's excitement faded as a frown crept in. "But what if they report you? You could be killed."

Mordecai hesitated briefly, then waved off the concern. "We've got time. If something goes wrong, Harvona will understand. We'll still be rewarded."

In the days that followed, Harvona ordered the guards to maintain perfect grooming—uniforms spotless, beards identical, weapons gleaming. The king, pleased, promoted Harvona to first-rank bodyguard. But beneath the surface, unrest brewed. Mordecai soon learned that Bigthan, a prominent door guard from a noble Babylonian family, was deeply frustrated. Had Babylon not fallen, Bigthan might have been a high-ranking minister or general.

The next day, Mordecai spotted Bigthan wandering the streets, frustration etched on his face. Sensing an opportunity, he approached carefully.

"God's blessings on you, Bigthan," Mordecai greeted softly. *I need to act before someone else exploits his anger—someone who truly wants the king and Esther dead.*

Bigthan stopped but didn't meet Mordecai's eyes. "The gods have forsaken me, your honor. I was meant for greatness, but now I'm just dust. Misery."

Mordecai's voice softened. "Things are really that bad? What happened? Maybe I can help."

"Since Harvona's promotion, he's been humiliating us," Bigthan muttered bitterly. "He insulted my honor, said I wasn't properly shaved. Damn him!"

"Is Harvona targeting others too?" Mordecai asked, leaning in.

"Yes, Teresh feels it too. Harvona's always finding ways to humiliate us."

Mordecai nodded thoughtfully. "The three of us should meet. Maybe I can offer a solution."

The next day, Mordecai met with Bigthan and Teresh in secret. The tension was thick as they huddled together, speaking in low voices. Mordecai wiped his sweaty palms on his robe.

"My master seeks to restore the glory of the past. Pride. Revenge. Will you join him?" Mordecai whispered, his words deliberate and tempting.

Bigthan and Teresh exchanged glances before nodding. "Yes. Revenge."

Mordecai exhaled in relief. *I've got them.*

"What does your master offer us?" Bigthan asked eagerly.

Mordecai smiled inwardly at their naivety. *Trusted officers? Fools. You'll dig your own graves.*

"He'll grant you command," Mordecai replied smoothly. "Each of you will lead five hundred soldiers as his trusted officers."

Bigthan's eyes lit up. "What do we need to do?"

Mordecai paused, letting the tension build. "When the time is right, I'll give you a poisoned arrow. As the king passes, shout 'Intruder!'—point toward the balcony, then stab him. Pretend to shield him, pull out the arrow, and my master will handle the rest. For now, follow Harvona's orders, and stay perfect. It may take time, but I'll guide you. Are you with me?"

Bigthan and Teresh nodded without hesitation. "Yes, your honor."

Mordecai's gaze hardened. "You know the risks. We might be killed."

Tears welled up in Teresh's eyes. "I've waited years for this. I prayed to Marduk, and here you are—Mordecai."

Bigthan nodded, determined, unaware they were sealing their own fate.

Bigthan's demeanor shifted—he appeared more content, impeccably groomed, earning praise from Harvona. Mordecai, confident that Bigthan and Teresh would *not* act without the poisoned arrow, waited ten days before asking Yavin, "Any news from Harvona?"

"Yes," Yavin replied, noticing Mordecai's frustration—that I did not report sooner—"Harvona praised your advice. Though there were initial challenges, since he spoke with the guards, everything has been perfect. They're all happy and following orders."

Mordecai frowned. "They haven't reported me. Their hatred and pride are still simmering, but they are loyal to me. It pains me to harm them. Should we give them two more weeks?"

"We can't wait. The situation is too volatile. We're protecting both the king and Esther," Yavin urged. "We need to act before they find another ally. We will inform Esther now, but it will still take time before she is summoned to the king."

Mordecai contacted Hini, instructing her to inform Esther that Bigthan and Teresh were related to Baanah and Rechab,[5] infamous assassins. Realizing they were plotting against the king, but Mordecai had not called for immediate action, Esther decided to bide her time until the king summoned her, choosing not to appear uninvited and risk her life.

Two days later, Alarmed Yavin reported back. "A shopkeeper told me Teresh requested poison. I've delayed the sale and instructed him to give a harmless substance with false instructions."

"Good. Keep a close watch—he might try elsewhere," Mordecai warned. "Watch Bigtan too."

"We're monitoring them closely. If necessary, we'll act," Yavin assured him.

Mordecai nodded. "The goal is to credit Esther with stopping the plot. Keep me updated."

Two days later, Esther was summoned to the king's bedchamber.

The next day, Harvona met privately with Mordecai. "Queen Esther informed the king, in your name, that Bigthan and Teresh were plotting to kill him," Harvona began gravely. "I overheard the conversation and stayed calm. The king tasked me with handling

---

5   Two commanders who killed King Ish-bosheth the son of King Saul. (Samual 2, 4:7)

it. I arrested the guards, and Yavin confirmed they planned to use a poisoned arrow. When confronted, they proudly confessed and even praised you, likely thinking you had been caught and forced to reveal the plot. Their confession sealed their fate. They were discreetly executed, and now the king and his guards believe the goddess Ishtar saved his life. The king has expressed his deep gratitude to you."

Mordecai responded coolly, "But you've failed as the head bodyguard. You disciplined Bigthan, believing you'd reformed him. Wrong. That's when he started working for me on the plot. If I had wanted, I could have orchestrated the king's death."

Harvona stared in shock, eyes wide.

"Never give disgruntled guards a second chance," Mordecai continued sternly. "They must be removed immediately. No excuses. Any discontent can lead to disaster—for the king and or you."

Harvona dropped to one knee, pressing Mordecai's hand to his forehead. "Thank you for giving me another chance."

Mordecai helped him up and embraced him. "I'll create a new protocol for selecting and managing the king's guards."

"Thank you," Harvona replied gratefully.

"Keep this confidential," Mordecai added. "Record my actions in the king's history book, but don't reward me. I want the king to remain in my debt."

Harvona nodded. "It will be done."

"Also, send me Bigthan's and Teresh's belongings," Mordecai requested.

"Why?" Harvona asked.

"I'll send their possessions to their families in Babylon, with a letter saying they died bravely, serving *their* king's honor, along with some money. It will give their families closure."

Harvona, still puzzled, asked, "Why?"

"They served me faithfully. This will ease their families' suffering."

CHAPTER 26

Esther embraced her leisurely life while staying mentally and physically active. She took pleasure in training her white horse, practicing jumps and high-speed galloping, often leaving Hatach struggling to keep pace. To keep her mind sharp, she recited the poems and stories Mordecai had taught her, and she expanded her knowledge by having Hegai borrow history books from the king's treasury. She started with Persian and Babylonian histories before delving into other renowned nations, relishing accounts of great wars and the lives of kings and queens.

To deepen her understanding, Esther commissioned a silk tapestry embroidered with a detailed map of the empire, featuring forests, mountains, seas, lakes, rivers, roads, cities, and temples. This visual aid helped her better comprehend the historical texts she studied.

She also invited foreign ex-contestants to share their stories and translate books for her. Though some initially resented her, believing she was the contestant who used the lion, Esther welcomed them warmly as representatives of their nations. Gradually, they appreciated her kindness and were honored to be invited.

"Hegai," Esther instructed, "to avoid the king's jealousy, I will wear only gifts I received from him. The ex-contestants may honor me with their national foods and drinks."

One woman from Corsica gifted Esther two special bottles of liquor—one made from myrtle leaves, the other from fruits[6]—in honor of Ishtar. Knowing the king's fondness for unique wines, Esther thanked

---

[6]   There are many types of myrtle plants the world over, many of which are poisonous.

her with a hug. Inspired by this, other ex-contestants began presenting their own distinct sweets and wines. Esther soon accumulated a wine cellar filled with expensive, renowned vintages. Eager to learn, she had her map updated with new details about their homelands and asked each woman to teach her phrases in their languages, including salutations and blessings, which she diligently wrote down and practiced.

Though Esther concealed her Jewish identity, she followed the Torah as closely as possible. She maintained a mostly vegetarian diet and refrained from working on the Sabbath, allowing her chambermaids to rest as well.

Summoned to the king's bedchamber about once a month, Esther knew King Ahasuerus desired a son, but she did not align her visits with her menstrual cycle, awaiting Mordecai's instructions. She feared that after bearing a son—or possibly a second to secure the line—the king's interest in her might fade. She longed for a child. She questioned whether her sacrifices were worth it. Each evening, she prayed for Mordecai's success and the blessing of motherhood.

Mordecai was taken aback when Yavin presented him with a personal letter from Egypt. Before opening it, he studied the handwriting—*amateurish yet elaborately elegant.* The letter was from Rebekah, the daughter of Zechariah. Trembling with anticipation, he paused before reading.

Rebekah expressed her growing love for biblical stories and detailed her efforts to learn reading and writing. She asked permission to write to him again, knowing how busy he was. She admitted the challenge of forming Hebrew letters but noted her improvement. She described her visits to the pyramids, sailing on the Nile, and her father's quest to locate the Sea of Reeds, where the Israelites had crossed. She hinted at a theory she had about the crossing and promised to share more once she had tested her idea.

Mordecai noticed a faint smear on the luxurious Egyptian paper. Was it a kiss? Tears? He examined it closely, catching the faint scent of narcissus oil, which made him smile.

She's certain we're engaged, Mordecai mused. *According to court customs, the gift of the page and their mutual touching the page, might signify a commitment. Now that Esther was married, I'm free to pursue a wife. Perhaps I'll write back; it could help her improve her writing*, he thought.

Curious, he pondered Rebekah's hinted explanation. *What could her theory be?*

Mordecai penned an encouraging response but decided not to send a gift, unsure of what would be appropriate. Later, he waved Rebekah's letter in front of Yavin.

Yavin blinked in surprise.

"Aha! You and Gdaliahu Ha-Nasi are conspiring behind my back!" Mordecai exclaimed with excitement.

Yavin laughed. "Lucky for you."

"And now, because she's educated, I *have* to marry her!" Mordecai said, half-joking.

"Not exactly," Yavin replied with a smirk.

"What do you mean?" Mordecai's voice raised in frustration.

"I can marry her," Yavin said with a grin.

"You can…? Ha! Over my—" Mordecai started, but then broke into loud, uncontrollable laughter.

Yavin grinned. "Got you, my master."

Mordecai, catching his breath, smiled warmly. "True. I forgive you, my dear Yavin. I appreciate your efforts. And you can keep hoping."

CHAPTER 27

A few years later, Mordecai observed Carshena, the king's head minister, struggling to make his way through the king's gate, moving slowly and appearing frail. The dignitaries bowed as Carshena passed. On another occasion, Mordecai saw him stumble, only to be saved by his assistant.

"It seems Carshena's time as head minister is ending," Mordecai said to Harvona.

Harvona nodded. "Yes, he's even falling asleep in the king's presence. The king has already asked about his health."

The next day, Mordecai invited Yavin to dinner, where they enjoyed grilled lamb and vegetables. As Yavin ate grapes, he waited for Mordecai to explain the formal invitation.

"It's time to find a replacement for Carshena," Mordecai said.

Yavin choked, coughing violently before gasping, "Why?"

Mordecai smiled. "Politics are like gardens—if neglected, they yield no fruit, and weeds take over. The king is weak and has appointed corrupt ministers. One could seize power and become a tyrant. We need to control the situation to protect the king."

"So, what's your plan?" Yavin asked.

"My goal is to prevent the Jewish people from assimilation or extinction. I decided to apply two solutions: the Prosperity route and the Pain route—P&P. We're in a time of sweet prosperity, but that can easily lead to assimilation if we don't act. We need adversity to unite us, the Painful route. Just as God used the slavery in Egypt. I plan to bring great danger to our people, then save them, create a new holiday to celebrate our victory, and re-establish the Torah as our guide."

"Adversity?" Yavin asked, still confused.

"Yes," Mordecai raised his voice. "Troubles will unite us. Victory will strengthen our faith." Mordecai slammed his fist into his other hand's palm. "Do you understand now?"

"I hear you, but I'm still dumbfounded," Yavin replied.

"There's no other choice. What worked for God will work for us," Mordecai said.

Yavin paused, still unsure. "But why *you* have to do it?"

Mordecai took a deep breath. "I am of royal blood, a descendant of King Saul. My grandfather instilled in me the duty to help our people, and Gdaliahu Ha-Nasi anointed me for this. I've identified the problem and the solution. Our people are strong and prosperous—the time is right. Please, help me."

"Tell me your plan, successor of King Saul and King David," Yavin said.

"We need to ensure Carshena's replacement is someone we can manipulate," Mordecai explained.

"So, what's the strategy?" Yavin asked.

"We initiated the 'beauty contest' that made Esther queen, and the 'assassin contest.' Now, we'll create a 'corruption contest.'"

Yavin laughed. "A corruption contest? What's the criteria?"

"We need the worst candidate—ambitious, corrupt, hungry for power. We'll set a trap, and the most evil minister will take the bait," Mordecai replied.

"Like chess," Yavin mused.

"Exactly. Sometimes you sacrifice a piece for victory," Mordecai agreed.

"And if no one takes the bait?" Yavin asked.

Mordecai burst into his loud laughter. "No one? Ha. Ha. Ha! None of the king's ministers? Ha. Ha. Ha." Mordecai wiped tears from his eyes. "You are joking, aren't you? Of course, one will hurry to snap the bait from his friends! Ha. Ha. Ha."

Yavin smiled. "All right, there are several, I agree."

"Good," Mordecai said. "Do you have any ideas for promoting one of them?"

"We'll let the corrupt minister do what he does best—rob and brobe (bribe)—he'll expose himself," Yavin suggested.

"Perfect. We'll dispose of him before he gains real power," Mordecai nodded.

Yavin continued, "I'll ask wealthy Jewish leaders to contribute jewelry and valuables. We'll make it look like treasure plundered from an Egyptian royal tomb, authenticated with an official seal. It'll be a wedding dowry, traveling from Egypt to India for a royal bride."

"Let's include a beautiful bride," Mordecai added.

"Does Zechariah have another daughter?" Yavin asked with a grin.

"You've been to Egypt—why ask me?" Mordecai retorted.

"I'll ask for a pedigreed Jewish bride," Yavin said, blushing. "For me."

"Why the pedigree?" Mordecai laughed. "You're my heir."

"A wise man plans for the future," Yavin replied, embarrassed.

Mordecai chuckled. "Hide some recently minted gold coins inside fake poison bottles. Add magical items to the treasure. We'll bait the trap."

Yavin agreed, still laughing. "The minister will be tempted to gift some to the king."

Mordecai nodded. "I'll contribute Esther's golden tiara and letters proposing new security measures and a property tax."

"But we'll be shut out and pay higher taxes," Yavin protested.

"Every one must pay taxes. Still, we have a Queen and a Rook inside the palace. Others are playing chess without," Mordecai said, smiling.

"I'll start the ball rolling," Yavin said, "and just look at this," Yavin handed Mordecai a letter. "Another private message for you."

Recognizing Rebekah's handwriting, Mordecai said, "Leave."

Yavin, hiding a smile, bowed and exited.

Mordecai broke the seal of the letter and was immediately greeted by the scent of narcissus. He marveled at how quickly it had arrived. Skimming the formal salutation, his attention caught on a passage where Rebekah wrote:

I luve our ancestral mother Rebekah vary much. I tried to understand why she dropped from the camel. It woz vary dangerous. She could have broken a bone. In my opinion she wonted to mark herself as the bride. She did not wont Isaac to start evaluating all of her beautiful maidens. In addition, she forced Isaac to come to her, and she covered her face with a scarf as a message: 'I am not yours. Earn me.' Only when he gave her Sarah's property, which included the power to command her husband, did she agree to be his wife.

Isn't it nice? And my name is Rebekah, too.

I tested my idea of how the children of Israel crossed the see. It woz a success.

Eagerly waiting for the invitation.

Yours only,

Rebekah

Mordecai smiled and leaned back in his chair. Sweet. Direct transcribing from vocal sounds. Amazing ideas. She revealed her feelings, writing: 'Love,' 'Earn me,' 'Waiting for invitation,' 'Yours only.' He wiped a tear and quickly wrote a response:

Salutation to Rebekah, daughter of Zechariah, heir of King David,
Your explanation is original, amazing, ingenious—a touch of female creativity.
Eager to hear about crossing the sea.
The invitation will come soon.
Respectfully yours,
Mordecai the Jew.

He hesitated. I wish I could sign it with love.

———✥———

Gdaliahu's nephew in Egypt was thrilled when he heard about the upcoming caravan and eagerly agreed to organize it. Following Mordecai's instructions, Yavin directed the merchants to send their valuable goods to Zechariah. The merchants, who held great respect for Mordecai and trusted his judgment, complied without complain.

With great enthusiasm, Zechariah set to work, carefully gathering the exquisite treasures into several ornate chests. He meticulously compiled an inventory list, recording each item in detail to ensure nothing was missed. The anticipation of the journey filled the air with excitement.

———✥———

In the twelfth year of the king's reign, a heavily guarded convoy carrying treasure from Egypt to India set off through the dangerous Amalekite lands. Notices were sent to local princes, offering payments for safe passage. Soon, word arrived from Zechariah that the caravan had departed Egypt.

"I sent Rebekah a letter. Have we heard from Rebekah?" Mordecai asked Yavin, concern creeping into his voice.

"No," Yavin replied firmly.

"No?" Mordecai repeated.

"No!" Yavin confirmed again.

Mordecai frowned, pacing anxiously. "This feels like a bad omen. Could there be trouble?"

Yavin watched as Mordecai struggled with his thoughts.

That night, Mordecai dreamt of a message in flames: *"Guard me, and I will guard you."*

The next morning, with renewed resolve, he shared discreet details about the convoy at the king's gate.

As the caravan entered Amalekite territory, the guards' chieftain demanded extra payment. Pressured, the convoy leader hid the treasure secured by ten guards, and left to find more funds.

A few days later, Yavin approached Mordecai with a lead. "I know our target. I saw the Agagite's sons, Parshandatha and Dalphon, leave town with a hundred armed men."

Mordecai scoffed. "Ah, him—the corrupt junior minister—rushing to seize the treasure. Predictable."

Yavin speculated, "Perhaps owning Pharaoh's jewels is driving him."

Mordecai nodded. "Thieves steal, cheaters cheat, killers kill. His actions are predictable. Because only a few guards will protect the treasure, do you think he'll suspect a trap?"

"No," Yavin reassured him. "His sons will boast about their 'victory.'"

"Find a Jewish slave in his household," Mordecai ordered. "Enlist him as a spy."

As days passed, Mordecai's anxiety grew. He paced Yavin's shop, tugging at his beard. "Any messages yet?"

"No," Yavin said, calmly watching. "We just have to wait."

Mordecai sighed, uneasy.

"Get some sleep," Yavin smiled. "I'll do the worrying for both of us."

———≈———

A few days later, N the Agagite Junior Minister's (JMN) sons returned triumphantly, leading the caravan straight to their father's palace. They boasted of their daring assault, claiming victory over two hundred guards, with only ten escaping. Beaming with pride, the JMN rewarded his sons with treasure chests for their bravery.

As the JMN inspected the treasure, he carefully selected several items to present to the king. One item, a magnificent tiara, caught the eye of his wife, Zeresh.

"May I have it?" she asked eagerly.

"No. This is my path to glory," he replied firmly.

"I want it!" Zeresh demanded, but he turned away, leaving her fuming.

An Egyptian priest translated the inscriptions on the treasures. Armed with this information, JMN presented the gifts to the king, emphasizing their illustrious origins and magical powers. He pulled out a glorious royal golden tiara. Harvona, watching, was visibly impressed. Among the gifts were bottles of lethal poison, which JMN described with satisfaction, "It kills immediately, the assassin too."

The king, impressed, ordered the gifts taken to his chamber. Holding the tiara, he called for Esther. As they waited, JMN seized the moment. "Your Majesty, too many trivial things take up your valuable time. If it pleases you, I could manage the gate the people would *present* and *read* their requests to me. I'll filter out trivial matters and present only the important ones."[7]

Before the king could respond, Esther entered. Smiling, the king extended the tiara toward her. "Come, my Queen Ishtahr. I have a gift for you."

JMN looked smug, but as Esther took the tiara, her heart sank—it was her mother's. Fear gripped her. *Had Mordecai been killed?* She collapsed in tears at the king's feet, masking her shock.

---

[7]   This references Jethro's advice to Moses.

Moved by her display, the king promoted JMN to Head Minister (HMN), instructing him to implement his security proposal.

Later, Esther urgently asked Hatach, her bodyguard, "Who was that minister?"

"The new Head Minister, N the Agagite," Hatach replied.

Esther's mind raced. *An Agagite... He must have stolen my mother's tiara. Did Mordecai let him steal it? Is this a message from Mordecai, warning me he's my enemy? Who can I trust? What do I do now?*

Mordecai heard about the promotion N the Agagite to the Head Minster position of Carshana, and he is now called in short HMN. Mordecai decided to call him an insulting name—"Hay-man."[8]

---

8 In an effort to erase the name of the Amalekites, we assume his true name is unknown and refer to him as 'HMN' or 'Hay-man.' It is possible that in the scroll, his name is a shortened form of 'המנובל' (the vile one) or 'המונה' (the counter or weigher of money).

CHAPTER 28

That afternoon, Yavin visited Mordecai. "Have you heard? Our 'Hay Man,' N the Agagite, the new Head Minister, has already set up an office at the king's gate. He's barring dignitaries from entering the palace without his permission and making them kneel, claiming, 'All dignitaries sitting at the king's gate must kneel to him, because so ordered the king to him.'"

"Good," Mordecai replied with a hint of satisfaction. "Our plan is progressing faster than expected. As predicted, he implemented the new security measures recommended in our letter that was included in the Egyptian treasury. And thanks to this and Esther's tiara, he was promoted to Head Minister. He's given me a legal way to provoke him." Tapping his fingers thoughtfully, he added, "He's isolating the king and usurping honors meant only for kings and gods."

"What will you do? Aren't we prohibited from kneeling by our Jewish laws?" Yavin asked, concerned.

Mordecai raised his hand. "Hold on. The Greeks don't kneel to men, but our laws only forbid kneeling to other gods. Aren't we prostrating to King Ahasuerus? He claims this was ordered 'to him' specifically, but without an official decree or royal seal, it sounds like hearsay. I believe the king authorized him to have us read before him, but he twisted it to mean 'kneel.'"[9]

"So, will you kneel?" Yavin pressed.

---

[9]   This is a word play. In Hebrew the words 'read' and 'kneel' sound similar – כָּרַע, קָרָא. Similarly the word 'אסתר' and 'עשתר', and the words 'לעבד' and 'לאבד'.

Mordecai shook his head. "No, I won't. I won't read, and I won't kneel. If 'Hay Man' complains to the king, it'll expose his lie and earn the king's wrath for impersonating royal authority. And he can't kill me without the king's approval—especially after I saved the king's life. The decree isn't legally sound: it only applies to dignitaries who sit at the king's gate—not you, since you're not a judge or dignitary. And no one, including me, is required to kneel if we are anywhere else. Does that sound logical to you? I think the decree is invalid—not issued by the king."

"Do you think he'll back down?" Yavin asked.

"Too late for that," Mordecai said with a grin. "He's trapped by his own decree, issued in the king's name."

Mordecai then shared his plan with Yavin. "If he kills me, will you carry out our plan?"

"I will. Proudly!" Yavin replied.

Mordecai smiled. "Thanks to you, I have even more reason to stay alive." His thoughts drifted to Rebekah.

Soon after Mordecai's conversation with Yavin, an announcement invited all the king's dignitaries to a celebration at HMN's palace in honor of his promotion. Despite extending an invitation to the king's generals, the generals politely declined.

Mordecai attended, impressed by the wealth HMN had amassed and displayed. Scanning the room, he noticed properties once owned by Jewish families, as well as items from the "treasure caravan." *At least HMN has good taste*, Mordecai thought.

HMN and his wife moved among the guests, greeting them with warm smiles and extended handshakes. The dignitaries, adorned in their finest attire, left gifts and letters for HMN, praising his home and family. Mordecai observed how HMN's wife subtly managed him with gentle nudges.

HMN then proudly introduced his ten sons, all between 15 and 30, and though he appeared a loving husband, his wife clearly took charge, often finishing his sentences. Amalekite elders, also present, were promised homes in Shushan by HMN, and together, they blessed their gods for their newfound fortune.

CHAPTER 29

The next morning, HMN approached the king's gate, flanked by twelve bodyguards. As he arrived, the leaders at the gate stood, stepped away from their worktables, and knelt in reverence. Suddenly, a brown, skinny street dog appeared, stopping directly in front of HMN. Mordecai's heart sank—a bad omen. Everyone held their breath as HMN paused. The dog, confused, tucked its tail and lowered its head.

Is the dog kneeling, too? Mordecai thought, finding it darkly amusing.

HMN raised a finger, and a bodyguard swiftly drew his bow, shooting the dog. It limped away, yelping in pain. Mordecai noticed the brief, satisfied smile on HMN's face, while the other dignitaries looked on in disgust. As HMN continued, basking in his power. Respectfully, Mordecai stood and bowed, a nervous thought creeping in: *Will he point at me next?*

But HMN, engrossed in conversation with an aide, ignored him. His guards exchanged surprised glances, stealing looks at Mordecai.

———⋙———

"I've definitely irritated HMN," Mordecai told Yavin. "I saw his frustration as he tried to ignore me. I was terrified, especially after he shot that dog. I kept my eyes open and held my breath!"

"You're so brave!" Yavin exclaimed.

"I'm fighting for our nation. I gave him the same honor we extended to Carshena. If the king had truly ordered this, HMN would have arrested me on the spot."

"He might still complain," Yavin warned.

"We have time. Harvona will inform us," Mordecai replied.

"What if he tries something else to force you to kneel?" Yavin asked.

"He might try dressing like the king or using the king's flag, but eventually, he'll run out of tricks. I won't give in," Mordecai said confidently. "He'll investigate first, but I already have a response."

Before HMN's rise, leaders had direct access to the king. Now, all requests went through HMN, who decided their fate. Leaders lined up before dawn, gold in hand, hoping to approach him. HMN's friends cut in line, getting preferential treatment.

The following day, HMN wore the ceremonial robes of Marduk, hoping to compel Mordecai to kneel. But Mordecai stood firm, refusing to yield.

He thinks my name will make me respect Marduk. You can't trick a trickster, Mordecai mused. *You're desperate, worried that other dignitaries will follow me, and the king will punish you.*

It's not my job to expose HMN's false claims, and the king might punish me for disobeying, even if HMN's command is illegal.

HMN's friends soon approached Mordecai, asking, "Why won't you kneel to the supreme minister?"

Mordecai simply replied, "Because..." and waved dismissively. Confused, they left. More cronies came with the same question, receiving the same vague answer. Word spread, and even those who had never visited Mordecai sought an explanation.

'Hay Man' is frantic, Mordecai thought. *He's weak, and his mistakes will soon show.*

Would he try to assassinate me? Mordecai wondered. *No, that would be futile; the king would simply appoint a new Jewish leader who would continue to defy him. I'm fortunate not to have a family, except for Esther,* Mordecai reflected. *He cannot punish any close relatives.*

One of HMN's allies discreetly offered, "I'll spy for you."

He is hedging his bets, ensuring survival no matter who wins, Mordecai thought. Unfazed, he replied, "God will reward you," and waved him off. Others followed suit, and Mordecai accepted their offers, knowing that more spies could only strengthen his cause.

Meanwhile, HMN solidified his power at the palace, promoting loyal guards to command positions. Harvona reported that HMN had even spoken to the king's bodyguards.

It's getting dangerous, Mordecai thought. Fortunately, he can't enter the women's quarters to recruit more loyalists. I need to act soon.

The next day, Mordecai gathered the leaders and announced he was ready to explain his defiance. With fear gripping him, knowing this could bring ruin upon the Jews, he considered kneeling to HMN. But this was his chance to set his plan in motion.

With a stern expression, Mordecai declared, "Because I am a Jew," then walked away, leaving the words to hang in the air irrevocable. Now, HMN knows it's about the Jews, giving him time to plan.

Would he try to verify my claim? No. I'm the Jewish leader; no one will challenge me. Mordecai reflected.

Mordecai's spy reported HMN's reaction: "When HMN heard, his face twitched. He paced his office, muttering, 'What do you mean, "because I am a Jew"? Yes, that explains everything.' Then he erupted, 'A Jew... all of them? I hate him. I'll kill him, kill all the Jews—men, women, children. I'll eliminate his nation, erase his God. It's all his fault. His position will be gone. A lesson will be taught!'"

HMN hammered his fist in rage, already plotting his revenge.

———❧———

The next day, one of Mordecai's spies embedded in HMN's camp sent a secret message. The spy reported that a Jewish man, Ason Ben Aser, had informed HMN that "there is no Jewish law prohibiting kneeling to men. However, Mordecai is the leader of the Jews, and his word is considered the final law." HMN inquired about Mordecai's family and learned he had a daughter named Hadassah, who was kidnapped during the beauty contest and never returned. She might be in the palace as a maid or an ex-contestant. He was told Hadassah had long, light brown hair, though not as stunning as the other contestants, and that she was educated—able to read and write.

"Hay-man will try to find Hadassah!" Mordecai exclaimed, worry etched on his face. "It will take him some time; gaining access to the House of the Women or the House of the Concubines is no easy task. Alerting Hegai could be counterproductive. Still, finding an educated woman in the palace may not be difficult—Esther might be the only one." He turned to Yavin and asked, "Do you know this man?"

"Yes," Yavin replied, raising a finger thoughtfully. "That backstabbing treator is one of our students. A local."

"Should we relocate him?" Mordecai inquired. "No," he quickly reasoned. "Relocating him would only draw attention to our spies. HMN would likely replace him with someone even more loyal. Instead, we'll keep a close watch on Ason and use him to mislead HMN."

CHAPTER 30

Mordecai was stunned to learn that several survivors from the treasure caravan were waiting in his palace. Panic surged—*what were they doing here? They could ruin everything!* His heart raced as he hurried home.

When he opened it, he froze. Standing before him were Zechariah and a young man holding a scarf. They were dirty, disheveled, worn from their journey through the desert—no, not a young man—it was Rebekah, her hair cut short, covered in dust and sweat. The smell of exhaustion hit Mordecai like a wave, making him recoil. His hands trembled, and his breath quickened as he stared at Rebekah's pale, fearful face.

"Oh no. Rebekah..." Mordecai's voice cracked in horror. "How did you get here?" he demanded, his voice rising in shock as his heart pounded.

"We came with the treasure caravan," Zechariah stammered. "We were robbed. Here—" he extended an inventory list.

"You did what?" Mordecai shouted, barely glancing at it. He collapsed to the ground, sobbing uncontrollably, fists pounding the floor. "Oh God, why? Why did you come? Why?!"

Zechariah and Rebekah dropped beside him, tears streaming. "I'm sorry! It's all my fault!" Rebekah cried. "I sensed something was wrong. I... I forced my father!"

"I thought you invited us... a wedding... bride... pedigree..." Zechariah sobbed, confused.

"Bride?!" Mordecai's eyes locked on Rebekah. "You could have been killed! The caravan was bait! You were the bait! What have I done?"

"The caravan was bait?" Zechariah shouted. "Why didn't you tell us?"

"Spies everywhere!" Mordecai apologized.

They wept together, the weight of the situation crushing them. Mordecai longed to hold Rebekah, but he resisted. Wiping his face, he finally managed to speak, his voice thick with emotion. "You've come at the worst time. I'm caught in a deadly power struggle. The head minister wants my head on a stick. I can't send you back, not even with an army. From now on, you do not exist! Do you hear me?" His fist clenched as he spoke.

Rebekah gave a small, inquisitive smile but stayed silent. Mordecai noticed. *Is she pleased by my emotion?* Bewildered, he could smell the sour sweat and desert dust on her, but then, a spark of love flickered in his eyes. The scent of blooming narcissus seemed to fill the air, and he relaxed, returning her smile.

From a pouch at her waist, Rebekah pulled out a glowing red-orange persimmon and offered it to him with an embarrassed smile. "This is from the Garden of Delicious Comfort. Ripe and ready!"

Like you, Mordecai thought.

Mordecai, having never seen such a fruit, cupped her hands as he bit it. "The fruit of Knowledge, good 'n bed," he mused aloud. His eyes widened in surprise. "Thank you, O God, for such joy," he said, smiling.

Rebekah blushed and lowered her gaze.

Mordecai then showed them up the tower, and explained how to escape by sliding down a hollow marble column using a rope. He called for Yavin. "Seal and conceal Rebekah in the tower. No light, no fire, no looking out! Guard her with your life."

"Of course," Yavin replied, eyes gleaming with determination.

"For me," Mordecai added sharply.

"Of course," Yavin answered with a faint smile.

CHAPTER 31

The next day, HMN visited Ishtar's temple for a private consultation. His slaves carried numerous offerings, and he swelled with pride as he was ushered in to pray with the high priest. Since Esther's rise to queen, the temple's prestige had soared.

"I need your advice," HMN said cautiously. "But this must remain confidential."

"Of course, supreme minister," the priest assured. "It will be between us and the goddess Ishtar."

"I must punish a small nation that disrespects our gods, but I need the king's approval," HMN explained.

"Could the king have already granted them an exemption?" the priest asked.

"I can't ask him directly," HMN replied. "But I can present their crime and see his reaction."

"The king cares most about money," the priest advised. "Frame it as a new tax plan."

HMN nodded, recalling a tax letter found in the captured treasure. *Did Ishtar send it to me?* He wondered.

"When does the goddess suggest I act?" HMN asked.

The priest, after a prayer, handed him a dice. "Roll and find your answer," he said.

HMN kissed the dice, closed his eyes, and rolled. "In the twelfth month, Ishtar will grant you victory," the priest declared.

HMN frowned—eleven months was too long. "Can we try again? That's too far off. I'll pay you again. Double."

"The chosen month cannot be changed," the priest warned, "without Ishtar's wrath on your head!"

Frustrated, HMN sighed. *At least the delay would help conceal the connection to Mordecai's defiance.*

———————

Harvona alerted Mordecai, "A plot is brewing!"

"What happened?" Mordecai asked.

"HMN told the king, 'There are people scattered throughout the empire with laws different from ours, and they don't follow the king's law. It isn't profitable for the king to let them rest.' HMN then paused, as if waiting to see if the king had exempted any nation."

Mordecai realized the significance. HMN now knew Mordecai wasn't exempt from kneeling.

Harvona continued, "HMN requested, 'If it pleases the king, let a decree be issued to oppress them, and I will weigh ten thousand bars of silver into the king's workers … to bring to the royal treasury.' The king handed him his royal ring, saying, 'The silver is given to you, and the people to do as you see fit.' HMN tried to bribe the king, but the king refused."

Later, Mordecai shared with Yavin, "This is escalating fast," showing a freshly signed decree.

**Let it be known,
on the 13th day of the 12th month,
anyone may destroy, kill, and oppress all Jews,
young and old, women and children,
and loot their wealth.**

Stamped with the king's signet, the message was clear.

"This is a simple, strong, and efficient move," Yavin said, frustration evident in his voice. "HMN tried to bribe the king to let him kill the nation that does not respect the king's law. The king waived the offer, and allowed HMN to proceed. Now, HMN has effectively given people legal immunity to kill us and loot our property, as approved by the king's signet. This is a catastrophe! We're already a small minority, and now everyone will turn against us!"

"Exactly. This is what everyone thinks." Mordecai nodded. "But remember, this is what we promoted him for. Now that he's done what we expected, we don't need him anymore. We can dispose of him, before he tries to revoke the 'killing decree' and plead for mercy.

"We knew he would eventually cause trouble for the Jews. He plans to kill us all, and without a nation, my position at the king's gate will be terminated, even if I survive. Because of the king's fear of assassins, he would be free to isolate the king in the palace, and rule outside."

"But..." Yavin's eyes lingered on the decree. "The decree expects each of them to kill one of us, and they are so many. How can you be so calm?"

"Not quite," Mordecai said, steady. "Don't despair. What appears to be a strength can often become a weakness. HMN only used the dice to select the month."

Yavin's concern deepened, but Mordecai remained confident.

"Using the dice shows HMN's weakness. He couldn't even choose the month on his own. Our God gave us time to prepare, mocking him."

"But the king authorized our destruction!" Yavin protested.

"No," Mordecai corrected. "The king only authorized 'oppression,' not annihilation. The killing wasn't explicitly authorized."

"What do you mean? The king let HMN proceed as he wished!" Yavin argued.

"Think carefully," Mordecai replied. "HMN said, 'If it pleases the king,' meaning only what is legal and pleasing can be done. The king heard no mention of killing, and he didn't waive any bribe."

Yavin frowned. "Can you prove this?"

Mordecai leaned in. "The king cares about two things: RESPECT and TAXES. HMN cleverly twisted his words to confuse people, making it seem like he was offering a bribe for punishing those who don't respect the king—like I disrespected him by refusing to kneel because I am a Jew. But since Queen Vashti's refusal, the king has never been exposed to a disrespectful act, except now with HMN. The king likely thought HMN was referring to a nation that doesn't obey tax laws. HNM proposed using royal funds to pay tax collectors, much like Joseph did in Egypt." Mordecai smirked.

"In addition," Mordecai said, "because, in financial matters, the top minister speaks first, unlike in matters of life and death where the junior minister speaks first, as in Queen Vashti's trial. Here, HMN, as the head minister, spoke first, so the king probably thought HMN was talking about taxes.

"Yavin, focus on HMN's wording. He asked to 'oppress,' a vague term which could mean 'destroying and killing,' or 'taxing and enslaving,' or 'deporting and scattering.' It can't mean 'scattering' since, as HMN pointed out, we're already scattered.

"In the decree, he was forced to explain 'oppression' as 'killing and destroying.' And we know he's twisting the king's words—as we saw in the 'kneeling decree.' So, such an interpretation must be wrong.

"Now, what about 'taxing and enslaving'? In order to confuse the king that he was talking about Taxes, HMN used terms like 'profit,' 'workers,' and 'rest,' all linked to money and labor. The king must have thought that the word 'oppress' means 'taxing' or 'enslaving,' and I will show you, from the king's words, that this is true.

"HMN took the bait and used my second letter about taxes to mislead the king to give him a free hand to collect fair taxes from those who fail to pay. Jews are merchants, and there's no tax on their wealth or profit in Persia. As the custom in Persia, people who fail to pay their taxes are enslaved.

"The king's response—'The silver is given to you'—confirms this interpretation. HMN was authorized to use royal funds—up to ten thousand silver bars—to pay tax collectors to gather taxes, not to murder us."

"Seems logical," Yavin agreed. "The king must have assumed this was about money."

"Exactly. The king gave his signet ring, thinking it was for a long, bureaucratic tax process, not a mass killing—single use. HMN has some leeway, but only within what would please the king."

"Are you sure the king doesn't hate the Jews?" Yavin asked.

"HMN never mentioned Jews specifically," Mordecai explained. "And the king knows I am 'Mordecai the Jew,' the one who saved his life. He keeps us at the king's gate, invites us to his feasts, and allowed us to rebuild our temple. There is no evidence he wants us dead.

"The king loves wealth and grand feasts. Who would believe he'd reject ten thousand bars of silver? I'm sure he didn't knowingly approve a killing decree. HMN likely kept the term 'oppress' vague in case the king questions him later, and what is the purpose of the word 'oppress' after 'destroying and killin? There is noting left to 'oppress.' It is all a manipulation."

"But the king's orders can't be changed, and we'll suffer," Yavin said grimly.

"True, but suffering will unite us and teach us to fight for our survival, without waiting for God's help. Once we show the king that this decree is illegal, he will help us win."

Yavin looked worried. "People might blame you for their troubles."

"They'll only blame me if they think I caused this," Mordecai replied. "Most will blame HMN. But you're right—we must keep this secret."

"The Amalekites will try to wipe us out," Yavin said.

"And erase our God, too," Mordecai added. "Without us, who will teach the world about Him? We must win—God has no choice but to help us."

"A lot of Jews might die. What if only a large portion of us perish, but not all?" Yavin asked. "Would His name still be tarnished?"

Mordecai paused, his mind racing. After a moment of silence, he replied, "Right now, before the nations have fully accepted Him, his name would be tarnished unless there is a total victory. We must protect God's honor, and that means fighting harder for His sake."

Mordecai placed a firm hand on Yavin's shoulder. "I trust you to defend us if I'm gone. Even if it means facing a torturous death."

Yavin swallowed hard, his voice trembling. "Th…thank you."

Mordecai nodded. "I'm going to visit Gdaliahu Ha-Nasi to reassure him that we have this situation under control. He's too old to grasp it fully on his own."

With that, Mordecai turned to leave, the weight of their conversation lingering in the air.

———✦———

The next day, Yavin rushed to Mordecai, worry etched on his face. "Looters have already begun robbing our people. They're trying to steal our valuables before others join in, and meanwhile, the king is drinking with HMN."

Mordecai frowned but responded quickly. "Yavin, send a letter to the Jews. Tell them to mourn together and temporarily close their businesses in a general strike. This will send a message to the governors and the public, showing them what will happen if we perish. Wealthier Jews must support the community and contribute to the defense fund. Also, collect the names of those robbing and killing us."

He paused before adding, "Ensure no one deserts the towns. Everyone must defend their homes."

"I got worse news," Yavin said. "The Jews in Sifon have renounced their Jewishness. They all converted."

Mordecai thought for a moment. "That's one solution. In their hearts, they're still Jews, and they will return if we win. But their children might learn the wrong lesson. Add to our message: Denouncing your Jewishness won't save you. The attackers have already marked their prey. Stand together, fight together, win together—or be enslaved and killed together."

Mordecai began pacing. "I'm in danger. HMN could use the king's new tax plan—which the king did approve—to accuse me of a violation and act without mentioning my name."

"Should I increase your guard?" Yavin asked.

Mordecai shook his head. "No...and yes. I need a double. Find a brave, loyal soldier who looks like me, and teach him to mimic me. In all my public appearances, he will act for me."

Yavin nodded. "HMN seems nervous lately, increasing his guards and rushing everywhere."

"That royal ring weighs heavily on him, afraid to lose it," Mordecai mused. "In the end, it'll hang him." He smiled. "I'll join the mourning Jews and let HMN think he's succeeded."

CHAPTER 32

M ordecai, the leader of the Jewish people, was inundated with letters from across the empire, detailing atrocities and pleading for the king's help. In response, he carefully wrote back: pray, act with caution, train young men for protection, avoid dangerous activities, and wait for further instructions.

He deliberately avoided bringing these letters to HMN's office, knowing HMN would twist them to justify the killing decree and might kill him. Instead, Mordecai mourned with his people, tearing his clothes, wearing sackcloth, and covering himself in ash.

As he cried in the streets, Mordecai thought, *This is the perfect disguise. I'm sure 'Hay Man' is relieved not having me in the king's gate, thinking I've been killed, fled, or died in shame.*

———≈———

When Esther's chambermaids reported Mordecai's unusual behavior, she was relieved to hear he was alive but puzzled by his mourning. It wasn't a Jewish fast, and she knew he wasn't grieving a close relative, as she was his only family. Concerned, she hesitated to send money and instead instructed her maids to bring him fresh clothes. However, Mordecai refused the garments without explanation.

———≈———

After sending Esther's chambermaids away, Mordecai met Yavin at his store.

"Esther still cares for us. It was amusing—she sent me clothes!" Mordecai chuckled. "I think she wanted to see if HMN's guards are searching her servants when they leave the palace. I refused the clothes and waited to see if they'd search the servants or the garments on their way back. I needed to test this because I plan to send Esther a copy of HMN's 'killing decree.' HMN probably thinks I'm as good as dead, so he's less vigilant."

Yavin, puzzled, asked, "Wouldn't it have been simpler just to tell her about the decree?"

Mordecai shook his head. "Why would I? She hasn't asked for anything yet. Besides, one of her servants could be spying for HMN or the king. She'll ask soon enough, likely sending Hatach. He's loyal, but we need to be cautious. I'll give him cryptic messages—he might misinterpret them, but Esther will understand."

Mordecai scratched his head. "Something's crawling on me. Check for lice?"

Yavin inspected. "No lice, just ash. Stop scratching—you're bleeding."

"Easy for you to say," Mordecai muttered. "I just hope Hatach arrives soon."

Before long, Hatach arrived, and Mordecai quickly updated him, including the detail that HMN and the king had sat down to drink after issuing the decree.

Handing Hatach an official Hebrew translation of the killing decree, stamped with the king's signet, Mordecai instructed, "Tell the queen that HMN offered to weigh silver into the king's treasury to oppress the Jews. Urge her to go to the king and beg for her people."

Without reading the decree, Hatach tucked it under his shirt, pressed it flat against his chest, then bought a few pieces of qandi—small crystallized sugar treats—and returned to Esther.

As Hatach left, Yavin turned to Mordecai. "You exposed the spy when you used those specific words—'to weigh silver' and 'oppress'—just as HMN said to the king."

Mordecai smiled slyly. "Exactly. It was my way of showing that I knew what really happened in that conversation. Even if Esther uses those words, the king won't be suspicious. Everyone believes Ishtar knows all, so no one will think of spies."

"But you essentially accused the king of accepting a bribe to authorize the killing of the Jews," Yavin said, concerned.

"That's what Hatach will assume, and it's what everyone already thinks. If I had said anything different, it would've raised suspicions. We have to be careful with Hatach's loyalty. He is a spy for the king and might be working for HMN," Mordecai replied calmly.

Yavin furrowed his brow. "Are you sure Esther will understand?"

Mordecai snorted. "Of course she will. She's my student—and my daughter."

"And if she doesn't?" Yavin asked.

Mordecai waved off the concern. "All I told her to do was read the decree, understand the bribe, go to the king, and beg for mercy. It's straightforward. If she has questions, we'll explain more later. By then, we'll know if Hatach is trustworthy."

Yavin hesitated. "Why didn't you just tell her to show the decree to the king?"

"That would've alarmed Hatach," Mordecai replied. "He might have gone straight to the king—or worse, to HMN. By not telling her to show the decree, Esther will understand that she mustn't. She'll figure it out."

"You're playing a dangerous game," Yavin warned. "You've just revealed to Hatach that the queen is Jewish."

"Not quite," Mordecai said with a grin. "She wears the unity crown. All nations are her people. But you're right—it might be time to disclose the truth to the king."

───────※───────

Hatach delivered Mordecai's message to Esther, who maintained a calm, stern expression as she smoothed the decree. Relief swept over her—Mordecai was alive and still pulling strings. But she couldn't show it. Mordecai, though unable to enter the palace and communicate directly with Hegai, clearly had spies. Esther trusted him completely, knowing he was fully informed.

As she read the decree, Esther scrutinized every word. *Something doesn't add up. HMN had been promoted and is close to the king. Still, my husband wouldn't wait a year to punish criminals, or allow killing and looting without a trial, nor would he permit criminals' property to be stolen without being delivered to the royal treasury. The decree doesn't fit my king's sense of justice.*

Mordecai gave me two key pieces of information: the killing decree and HMN's conversation with the king, when one would have been sufficient. These must be conflicting pieces of evidence. HMN had asked to "oppress" the Jews, but the decree stated "destroyed, killed, and oppressed." This requires clarification. It must be that what the king agreed to was likely different from the decree—my king wouldn't have authorized a mass murder.

The king must have understood that "to oppress"—as the Jews had been in Egypt—could not be 'dispersed and lost,' as the Jews are already dispersed, so it must mean 'to enslave.' HMN must have used the king's signet ring and altered the decree after the king's approved 'to oppress,' publishing decrees in the king's name, acting as if he were the king himself. This isn't just a plot against the Jews—it is treason.

Esther's determination solidified. *HMN has to be stopped, and fast.* She summoned Hini, the supervisor of her maids, and told her to tell Mordecai: Hatach's messages, and Esther's responses, ensuring Hatach is accurate and loyal.

When Mordecai received Hini's report, he was satisfied with Hatach's accuracy and loyalty. Meanwhile, Hatach, still en route, was unaware of Hini's mission. When Hatach arrived at Yavin's store, he relayed Esther's message, mimicking her angry tone:

"Don't you know what everyone knows? The law states that whoever goes uninvited unto the king into the inner courtyard shall be executed unless the king holds out his golden scepter. And I haven't been invited to the king's bed for the last thirty days."

Hatach delivered the message faithfully, and kept the conversation private. Mordecai felt relief—*Hatach is loyal, one less concern.*

With a stern expression, Mordecai quickly replied, repeating the words sent earlier through Hini: "Tell the queen: 'Don't think you can hide in the king's house. If you stay silent, we will be silenced, but salvation will come from another place. However, you and your father's family will be oppressed. Who knows if you became queen for such a time as this?'"

The intensity of Mordecai's tone startled Hatach, causing him to step back and instinctively touch his sword. Mordecai, undeterred, knew Hatach's loyalty was to Esther. *He understands the danger*, Mordecai thought. *Hatach would die defending his queen.*

After Hatach left, Yavin offered his insight. "Hatach believes Esther fears the king no longer loves her, and she's afraid to go to him uninvited. She is asking to wait until she is invited to his bed, presumably soon.

"She misquoted the law," Yavin continued. "It states, 'Any man or woman who comes uninvited to the king—wherever he is— **or** to the royal court—even if the king is not there—shall be executed unless the king extends his golden scepter.'"

Mordecai nodded. "Why did she misquote it?"

"She's protecting herself," Yavin explained. "Her real concern is the king may not be in the royal hall when she arrives, and he wouldn't be able to save her. She fears HMN might suspect something if she has to keep returning. When she insulted you about the law, she was actually asking whether you can ensure the king will sit on his royal chair when she goes.

Mordecai smiled. "Very good so far."

"And when you shouted at her, it meant, 'Yes, I can handle that.' You warned her that she and her father's family—meaning you and her only—are in imminent danger. You hinted that HMN is after you, and your daughter, who was a contestant—as Ason informed him. You urged her to go to the king as soon as possible and implied you wanted to know when it would happen."

"Excellent," Mordecai agreed, smiling. "But what about the thirty days?"

Yavin frowned, thinking. "That's a harder puzzle. I'm sure it's not about the king not loving her. There's something more. I'll have to think about it. Don't tell me yet," Yavin pleaded.

Mordecai's smile widened. *Esther's message was more ingenious than even Yavin realized, stirring powerful emotions and motivations that would soon unfold.*

By the time Hatach delivered Mordecai's message to Esther, she had already heard it from Hini. However, she maintained her composure, acted surprised, and calmly gave her response to Hatach, sending him back to Mordecai.

———⇜———

"Hatach has returned," Yavin announced. "She didn't send Hini this time. It seems she trusts him now."

Hatach relayed the queen's message: "The queen says, 'Tell the Jewish community in Shushan to fast on my behalf for three days and nights without food or drink. My maids and I will do the same. Then, I will go to the king, even though it's against the law. If I am to be oppressed, then I will be oppressed.'"

Mordecai nodded, dismissing Hatach without further comment.

"She's sharp. She understood everything, wouldn't you agree?" Mordecai asked.

"Yes," Yavin replied. "Let me break it down. She's instructing us to tell the Jewish community the queen is Jewish and to fast for her because she's going to the king uninvited. But she cleverly misled Hatach into thinking everyone already knows, so there's no need to tell anyone.

"No one can truly go three days and nights without drinking, so she's saying the opposite—don't tell the Jews. If the Jews hear that the queen is Jewish and is going to the king to plead for them, they will end their fasting and celebrate hysterically. HMN will hear—likely through Ason—and attack. What she's really saying is that in exactly three days from now, she will approach the king, signaling you must ensure the king is seated on his throne at that time."

"Good," Mordecai said. "Mark the present time."

"She said, 'If I am to be oppressed, then I will be oppressed,' showing she understood the key word 'oppress' and its double meaning.

"For the next three days, you should hide. Shall I give a fake eulogy for you in the Jewish high court to fool Ason?" Yavin asked, grinning.

"No," Mordecai replied. "That would hurt his credibility and our people's morale. I don't want to imagine what Kaffir-Ariot would do next."

"I was joking," Yavin reassured him. "You did not answer. She caught on to your concern about 'oppress' and responded clearly. No need to add a word, that might tipped off Hatach."

Mordecai smiled. "Blessed are her parents. We're lucky HMN has taken on so much of the king's work, giving us the time to adjust the king's schedule, and keep HMN away from him. In three days, we'll further overwhelm HMN."

CHAPTER 33

HMN, noticing Mordecai's absence at the king's gate, walked with a lighter step, head held high, smiling and nodding to the kneeling dignitaries. Mordecai's absence also eased his workload.

———❧———

Esther and Lucky sat together on the balcony, watching the world below with quiet tension. Esther scattered wheat seeds on a high shelf, just out of Lucky's reach, while the cat squeaked in excitement, trying to lure the birds closer. Both enjoyed the evening sun and the birds—but with very different intentions.

"We're in a similar situation," Esther said with a soft laugh, glancing at Lucky. "We're both setting traps, waiting for our prey to step in. Tomorrow is crucial. I'll pray for you if you pray for me."

Lucky responded with, "Miaau."

As Esther watched the birds, her mind turned to the weight of the task ahead. Approaching the king uninvited was a dangerous gamble—a collision of personal risk, legal boundaries, and political maneuvering. The stakes were high, and HMN was watching everyone's move. But excitement stirred within her, fueled by the urgency of Mordecai's call to action. She would stand before the king, pleading for her people, just as Moses had stood before Pharaoh.

She couldn't afford any mistakes. If HMN discovered her plan, he could act swiftly, bringing guards to kill them all. She had to be strategic and unpredictable.

"I won't follow Mordecai's instructions to the letter," she decided, a sly smile forming. "I'll do what he would—outsmart them all. Like when he tricked Shimon and rescued me. I'll be unexpected."

She chuckled at the thought, imagining herself as Ishtar descending into the underworld, preparing to face Satan. And hopefully, the king or Mordecai would play the role of Marduk and save her.

"Hini," Esther asked, her thoughts shifting, "what should I wear when I approach the king uninvited?"

"Your Ishtar dress, of course," Hini whispered, blushing slightly. "But leave off the belt and dagger. Show your stomach. Pad it, my queen."

Esther smiled, appreciating Hini's advice.

Three days later, exactly as she had planned, Esther was ready. Her seven maidens lay prostrate, weeping and praying for her safety.

As Esther approached the king, she fought to keep her fear at bay. *Does he love me enough? Will I die today? What will happen to me?* But she pushed the doubts aside, reminding herself that she shared the fate of her people. HMN would stop at nothing—not even killing the king—so she had to act. The king adored her, and she trusted in God's protection.

Relax, she told herself. *God is my shepherd. I will not fail.*

With her fully armed shadow, Hatach, Esther crossed the outer courtyard without issue. As she and Hatach, carrying her flag mounted on an iron war spear, approached the closed gate of the inner courtyard, the door guards presented their weapons and opened the gate.

Esther hesitated for a moment. *My next step could be my last.* She was about to break royal law, intruding on HMN's power and exposing herself to great danger. *If I don't retreat now, I seal my fate.*

She took a deep breath, scanning her surroundings. No one seemed alarmed. *I am the queen, after all.*

They moved forward, the crunch of gravel underfoot. The guards saluted and opened the golden doors to the royal hall. *They think this visit is prearranged,* Esther realized. *This is it. I won the crown here, and I may lose it here.*

Wearing the diamond necklace the king had given her and her unity crown, Esther stepped inside. She had deliberately placed the

Jewish stone to the side, but in her heart, she believed God was still with her, protecting her.

The king, seated on his throne, raised his eyes to watch her closely, though his head remained tilted downward.

Esther signaled subtly. Hatach planted the spear into the ground with a decisive thud and knelt beside it. Esther took seven deliberate steps forward and bowed her head. Hatach tilted the spear down until the queen's flag almost touched the floor, while the sharp tip pointed toward the king's head in a gesture of threatening submission. When Esther finally raised her eyes, she locked onto the king's gaze, silently pleading for him to acknowledge her.

After a moment, on his own initiative, Harvona bellowed, "A...tten...tion!"

Esther flinched but stood firm. The king's guards presented their weapons. *Are they warning me? Or honoring me?* she wondered, feeling a flicker of relief when no further action followed.

The king slowly lifted his head, his eyes sweeping over her, pausing at her midsection. She was relieved she had left her dagger behind.

He seemed pleased, noting the gifts he had given her. Since her ascent to queen, his empire had thrived. Esther knew he believed Ishtar's blessings came through her.

According to protocol, the king had two choices: let her approach or have her killed. Esther prayed he couldn't see how her legs trembled or hear her heart pounding. She forced a smile.

The king, remembering that he hadn't seen her for more than a moon cycle, studied her rounded belly. *He's watching my belly,* Esther thought, feeling her tension eased. *He thinks I'm pregnant—with his child—two weeks late—risking my life to give him great news. I am safe.*

The king returned her smile and extended his scepter, signaling her to come closer. Esther stepped forward, gently kissing the golden head of the scepter.

"What is it, Queen Ishtahr?" the king asked. "Whatever you want—up to half the empire—it will be yours."

He's convinced I'm pregnant, Esther thought, *The gift is really for his child within me—half his reign. Naming HMN as a guardian or regent will make perfect sense to him.* She knew the king's offer—up to half his empire—could mean anything, even as small as a single coin.

The king's joyful expression reassured her, but a cold dread gripped her heart. *What will happen when he discovers the truth? Will he be angry? Will he kill me then?* Her mind raced, but she steadied herself, savoring the moment. *He called me by my godly name,* she thought, feeling a surge of confidence. *He truly does love me.*

Everything seemed to be falling into place. *Mordecai has succeeded. HMN didn't stop me, and the king hasn't killed me. Yet.*

Esther licked her lips, speaking in a voice as sweet as the purr of her cat, "If it pleases the king, let only the king and HMN join me today for a wine banquet I have prepared in my chamber."

As she spoke, Harvona noticed a guard discreetly slipping away from his post. *I'll need to watch him,* Harvona thought. *Is he working for HMN?*

Without responding to Esther directly, the king turned to one of his bodyguards. "Fetch HMN immediately and bring him to the queen's banquet," he commanded.

———✥———

HMN was stunned by the invitation to join the queen and the king in her chamber. It was an unprecedented honor, one that swelled his pride. To his knowledge, no minister had ever been granted such a privilege, and being named directly by the queen made it all the more distinguished.

Rumors had already reached him that the king had offered Esther "up to half" of his empire. As the holder of the king's signet, this news piqued HMN's interest even more.

She must be pregnant, HMN mused, a sly smile creeping across his face. *Perhaps I'll be named regent.* The thought thrilled him. *If or when the king dies—sooner than later, I hope—I'll be the one to rule the empire for the young prince.*

His mind racing with ambition, HMN hastened to join the king, his heart filled with visions of power.

———◈———

HMN won't even consider that I risked my life by going to the king uninvited, Esther thought, suppressing a smirk. *He likely assumes I'm just seeking his "wise" counsel. The breach of protocol won't even cross his mind—he'll be too flattered by the invitation to question it.*

She felt a sense of satisfaction. *A little praise, and he turns into such a fool. But will he assume I'm pregnant? Does he really think he could be named regent?*

Uncertainty tugged at her, though. *So many layers to this game—it's dizzying.* Esther took a deep breath, trying to steady her swirling thoughts. *This has to work.*

Chapter 34

Esther returned to her quarters, where her guards saluted and opened the door for her. Inside, her maids, still prostrated on the floor, leaped to their feet the moment they saw her, hugging one another and dancing with joy. Esther smiled warmly, nodding as she waved them off to continue preparing the room for the king and HMN, the head minister.

Meanwhile, HMN hurried to meet the king, leaving his bodyguards behind at the king's gate. The rush left him breathless and sweating. They went to the queen's chamber. The king instructed his own uninvited bodyguards to remain in the garden outside close by.

When her esteemed guests arrived, Esther personally opened the doors. "My lord, who shares the powers of the gods, the great King of Kings, the Great Lion of Persia," Esther announced, bowing gracefully to her husband.

"Be blessed, Ishtahr, my queen," the king replied.

HMN visibly flinched at hearing the king call Esther by her godly nickname, honoring the goddess Ishtar. He knelt on one knee before the queen, his breath quickening as beads of sweat formed on his forehead. His hand trembled slightly as he wiped them away, clearly unnerved by the exchange.

Instead of wearing her unity crown, Esther had chosen her tiara—honoring her Jewish heritage, her mother, and the king. HMN's eyes darted to the tiara, and a subtle smirk of satisfaction crept onto his face. He recognized it immediately—it was the one his sons had stolen from an Egyptian treasure caravan, and he gifted it to the king, who had, in turn, given it to her.

Esther smiled inwardly as HMN misinterpreted her gesture. *He thinks I wear it to honor him*, she thought. HMN, *why don't you tell the king how you really acquired my mother's tiara?* But she remained silent, ushering her guests into her chamber. Hini quickly closed the door, ensuring even the king's bodyguards stayed outside.

The room was softly lit by candles made from whale fat, imported from China, their flickering light casting gentle shadows across the walls. The air was rich with the scent of blooming jasmine, and soft music played in the background, enhancing the serene atmosphere.

Esther had thoughtfully sectioned off a private area within the chamber using Persian carpets as makeshift walls. In front of her bed, three low pillow seats were arranged, the one closest to the entrance draped elegantly in white silk with braided gold, and slightly higher. With a graceful gesture, she guided the king to the elevated seat and invited him to sit.

The other two pillow seats were low, and it would be challenging to rise from after indulging in too much wine. With a subtle gesture, Esther invited HMN to choose his seat. Smiling, he selected the one with the thicker pillow, a clear display of his self-importance or medical condition.

Perfect, Esther thought. *I knew you'd pick that one. Hatach, my loyal bodyguard, is hidden behind you, ready if needed. But you're still dangerous—perhaps with poison or a concealed dagger.*

Lucky, her cat, silently appeared and jumped onto the king's lap. Repeatedly, the king stroked her back, and let her tail slide through his fist. Both of them enjoyed the gentle touch, finding a moment of calm amidst the tension.

Esther had strategically placed a long, thin candle nearby, marked to track time discreetly. As the evening unfolded, the music would occasionally swell, giving Hatach cover to stretch or adjust his position, ensuring HMN remained unsuspecting.

Two of Esther's chambermaids unrolled a large carpet map of the empire at the king's feet, spreading it out across the floor. The commotion frightened Lucky, and she jumped off the king.

The king adored his territories, seeing them as a testament to his glory. The map highlighted roads, bridges, and dams constructed by the king and his ancestors, even showing the diversion of the Euphrates—a tribute to his grandfather's military brilliance. It was the perfect map for discussing military campaigns. The king smiled cynically, and Esther smiled back. *He thinks I'm going to ask for my half. He'll give it to me, as long as I remain his.*

HMN watched the king's face intensely, likely contemplating how Esther's request for land or people might impact his killing decree.

Esther's chambermaids then brought in several notable bottles of wine from her private collection, each bottle stamped with the seal of a famous king. They were works of art in themselves, with intricate descriptions of their origins and the historical events they commemorated. Esther's maidens placed each bottle on the map near its capital city of origin, symbolizing the empire's vastness, wealth, and power.

The king, intrigued, rubbed his hands together and adjusted his seat.

I've created a barrier between HMN and the king, Esther thought, *one that HMN won't dare cross.*

Esther began the evening by toasting the king with a wine made from myrtle leaves, a gift from the Corsican ex-contestant, in honor of the goddess Ishtar. After they finished, she handed the king a coin. "Wherever the coin lands, that's the next bottle we'll taste," she explained, knowing how much the king loved games of chance and believed the gods always favored him.

For the occasion, Esther had carefully selected her attire: a silk shirt and wide pants with long slits on the sides, both loose around her arms and legs but tight at her waist, wrists, and ankles. The outfit was adorned with delicate silk needlework, featuring bright flowers along the lower part of her dress and butterflies fluttering across the upper part. The lightweight fabric flowed elegantly as she moved, casting an enchanting air around her.

The king tossed the coin, striking one bottle, and hit several others with a melodious chime. The sound echoed like mysterious music through the chamber. With effortless grace, Esther danced between the bottles, her movements fluid and deliberate, until she finally picked up the first bottle the coin had touched. She announced the nation it represented and the name of its king, handing the bottle to her husband for inspection. As he examined its external quality, Esther transformed her demeanor, embodying the nationality of the land the bottle represented. The musicians shifted to play music from that region, setting the perfect atmosphere.

In character, Esther saluted the king with the traditional gesture of that nation, blessing him in its language with an accent so perfect that she savored the unfamiliar words as they rolled off her tongue. The king, delighted, laughed heartily at her performance. Esther then repeated the greeting in Persian, cementing her command of both cultures.

The bottle was uncorked, and one of the chambermaids took a small sip to ensure it was safe, following Mordecai's old warning: *"One never knows about one's own wine, let alone a foreign king's."* Satisfied, the wine was returned to the king.

New, elegant goblets were brought for Esther and her guests. The maid poured the wine, and the three guests—king, HMN, and Esther—each selected their glass. They held the goblets up to the light, observing the wine's clarity and body, then smelled it, letting its rich aroma envelop them. After taking measured sips, they swirled the liquid in their mouths before spitting it into large jars placed nearby. *No need to be intoxicated*, Esther thought, smiling discreetly.

While savoring the lingering flavors, Esther launched into a carefully chosen story about the wine's origin and the nation that produced it, weaving tales designed to evoke pride in the king for his vast empire. Her stories delved into the emotions and struggles of the characters, highlighting the causes of their triumphs and downfalls. The trio nibbled on small pieces of bread, salty olives, and sipped water to cleanse their palates between wines.

When the coin landed near a bottle from Edom, Esther gracefully approached it but calmly selected a bottle from Judea. She blessed the king in Hebrew, invoking the name of God, before tasting the wine. The atmosphere grew solemn as Esther recounted one of King Solomon's famous trials.

"Young King Solomon had just ascended the throne when two beautiful women came to him, seeking justice. They were prostitutes, living together without husbands, in a house they owned jointly. Their families had disowned them in shame, but the women found solace in each other's company. They had made a plan—to have babies together so each can feed both babies, while her friend works. Both gave birth to boys almost identical, three days apart.

"These boys, destined for a hard life, would typically have been cast away at birth. But these women, against all odds, loved their children fiercely and cared for them together.

"A couple of days later, at night, one of the women woke to feed a crying baby and found the baby beside her lifeless. Heartbroken, she took the crying baby, fed him, and placed him in her bed, while putting the dead boy in her sleeping friend's arms.

"In the morning, a bitter argument arose—each woman claimed the living child was hers."

Esther paused dramatically, taking a small sip of wine to heighten the tension in the room. The king, captivated, leaned in with a smile. "Continue," he urged.

Esther nodded. "Both women went to King Solomon's court to resolve the matter. Neither accused the other of lying, but each insisted the living child was hers. Solomon studied them carefully, noticing how similar they were, and he thought the same man must have fathered both babies." She glanced at the king and HMN, both listening intently.

"I imagine the babies were likely switched more than once during the night," King Ahasuerus interjected. "The women themselves probably didn't know whose child it truly was. In court, both may have *lied* or *withheld the full truth* to the king. Either way, they were subject to the death penalty."

Esther allowed a pause, giving the king time to reflect on how he might have approached the situation. She lowered her eyes, embodying the humility of one of the mothers. When the king gestured for her to continue, she said, "In Judea, possession is seen as strong evidence of ownership, and the other party must prove otherwise. But there was no proof here. When ownership can't be resolved, the item—whether it be property or a child—must either be equally split or sold, with the value divided equally."

"'Bring me a sword!' King Solomon commanded his guard. 'Let each woman hold one leg of the baby. On my signal, cut him in half, and each can take her share.'

"The guard held the baby, who screamed in terror, and instructed the mothers to step forward and take the baby's legs."

The king and HMN's eyes widened, and the room grew still. Even the musicians had stopped playing, eager to hear the resolution. The king raised his chin, motioning for Esther to continue.

"The first woman immediately refused, shouting, 'Please don't kill him! Give the baby to her!' She collapsed to the ground, sobbing. Opposing the king's order was dangerous—a capital offense. Some of Solomon's courtiers clapped and cheered, impressed by the scene."

HMN grinned. "She's the real mother."

King Ahasuerus scratched his ear thoughtfully. "Not so fast. That could be an admission of guilt—an attempt to sacrifice herself to save the baby."

Esther's breath caught. She felt as though she, too, was pleading for her people's salvation, standing in the place of the desperate mother. She continued, "King Solomon silenced the crowd and turned to the second woman. She now held all the power. She could have simply said, 'Thank you, I'll take the baby,' but she knew that might lead to the execution of her friend, who had admitted her crime. Or she could confess, 'Yes, I stole my friend's baby,' saving her friend and the baby, but be executed herself. Or she could say, 'Don't kill. Let her have the baby,' which would annoy the king by showing his inability to prove who the true mother was, and risk both being killed.

Additionally, raising the child alone would mean she couldn't work. So, she faced a dilemma—how to prevent any death. Refusing to assist in the killing, she finally declared, 'Neither for me nor for her. You **cut** the baby yourself.' By saying 'YOU,' she was essentially saying, 'I won't help you. The blood will be on your hands if you cut.'"

The king nodded, his expression still uncertain. "She clearly didn't want to participate in the killing, but that doesn't necessarily mean she was guilty—it just means she didn't want to assist the king. It was her gamble that Solomon, in his wisdom, would realize, that based on the known facts, there is no way he can decide who is the true mother—especially because the mothers themselves didn't know. His options were either release or kill both."

Esther smiled and nodded in agreement. "King Solomon waited, but then the first woman, with tears streaming down her face, lifted her head and pleaded, 'Please don't kill him! I'm begging—please, I will take the baby!' The courtiers fell silent, awaiting Solomon's final judgment."

King Ahasuerus said, "There's no way to truly know who the real mother is, but the first woman showed more love."

Esther nodded and continued, "King Solomon pointed to the first woman and declared, 'Give her the baby; she is the mother.' The women embraced, wept, and took the baby home together."

"No cutting!" the king exclaimed with satisfaction.

Esther smiled. "But King Solomon did cut something—he cut his workload. His ruling sent a clear message to all litigants to resolve their disputes before daring to come before him."

HMN grinned broadly, nodding and subtly shimmying his shoulders.

He thinks he got it right earlier, Esther mused. She had deliberately used the word "*begging*" to gauge the king's reaction, as Mordecai had instructed her to *beg* for her people. King Ahasuerus had wrinkled his nose when she used the word but then smiled approvingly.

The king prefers to rely on 'law and justice' over begging for mercy, Esther thought. *Good thing I didn't follow Mordecai's advice exactly. The king would have demanded an investigation.*

Esther also noticed HMN raise his eyebrows at the king's reaction. *Another step accomplished. HMN will hesitate before begging*, Esther thought.

"People assumed it was a trial to find the true mother, but in reality, it was about friendship and motherhood," Esther explained. "King Solomon never learned who the true mother was, so neither woman was executed. The second woman's wisdom saved not only herself but her friend and the baby."

After a brief pause, King Ahasuerus clapped. "Excellent! Let's drink!" They raised their glasses and drank the wine from Jerusalem.

HMN asked, "Would King Solomon really have killed the baby?"

Esther paused, thinking: *Look at you, the man who signed a decree to kill women and children, now pretending to be the concerned advisor. Yes, you are angling to be regent and care for my baby.* Out loud, she said, "King Solomon turned a heartbreaking tragedy into a clever test, letting the mothers reveal the truth themselves. That way, the responsibility for the baby's fate would rest on their hands, not his."

HMN nodded thoughtfully, stroking his chin. Esther's gaze lingered on him as her thoughts churned: *Don't you see? This is the same situation between our nations. But unlike Solomon's case, there's no peaceful solution in sight.*

The king, now more at ease, leaned back on a thick pillow, enjoying the stories that accompanied each wine. Some wines brought flavors he had never experienced, while others, despite great anticipation, failed to live up to their reputation. Yet the evening was rich with history, surprise, and indulgence.

Esther noticed the king's growing pleasure, but she was aware the hour was getting late. She saw HMN's eyes flicker toward the bottle from the Amalekites. She was ready, armed with a tale that would celebrate their contributions to the empire while subtly exposing their underlying treachery.

The king, impressed by her deep knowledge of history, praised her. "Your stories are remarkable, full of wisdom and insight. Whatever your wish or desire—up to half my empire—it shall be yours."

Esther stood, bowing deeply. "Oh, great king, if it pleases you, and if you truly love me, please come again tomorrow with HMN. I'll prepare another banquet, and then I will make my request."

A faint smile crossed the king's face, though he remained silent in response to her invitation.

Good, Esther thought. *He didn't demand an answer now, nor did he end the game. If he comes tomorrow, it will prove his love.*

She glanced at HMN, whose smug satisfaction was unmistakable. *Look at him,* she mused, *so proud to be invited again. He has no idea I've just served him a subpoena to appear. The king will be my witness at the next banquet. HMN is trapped—if he doesn't come, it will be an admission of guilt.*

Esther smiled inwardly. The pieces were falling into place.

CHAPTER 35

While Esther hosted her banquet, Mordecai ended his mourning and returned to his post at the king's gate. Most dignitaries had already gone home, but Mordecai remained restless, eager to hear if Esther's plan had worked and if HMN had been brought to justice.

At HMN's palace, his wife, Zeresh, had heard of the great honor bestowed upon her husband—drinking with the king and queen in her private chamber. Her face flickered with a mix of emotions—pride, suspicion, jealousy—but she quickly ordered a celebration, inviting HMN's allies. The table was lavishly set with food and wine.

HMN left the banquet smug, twirling his golden belt. Approaching the king's gate, he spotted Mordecai calmly sitting at his desk. HMN's smile faltered when he noticed Mordecai hadn't stood to greet him, treating him as though he were invisible, servant, ghost.

Fury surged through HMN. His blood boiled, but he kept walking, quickening his pace, determined to hide his rage.

———❧———

Mordecai grew alarmed as he saw HMN smiling while passing the king's gate, his footsteps echoing in the quiet night. Did Esther fail? Mordecai wondered. He's still trapped, but this is dangerous.

An hour later, one of HMN's friends arrived, visibly shaken. Mordecai motioned for him to sit. Soon, another spy entered, followed by two more. Each seemed startled by the others' presence. Mordecai observed them closely—*traitors to HMN could easily betray me as well.*

Finally, the first spy broke the silence. "It's urgent—you need to hear this."

Mordecai stepped outside to instruct Yavin before returning. "For your safety and your families'," he warned, "a guard will be assigned to each of you. Behave as usual, but betray me, and all of you will suffer."

He then interviewed the spies separately. The first spy revealed, "At HMN's home, his friends greeted him with 'Ishtar's blessing, supreme minister,' but HMN seemed disturbed, like he'd come from a funeral. He muttered about his wealth and sons."

Mordecai thought, *He's preparing his Will and Testimony, seeing the angel of death.*

The spy continued, "HMN boasted about his promotion to head minister, guardian of the king, and his full authority outside the palace. He announced he's the king's drinking companion, dining with both the king and queen at the women's house, and, to top it off, he's been invited to another banquet tomorrow with them."

Mordecai raised an eyebrow. *Strange,* he thought. *He didn't mention his greatest achievements—that all the king's dignitaries are kneeling to him, the royal signet, or the decree to kill the Jews. He knows that if the king discovers his power grab, he's finished.*

The spy hesitated, then added, "HMN said it was all worthless as long as Mordecai the Jew *sits* at the king's gate."

A surge of satisfaction swept over Mordecai. *'Sit' HMN told his wife and friends about me—for him, it means: 'I sit, not dead, I still hold my position at the king's gate, and I sat without showing him any respect.' HMN is fully rattled. He's unhinged, willing to sacrifice everything just to get rid of me. He will sacrifice everything very soon.*

"HMN looked exhausted," the spy continued. "He refused to answer any questions."

He's already exposed his weakness, Mordecai thought. *Let's hear what advice they gave him. He's too shaken to object, and his friends must sense the danger.*

The spy's voice lowered. "Zeresh, his wife, stood up, angry and confused. She stared at us in silence before turning to her husband and spitting, 'Make a tree fifty feet high, and in the morning, tell the king to hang Mordecai there!' Everyone agreed, but HMN just sat there, covering his face."

She's furious HMN hasn't acted yet, Mordecai smirked. *But she doesn't realize HMN can't order the king to execute me without a hearing.*

The spy added, "I don't know why the tree needed to be so tall. It seemed excessive."

Fifty feet? Mordecai thought. *That's not just a punishment—it's a spectacle. She wants to make an example of me. But HMN is too weak to follow through. He's trapped, unable to explain.*

Suddenly, the sound of chopping wood echoed through the city.

Moments later, the fifth spy arrived, breathless. "HMN ordered workers to chop the branches of a fifty feet tall cedar tree in his yard, leaving a few branches at the top. He's planning something. As they worked, he sang, 'So shall be done to the man whom HMN delights to dishonor.'"

HMN is happy, Mordecai thought, *because he has finally realized how to get the king's approval to kill me without mentioning my name, by using the new tax plan the king approved.*

Mordecai's mind raced. *He wants more than the king's signet—he craves the power to execute his enemies as sovereign. The tree height is for crows, to feast on my live body up there. And his wife—such a 'kind' soul—helped hatch this plan.* A shiver ran down Mordecai's spine.

———≈———

Mordecai remained at his post, listening to the sound of axes chopping wood echoing through the night, reaching even the king's palace. *He's in a hurry,* Mordecai thought, *and so must I be.*

Sensing the urgency, he used a secret tunnel to the royal palace and quickly sent precise instructions to Harvona. When Yavin returned, Mordecai wasted no time. "Yavin, seal off HMN's palace. No one enters—no exceptions, no questions. Arrest or kill objectors. Use men disguised as Amalekites."

Yavin nodded and disappeared into the shadows, ready to act.

CHAPTER 36

It was early spring, and the crisp morning air filled the dawn. The sound of axes chopping wood mingled with the songs of birds calling to their mates, reaching even the king's bedroom. Harvona, the first bodyguard, instructed a servant to whistle, mimicking a bird's tune. The king loved the sound of birds and was never disturbed by their cheerful songs during his light sleep.

But today, King Ahasuerus found it hard to fall back asleep. His mind raced. Could my queen be pregnant? Shall I appoint HMN to be a regent? Excitement fluttered in his chest.

At Harvona's suggestion, a servant began reading aloud from the royal history book. By chance, the servant selected the account of Mordecai's brave act in saving the king's life. As the king listened, he reflected on details he hadn't fully appreciated before.

Since his banquet with the queen, the king had gained a new perspective on analyzing situations. He was now more impressed than ever by Mordecai's loyalty and quick thinking. At the time, the king hadn't grasped why Mordecai had informed the queen, nor had he investigated further. But now, the story hinted at a greater danger he had overlooked. The king also admired the security protocols Mordecai had put in place to protect him.

Rising from his bed, the king asked, "Other than recording it in the royal history book, was anything done to honor Mordecai?"

"No, Your Majesty," the servant replied.

"Not even a small gesture? Nothing?"

"Nothing at all," the servant confirmed.

The king thought for a moment. "I need an objective advisor. Who is in the outer courtyard?"

The servant quickly left and returned moments later. "HMN is standing in the outer courtyard, Your Majesty."

The outer courtyard, not the inner. Standing, not sitting, Harvona noted, intrigued.

"Bring him in," the king commanded.

CHAPTER 37

The head minister entered the king's royal bedroom, humming cheerfully, his steps light and a wide smile spread across his face. He stood quietly before the king, his confidence palpable.

Look at him, Harvona thought, observing HMN's demeanor. *From the queen's chambers to the king's—he's certainly climbing fast!*

Without mentioning Mordecai's name, the king posed a question to HMN: "What shall be done for the man whom the king delights to honor?"

Surprised and thrilled, HMN clapped his hands together, bringing them to his chest. He slowly repeated the question, "A man... whom the king delights to honor...?" He stretched the words 'man' and 'honor,' waiting expectantly, barely moving.

He's fishing for the name, Harvona speculated, watching the minister's eager anticipation.

The king remained silent, letting the tension build. HMN, assuming the question was about him, pondered the implications. Traditionally, such honors would be reserved for someone who had earned a significant promotion, saved the king's life, or achieved a great victory. *Recently, however, only I have been promoted*, HMN thought, grinning inwardly.

After a moment of thought, HMN leaned forward, his excitement barely contained. In a clear, confident voice, he proclaimed, "Let the man be dressed in the king's royal robes, ride the king's horse—with the crown on his head—paraded through the main streets, and have a *noble minister* announce, 'This is what is done for the man whom the king delights to honor!'"

What a clever and cost-effective idea, Harvona mused. *He's so wrapped up in his excitement that he forgot to say, '**if it pleases the king.**' He's convinced the honor is meant for him!*

The king, delighted by the suggestion, smiled and turned to HMN. "Take the horse and the robes, and do *exactly as you have said*—for Mordecai the Jew, who sits at the king's gate."

Harvona mused, *"Exactly," the king said, as if slapping HMN!*

Harvona noted, as HMN's jaw dropped in shock.

Harvona thought, *It annoyed the king that HMN hadn't said, 'if it pleases the king,' leaving room for HMN to act as he pleased, even if it didn't align with the king's wishes. Therefore, the king strictly limited HMN to his own recommendation. HMN had intended for a 'noble minister' to serve the 'man,' as if he himself were above it—'second to the king.' But when the king ordered him to carry it out, the king made it clear that, in his eyes, HMN is merely a minister, nothing more.*

Harvona quickly assessed the situation. *Although the king had subtly put HMN back in his place as a minister, he still granted him the significant task of organizing the parade and ensuring the safety of a man presented and honored like the king. But this also meant Mordecai would now be vulnerable to HMN's hatred, paraded under HMN's direction. The king didn't specify that the parade had to be for a living Mordecai,* Harvona thought, sensing the danger.

"May I assist HMN in the parade?" Harvona asked, ensuring the king missed HMN's crushed expression.

The king nodded in agreement.

————⋙————

Shortly after, HMN arrived at the king's gate with a group of the king's guards bearing the royal lion flag. HMN waved dismissively, trying to stop the dignitaries from kneeling to him. Yet all—except Mordecai— knelt. Mordecai remained seated, feigning indifference, though his heart pounded with fear.

As HMN strode directly toward him, panic surged through Mordecai. *My plans have failed. I'm finished.* He had survived the previous night's banquet with the queen and evaded Harvona's trap. *He's like a cat with nine lives, this 'Hay Man.' What now? He's coming to hang me alive on that tree!* Every instinct screamed for Mordecai to flee, but he stayed rooted, his eyes darting to the smirking dignitaries. He made a mental note of who they were.

Then, Mordecai spotted Harvona's puzzled expression. A sliver of tension eased. *Why is Harvona confused? Is he questioning why the dignitaries kneel while I sit?* Mordecai could only hope that Harvona would inform the king. *The noose is tightening around HMN's neck. Will he try to silence Harvona next?*

"Follow me," HMN ordered in a stiff tone, not even using Mordecai's name. *Disrespectful,* Mordecai thought. *But not arrested— yet. Am I being taken to trial?*

As some of HMN's allies smirked and clapped, murmurs spread among the dignitaries, speculating about Mordecai's fate. On the way to the palace, Mordecai made sure to keep Harvona between him and HMN, a small but deliberate move for protection.

The tension lifted when HMN dressed Mordecai in royal attire— excluding the king's crown—and helped him onto the king's white Cilician horse. As HMN announced, "So shall be done to the man whom the king delights to honor," Mordecai smiled, aware of HMN's frustration.

The procession, enhanced by Harvona's presence, caused dignitaries to kneel, uncertain whether to honor the king's garments, the king's flag, HMN, or Mordecai himself. Mordecai intended to keep HMN occupied until the queen's banquet, preventing the possibility that HMN would withdraw the 'killing decree' against the Jews.

To prolong the moment, he slowed the parade, greeting citizens and conversing with foreigners in their languages, subtly mentioning HMN's name to imply he was the topic. HMN, blistered and weary, had no choice but to endure as a crowd gathered to touch Mordecai's royal clothes.

Noticing HMN's friends whispering, Mordecai felt a surge of satisfaction. After hours of parading, he signaled to conclude the event and return to the palace, prompting HMN to quickly discard the royal attire and instruct Mordecai to resume his post at the gate.

HMN rushed home, avoiding the dignitaries at the king's gate who were gathered around Mordecai, praising his leadership.

After a while, Mordecai noticed the king's guards ushering HMN toward the second banquet. While he waited for the banquet to conclude, one of Mordecai's spies approached him.

"I just came from HMN's palace," the spy reported. "His wife, Zeresh, and their friends were eagerly awaiting news of how things went with the king. When we saw HMN's sad face, we knew it hadn't gone well. He shared everything that happened, and we were all shocked. Zeresh asked how it was possible that the king had honored Mordecai the Jew, by name and nationality, after issuing the decree to kill the Jews. She noted that once he had fallen before the Jew, he was doomed. HMN refused to respond. Zeresh stomped her foot, turned around, and left the room. I also saw your other spies there."

The spy continued, "A wise adviser told HMN that the hanging tree had lost its purpose and should be dismantled. HMN looked around, as if searching for his wife's approval to erase any signs of the tree. But he stubbornly resisted, gritting his teeth as he said, 'No! The king honored him for some unknown service, and now he's getting his due. I can still ask the king to execute him.'

"One adviser tried to argue, 'The only proof against you is the hanging tree. Please reconsider. Don't be arrogant. Once the king approves the execution of Mordecai, you can hang him on the official tree or anywhere else.'

"I immediately told HMN, 'The king trusts you.' He turned red and replied, 'I do have influence over the king. The queen needs me. For all the harm Mordecai has caused me, he must suffer greatly... on that tree.' Then, the king's guards arrived to take him to the queen's second banquet.

"After HMN left, Zeresh came in and asked what had happened. The wise adviser recounted the events and announced that although HMN had refused his advice, he intended to cut down the tree. Zeresh warned him that he would be punished if he dared to get out of his chair."

Mordecai replied, "Thank you. HMN has received sufficient warning."

CHAPTER 38

The time for the queen's second banquet had come and gone, yet HMN was nowhere to be found. Irritated, the king commanded, "Fetch him."

Harvona directed six guards to take the king's flag and bring HMN, even by force if necessary. They swiftly entered HMN's palace, ordered his guards to stand down, and found HMN conversing with friends. With minimal pleasantries, they instructed him to follow and hurried him to the king. On the way, the guards caught sight of the hanging tree, its large noose swinging ominously in the breeze, and exchanged silent glances.

Harvona signaled the lead guard to approach and report. Leaning in, the guard whispered about the tree and the friends at HMN's palace. Harvona nodded, smiled, and relaxed his shoulders. "Thank you," he said. "Everything is fine. Ensure that you and your men say nothing."

Apparently, Mordecai's outrageous claim about the hanging tree was true, Harvona thought.

The king and HMN hurried to Esther. As before, the king left his bodyguards outside the queen's chamber. The decorated bottles of wine were already arranged on the glossy silk carpet, emphasizing the glory of Persia.

The king arrived. He loves me, Esterh thought with satisfaction. *I am ready.*

HMN settled into his favored pillow seat, smiling, though his eyes appeared sad and weary. He looks drained and exhausted, Esther observed. Something dreadful must have happened to him since yesterday.

Esther's good-luck black cat, Lucky, approached HMN, ready to jump onto his lap. HMN shooed her away, pushing her with his leg. *Evil man. It seems black cats bring bad luck to the Amalekites*, Esther noted. Lucky weaved gracefully among the bottles, her tail high, wiggling in the air before leaping onto the king's lap. The king petted the purring cat, cupping her face. Lucky stretched her front paws, exposing her sharp claws, and gently pushed against the king's stomach. *Thank you, partner,* Esther thought. *Go on, help me make this party a success.*

After three tastings of wine, the king fidgeted in his seat. He took a deep breath, as if about to speak, paused, sighed, and finally said, "Whatever your wish or desire, Queen Ishtahr, up to half my kingdom, shall be done."

Esther's heart raced. She stood up, took a deep breath, and replied, "Oh, great King of Kings, may you live long and prosper. If it pleases the king, grant me my life and the life of my nation."

The king chuckled and stretched his legs. That seemed an easy request to grant. He tried to recall Esther's nationality but could not; as she had been a contestant, he assumed her nation was already under his control. There would be no need to go to war in her honor.

"Because," she continued, "my people have been sold into destruction, death, and oppression. If we had been sold only into slavery, I wouldn't have troubled the king."

HMN gasped at the queen's accusation. He couldn't believe she was blaming the king for taking a bribe, selling his reign, and running a corrupt court. Not to mention, she didn't even appear frightened. Confused, he wondered why Ishtar would defend the Jews as her own. A cocky sneer crossed his face as he kept his gaze on the king while subtly shifting his body toward the exit.

Hini, Esther's head maiden, moved to stand by the exit door.

Esther was alert. With the signet ring in hand, HMN could kill the king and crown himself. *I vow, a free man, you will not leave this room.*

Hatach looked startled, ready to pounce.

The king shook his head, a puzzled expression on his face, and roared, "Where is this arrogant heart that dares to act in my name?" Lucky jumped off his lap as the king sprang to his feet, folding his arms and standing with his feet apart, his gaze fixed on Esther.

He acts as if he knows nothing about the killing decree, Esther thought. *That's good. I don't have to cry at his feet and beg for mercy.*

Cautiously, aiming to avoid accusing the king and evading his direct questions, Esther pointed at HMN and declared, "This evil HMN is a troublemaker and an enemy!"

The king froze.

———❧———

HMN's eyes darted around the room, panic coursing through him. The wrath of the goddess was upon him; the prophecies of his wife and friends had come true. Ishtar was against him, and he felt doomed! He was not a soldier but an adviser, and a drunken one at that. Sore from the long parade and from working all night, his cramped muscles prevented him from getting up. He trembled and dropped his glass goblet, which shattered on the marble floor, sending shards and droplets of red wine spraying like spilled blood.

I caught you alone, without your guards! Esther thought.

Startled, the king raised his hand to shield his face and blinked in disbelief.

Esther maintained her stern expression as she noticed the horror on HMN's face—a look that could easily be interpreted as an admission of guilt.

The king, too, recognized the terror in HMN's eyes and realized he had entrusted his signet to him. A chilling thought struck him: *He might attack or use one of his deadly poisons to kill me!*

With wide eyes, the king scanned the room, searching for a guard. But none were available; he had left them all outside. Grasping his robe, he hurriedly made for the entrance. Hini opened the door for him, and he sped out, slamming it shut behind him with a loud bang. A cloud of dust swirled in the air, glimmering in the afternoon sun's rays. The room fell silent.

He slammed the door—effectively arresting us, Esther thought. *He escaped and left me alone with my enemy. He is confident that HMN will not harm me, knowing it would only lead to a slower and more painful death for HMN and his family.*

Outside, the king found his guards and began to calm down. The guards positioned themselves at his side as he sought a lavatory to relieve himself, offering a convenient explanation for his hasty departure. Harvona, having heard the slamming door, understood the situation. The king returned to the queen's chamber, and Harvona followed without objection.

———≈———

Esther looked at HMN and thought, *You are tired and drunk. You are trapped, with nowhere to run. You are alone. Except for me, no one can help you. Admit it and submit.*

HMN slid out of his chair and collapsed to the ground.

The king will be back shortly. You could leave my chamber and beg for mercy, Esther thought. She moved away from HMN and the entrance door, made her way to her bed, stretched out on her side, and began petting Lucky as she waited.

HMN lowered his head, gazing at Esther with desperate eyes. *Desperate. Now, he truly believes I am Ishtar and that I am punishing him.*

He approached her on his knees, leaning against the bed. With tears in his eyes, he begged, "Ishtar, please spare my life. I beg you. Save me. I will donate ten thousand bars of silver to your temple."

Esther remained silent, hardly holding her laughter.

HMN's voice trembled as he continued, "I was the one who gave this royal tiara to the king for you. I only wanted to please the goddess."

Esther said nothing.

"The king specifically ordered me to oppress the Jews. Here is his royal signet as proof that I was only following orders!"

Esther waited, her expression unreadable.

"Trust me, I did not instruct all the leaders of the nations to kill the Jews. I don't know who ordered their oppression or the decree to kill them. Please, your highness, how can you blame me for what Mordecai wrote? I cannot read Hebrew."

Esther remained silent.

"Believe me, I love the Jews. Praise Mordecai the Jew," HMN whimpered. "I exempted him from kneeling to me, and I suggested that the king honor him with a royal procession. We paraded together just this morning!"

Esther tightened her lips. *Is it possible? No, liars always start with 'believe me' and 'trust me.'*

"I promise I will have the king's order rescinded," HMN said, desperation creeping into his voice. "I promise to pay the king's treasury all the taxes he imposed on the Jews. Please save my life!"

Esther sighed, and a joke came to mind: *a man borrowed a neighbor's vase and returned it damaged. When confronted, he claimed, "First, I didn't take it. Second, when I did take it, it was already broken. And third, when I returned it, it was whole."* Esther couldn't help but smile.

"I accept your explanations," she replied coldly. "I will ask the king to sanction your head."

HMN relaxed, taking Esther's hand and kissing it repeatedly.

He is kissing my hand endlessly. Is he waiting for the king to see him like this? Esther assessed the risks and benefits of such exposure to the king. *Perhaps he wants to demonstrate to the king that he still believes I am the goddess Ishtar and that I have forgiven him. But what will the king think when he believes I am pregnant?*

At that moment, the king and his guards returned. The king opened the door and stepped in first, immediately spotting HMN in an awkward position at the queen's bedside, still kissing her hand. *A regent? Conspiring? My wife?* The king felt a rush of confusion and watched for a moment.

"This too?" the king barked, his voice firm. "Seducing my queen in my own home, with me present?"

Esther panicked. *I am forbidden from helping HMN, or the king will kill me, too.*

My plan has failed, she thought in alarm. *Under Persian law, even the king must find more than one capital offense before ordering an execution. The king has not mentioned HMN's usurpation of royal power, and this is the only crime his guards have witnessed. He will have to conduct a further investigation, which could allow HMN's loyalists to kill the king.* Stricken with fear, Esther searched her mind for additional crimes HMN might have committed, careful to avoid sounding apologetic or guilty. Her thoughts froze.

"No, I was just... I never..." HMN stammered, backing away from Esther and covering his face with his hands.

Before HMN could order his loyalists among the king's guards to attack, Harvona interrupted without seeking permission to speak. He had been waiting to announce HMN's additional offenses since that morning. "HMN has also constructed a fifty-foot-high hanging tree at his palace to hang Mordecai, a loyal servant of the king," he declared.

Good move, Esther thought with relief. *None of the other guards, even if loyal to HMN, will support him now, and the king has enough evidence to execute him.* She wondered how long Harvona had known about the tree and why he had risked the king's life by allowing him to come alone to her party, fully aware of the situation. *The king might punish him! But certainly not right now.*

As Harvona spoke, Hatach emerged from his hiding place to protect the queen, the king, and Harvona. Esther noticed the puzzled expression on Hatach's face. *Now, he's starting to grasp what Mordecai really told me.*

The king looked at Hatach with hidden anger. *You were here the whole time and did not step out when I fearfully ran from the room?*

King Ahasuerus pondered. *Did HMN crown himself and establish an official hanging tree on his property? Did he attempt to kill Mordecai, who protected me, after I bestowed such great honors on both of them? Is he purging the court of my supporters?* Aloud, the king turned to Hatach and ordered in a measured, clear voice, "Hang him thereon."

'Thereon'? Why limit it to just that specific tree? *Is there a legal issue here?* Esther thought.

Esther smiled with appreciation. *My king is so smart, a real judge. Without investigation and hearings, he cannot conclude that HMN published an unlawful 'killing decree' and intended to kill Mordecai. He knows HMN did not seduce me, but the king will use it as the first offense. He needs a second one. The only definitive proof of HMN's crimes is the tree. If it exists, all of HMN's offenses are confirmed and HMN will be hanged; if not, HMN must be returned to the king for further investigations.* She glanced at Harvona and Hatach, realizing they were thinking the same thing.

HMN knew the tree was still there. The head minister knelt, his forehead touching the floor, and relaxed his limbs, resigning himself to his fate.

He is lucky, Esther thought. *The king ordered his death alone and spared the lives of his wife and sons.*

But what about me? Is he going to punish me for misleading him about the pregnancy and exposing him to this dangerous meeting? Still he will have to admit my plan was wonderful—I exposed Haman and protected him!!!

CHAPTER 39

Harvona was to remain with the king and queen until all the guards' loyalties were reevaluated and their personal quarters searched for evidence of contact with HMN. HMN was to be secured by particularly loyal guards, as there was a distinct possibility he would try to bribe them on the way to his execution.

Together with soldiers from the king's harem, Hatach moved swiftly with his prisoner, aware of the danger, as HMN's supporters might attempt to rescue their leader.

The dignitaries at the king's gate were bewildered by the scene unfolding before them. They saw HMN, devoid of his personal guards, being escorted out of the palace by the queen's bodyguard, who bore the king's emblem. HMN appeared broken, walking with his head down. The dignitaries remained seated, confused, until Mordecai rose and bowed his head, offering HMN a final show of respect. One by one, the other dignitaries followed Mordecai's lead, honoring HMN as well.

When Hatach spotted the hanging tree towering over HMN's palace, he felt a sense of relief. Harvona had spoken the truth, and the execution must proceed. He knocked on HMN's gate with the handle of his sword. "In the name of the king, open up!" he shouted.

HMN's guards opened the gates with unsteady hands, clearly unaccustomed to such alarming official visits—this being the second in one day. Though HMN had ten times more guards in his palace than Hatach had brought, Hatach carried the king's authority, which quelled any desire to resist.

Despite this, the situation remained volatile.

"Remove your weapons, lay them on the ground, move over there, and stand in military formation," Hatach ordered.

HMN's guards exchanged glances with him. He nodded sadly, and they complied.

Zeresh exited the house and rushed toward Hatach, flanked by her personal guards, loudly demanding an explanation for the intrusion. Hatach shot her a fierce look, raising his hands to signal her to stop and submit. Seeing her husband, she collapsed.

Hatach dispatched some of his guards to secure the main gate. One guard led HMN to the tall hanging tree, placing the large noose over his head and arms, tightening it around his chest, and binding his hands behind his back.

HMN looked at Hatach, his eyes pleading for mercy.

Hatach glanced at the guard and shook his head. He raised his palm toward HMN and gestured upward slightly.

The guard released the noose, tightening it instead around HMN's neck. HMN thanked, relieved that he was avoiding the torturous death he had planned for Mordecai.

"Look here, he carries the king's signet on a string around his neck," the guard said.

"Incredible. Give it to me," Hatach ordered, while Zeresh, surprised and shocked, covered her face as she knelt on the floor. *Did he steal it? Am I going to be killed too?*

Turning to HMN's supporters, Hatach shouted, "Everyone must vacate the house immediately and assemble in the courtyard."

Several hundred Amalekite friends, assistants, servants, and young apprentices poured into the courtyard.

Pointing at HMN's private army, Hatach declared, "From this moment on, you are soldiers of the king and subject to his absolute authority under my command!"

"Attention!" the sergeant of the guards shouted.

Every soldier folded his right hand into a fist and held it over his chest, elbow horizontal. The king's lion flag was raised above the house.

Silence enveloped the courtyard. Crows perched atop the hanging tree and cawed a few times before taking flight as a soldier struck the tree trunk.

Hatach proclaimed in a loud voice, "In the name of King Ahasuerus, the great King of Kings, the head minister HMN has been found guilty of: one, attempting to seduce the queen in the king's house; two, constructing an unauthorized hanging tree at his residence; and three, conspiring to execute a loyal servant of the king."

HMN's relatives stood stunned in silence, praying they wouldn't be next to face execution. The stench of sweat and urine hung heavily in the air.

A monotonous drum beat announced the beginning of the execution.

"Height I sought; here I rise!" HMN shouted defiantly. "I won immortality!"

"HMN, you are erased! You will be remembered as 'Hay Man!' Your descendants will suffer for your sins!" Hatach retorted.

Hatach signaled to the executioner regarding the height to which the rope should be pulled. He raised his hand, and the drummer increased the tempo and volume.

When Hatach dropped his hand, HMN was swiftly yanked up the tree by his neck. His feet dangled just a finger's width above the ground, leading to a long, agonizing, choking death. The head minister's body convulsed, deprived of oxygen, twitching and writhing until it finally swung limply. Soft lamentations and prayers rippled through the crowd.

Hatach appointed a guard to manage HMN's property, instructing him to secure the house. He ordered the servants and slaves back to their duties as if nothing had changed. Then, he commanded HMN's wife, Zeresh, her family, and the rest of the household to vacate the property. They were not permitted to return or take anything with them, as Hatach did not want to risk vandalism or arson.

HMN was left swaying in the wind, hanging from the tree.

Hatach compiled a list of Amalekite elders and leaders who had been in HMN's palace and forbade them from leaving the city without the king's permission. He ordered them to register and appear weekly at the king's gate. If anyone should disappear, their entire family would be punished. Parshandatha, HMN's eldest son, promised Hatach that he would secure the Amalekites in his palace and take care of them.

Zeresh, realizing that her advice had led to her husband's tragic fate, nonetheless thanked the king for sparing her sons as she hurried off the property. She knew that the children of condemned men often harbored grudges and sought blood revenge, making them a threat to the king. However, in this case, the king had made it clear that HMN had acted against his family in his attempts to seduce the queen. *I knew it,* Zeresh thought, *that tiara.*

HMN's sons learned about the tiara their father had given to Esther after refusing to give it to their mother, which seemed to indicate his intention to seduce the queen and abandon their mother. They also understood that if their father had married the queen, she would have likely killed them all. Still, the sons were afraid to leave Shushan without permission, as it could be seen as an admission of guilt.

Hatach reported to the king that HMN was hanged on the fifty-foot-high tree in his palace.

Parshandatha then emerged as the new leader of the Amalekites at the king's gate.

CHAPTER 40

"**Y**ou tricked and shamed me, Ishtahr, making me scurry in fear from your chamber," the king said, raising an eyebrow and tilting his head. His stern expression was punctuated by a pointed finger aimed directly at her.

Esther recoiled, a chill of fear washing over her. *Is he going to punish me?* "I had to verify who ordered the killing decree. And... I could not trust your bodyguards. I had to sequester HMN. You were safe in my care. My bodyguard..." Her voice trailed off as tears filled her eyes, and she lowered her head, bending her knees as if ready to collapse.

But when the king saw the crumpled look on Esther's face, his anger began to dissipate. "Yes, I understand why you did it. It was a clever solution to isolate us," he said. "I promised you up to half my kingdom several times. Your people, and HMN's palace are now yours." A smile spread across the king's face as he caressed Esther's cheek, banishing her sadness and restoring her lovely smile.

Far less than half his kingdom, yet still a magnificent gift. Is he banishing me from the royal palace? Is he testing my loyalty? Esther wondered. *Can I refuse such a gift? What am I to do?*

Of course, I cannot move to HMN's palace. It's merely a property to hold, she thought. *But this is wonderful! Now, I can travel from the royal palace to my property in the city. I can leave the harem and command a protective royal battalion. I can manage my own time and expenses. I am the powerful queen on the chessboard!*

"Thank you, my honored king," Esther replied joyfully. "Thank you forever and ever." A radiant smile lit up her face. "If it pleases the king, I will appoint Mordecai to manage my palace."

The king narrowed his eyes with suspicion as he regarded her. "What is Mordecai to you?" he asked, a hint of sarcasm lacing his tone.

Why does he ask me this way? Does he think I was Mordecai's wife? I must stick to the truth but say as little as possible, Esther thought. "I became an orphan at age ten. Mordecai, my cousin, took me into his home, adopted me as his daughter, and educated me. I was the one who suggested the Jewish stone for the unity crowns, in honor of our God, to bless and protect the king. …He sent me to the beauty contest and guided me to victory, …bringing great glory to you, your majesty. He saved your life from the two assassins, … and also informed me of HMN's treachery against your power. Mordecai is a very powerful man. He is doing much, though I do not know the details."

"Bring Mordecai," the king commanded.

When Mordecai arrived, the king was astonished to hear about HMN's promotion, the truth behind the queen's tiara, and how HMN had deceived him into publishing the killing decree. Ecstatic, the king learned how Mordecai had cleverly utilized the court messengers to establish his own private information bureau, ensuring prosperity for the empire.

"This is one of the Egyptian poison bottles that HMN gave you," Mordecai asserted, pointing to a bottle he had prepared for the treasure caravan.

"Yes," the king replied. "Be very careful. It is highly poisonous."

Mordecai took the bottle, verified that the seal was unbroken and the gold coin visible at the bottom, and said, "I'm going to break it open."

"No!" the king shouted.

But Mordecai had already smashed the bottle against the marble table. Instead of releasing poisonous gas, a sweet scent of honey wafted through the air. Carefully, Mordecai dipped his finger into the sticky residue and extracted a coin minted by King Ahasuerus in honor of the

Royal World Fair. He licked the coin, and while showing it to the king, he let out a loud, boisterous laugh.

Initially stricken with fear, the king couldn't help but join in the laughter. "Your story is good enough to be one of Esther's banquet tales," he proclaimed. "In fact, it may be the best one of all. All the stolen gifts I received from HMN shall be returned to their rightful owners."

"Thank you very much. Now that I have accepted them, those glorious gifts of the Jews are legally bestowed to our beloved king," Mordecai said. "Please keep the poison bottles, but remember, they are all fake. This ensured that HMN's murderous attempt, as well as any other court assassin's, would fail."

King Ahasuerus looked at Mordecai, contemplated for a moment, then shook his head. "You knew what HMN was authorized to do. I hereby appoint you as my head minister, the holder of the king's signet, and command you to execute my prior orders to please me."

Mordecai knelt before the king and kissed his ring. "Thank you, great king, for the honor you have bestowed upon me."

"Mordecai, do you intend to continue manipulating the crown?"

Mordecai smiled. "With this signet in my hand, I do not need to."

"Ah-ha. Really?" the king laughed.

Mordecai raised a finger. "But if I ever do, I promise to inform your majesty immediately after the matters are successfully executed and recorded in your history book."

"Do you want to use your new power right now?" the king asked.

"Yes, your majesty. As our lives are sheltered within his hands, with the power vested in me in favor of the king, I hereby declare that Harvona shall be allowed to wear a royal purple ribbon in recognition of excellence," Mordecai announced.

The king nodded. Harvona, standing behind him, blinked in surprise.

CHAPTER 41

Meanwhile, Rebekah, locked away, secured with her father in the tower of Mordecai's palace, heard a commotion downstairs, followed by men rushing up the stairs. She grabbed her father's hand and pulled him away. It was too late to escape through the hollow column. Shaken, they hid behind the bed, silently praying.

Mordecai sped home, dashing up the stairs two at a time. He hastily opened the door to find the room empty. *Where are they?* He thought, freezing in fear.

"Hallelujah?" he panted, trying to encourage them to show themselves. He spotted Rebekah and Zechariah rising from behind the bed, still trembling. "Hallelujah!" he cried. "Your imprisonment is over! You are free—free to come out!"

"What happened? You look elated," Rebekah said, excitement shining in her eyes.

"Yes," he gasped. "The king loves Queen Esther, my daughter Hadassah. HMN has been hanged, and I've been appointed second to the king! Look— the king's signet on my finger. Hallelujah!"

"We must celebrate!" Zechariah shouted though it sounded more like a question.

"I am ready," Mordecai proclaimed.

"Ready?" Zechariah asked.

"Ready to ask for—"

"—I agree—" Rebekah blurted out, moving closer to Mordecai. "—Rebekah's hand," Mordecai declared.

"Wait! I have to agree first," Zechariah interjected. When both Mordecai and Rebekah looked at him expectantly, he laughed and added, "I agree."

"Thank you," Mordecai and Rebekah said together.

Mordecai turned to Rebekah. "May I kiss my bride?"

Rebekah's eyes sparkled with joy as she leaned forward, extending her arms to hug him. Mordecai took her right hand, bent down, and kissed it tenderly. It was a long kiss, and when she placed her other hand on his head, he pulled back, leaving a warm, salty mark on her hand. "We cannot celebrate our engagement just yet. No one should know you are my fiancée. It's not safe. I have too many enemies who might hurt you to get to me. If we survive the impending war, we will marry. In the meantime, you'll join Sarah's class at the Jewish Academy and live with her. I cannot let you return to Egypt. My heart would break if I lost you," Mordecai said, his voice trembling.

"In the meantime, until Yavin can take you to Sarah's house," Mordecai requested, "please tell me how the children of Israel crossed the Sea of Reeds. You promised to tell me but didn't."

"I waited to tell you in person," Rebekah blushed. "To keep you eager."

"You succeeded. And…"

"I found it was possible. Near our house, there was a water canal about forty feet wide, filled with pressed-together reeds standing twenty feet high. One day, a strong wind bent the reeds almost all the way down." Rebekah demonstrated with her fingers how the reeds swayed.

"I took a long, flat plank and pushed the reeds down to float on the water, stepping on them as I went. I considered tying them together, but it wasn't necessary. I walked on the reeds—they hardly sank. Only when I reached the other bank did I step slightly into the water. I think when the Egyptians' chariots traveled over the reeds, their wheels separated them, causing the chariots to sink. What do you think?"

"This is an ingenious idea! I've never heard such an explanation," Mordecai declared, moving closer to kiss Rebekah's head. She glowed with pride.

"The wind flattened only a narrow strip, while the reeds on either side stood tall like green walls, swaying gently with the green water of the swamp. It's possible the children of Israel learned to do this while living in the swamplands of Goshen."

Mordecai and Rebekah sat together, holding hands, until Yavin arrived with a group of soldiers, bringing uniforms for Rebekah. She quickly dressed as a soldier, her hair short like a boy's. Rebekah soon learned to match her steps with the soldiers as they made their way to Sarah's house, where she would be safely left.

———≈———

With the king's approval, Esther appointed Mordecai to manage HMN's palace. Though he accepted the responsibility, he left the king's flag flying over the property. Mordecai terminated all of HMN's servants and freed his slaves, ensuring they received payment for their service. The freed slaves expressed their gratitude to Mordecai, with several of them beginning to speak Hebrew with him. Delighted, he embraced them and asked for their names and family affiliations. He promised to compile a full report of their efforts and appointed them to help manage the palace in his absence.

Before night fall, Mordecai ordered to respectfully bring HMN's body down from the tree and deliver it to HMN's eldest son. Afterward, Mordecai instructed the gardener to care for the heavily pruned tree, hoping to revive it.

Mordecai enlisted the freed Jewish slaves to sort through and record the contents of the looted jewelry boxes in HMN's palace. Over time, he discovered most of the missing treasures from the caravan. However, he estimated that five chests were still unaccounted for and suspected that some might be with HMN's sons. Among the treasures in HMN's house, he found jewelry that had belonged to Esther's parents—the very parents who had been beheaded on their way to Jerusalem.

Summoning the Jewish high court, Mordecai ordered Yavin to attend. "Yavin, I am appointing you to take my position at the king's gate," he said.

Yavin knelt before him. "Thank you, great leader."

Mordecai continued, "Return the gifts to their original owners, along with a thank-you letter signed with the king's signet. Provide them with additional gold equivalent to the value of their gifts. For the owners of the missing gifts, they shall receive triple the value of their contribution and a signed letter explaining that if their gifts are found, they will be returned. Those whose gifts the king kept shall receive quadruple the value of their contribution, along with a letter honoring them for their generosity and stating that the king cherished their gifts. As for me, I've received my payment: a bride!" Mordecai smiled, his heart full.

———≈———

Mordecai continued his search through HMN's house for any documents and correspondence. He discovered a stack of letters and meticulously recorded the names and locations of HMN's supporters and co-conspirators. To protect this valuable information, he refrained from alerting the servants to its contents. Instead, he left the documents undisturbed, making them appear inconsequential so that HMN's friends wouldn't be warned of their exposure and the impending consequences.

CHAPTER 42

Esther designed a new flag for herself, featuring the royal lion of Judah carrying the unity crown adorned with the stone of Judea. Now free to leave the royal palace, she was escorted by twelve bodyguards under Hatach's command. In public, Esther wore her golden dagger at her hip, and she and her bodyguards rode beautifully decorated white Cilician horses. She also joined Mordecai in overseeing the king's dignitaries, governors, and generals.

Despite Mordecai's promotion to second-in-command, the killing decree remained in effect. Jews throughout the empire continued to face insults and assaults, and letters pleading for help flooded in, detailing the atrocities they endured.

"How long are you going to let this continue?" Esther asked, frustration evident in her voice. "Don't you hold the king's signet?"

"A little longer," Mordecai replied, his voice tinged with a mix of pain and excitement. "God allowed the children of Israel to suffer slavery in Egypt for more than seventy years during Moses's life before sending him to Pharaoh. We will wait just seventy days—one day for each year. Suffering unites us and motivates us to rise and help ourselves."

"Sad to hear," Esther commented.

"I did instruct Yavin to assist the Jews in some areas," he added. "This delay will also help us see if Parshandatha, the new leader of the Amalekites, intends to mend our relationship out of goodwill rather than fear."

"What if he does?" Esther asked, alarm creeping into her voice. "That could ruin your plan."

"His people are too unruly for him to control. If he tries to deprive them of their loot, they might turn on him. We'll see what happens. Perhaps God will harden his heart," Mordecai said, a smile crossing his face as he recalled Esther's speech at Passover all those years ago.

"Let us go and pray with the mourning Jews," he urged.

"But you are the one keeping them in suffering," she countered.

"Exactly. That's why I must join them and pray even more," Mordecai insisted. "Do not think I do not suffer too. The burden is unbearable, but timing is everything."

———≈———

When the seventy days had passed, Esther turned to Mordecai and said, "It's time to act. Who will speak with the king?"

"It would make me very happy if you would do it," Mordecai joked.

"Me? Again? Going uninvited?" Esther replied, a hint of anxiety in her voice.

"I'm sorry, but you were crowned for this purpose. You asked the king to save your nation. He gave them to you. They are yours, and you are theirs," Mordecai explained.

"I will do it," she said, determination in her tone. "I will ask the king to be wise and loving toward me and to rescind HMN's killing decree, even knowing he might not be able to do so. It's better than demanding a free hand, which we desire but cannot ask for directly."

"That's a good plan," Mordecai agreed. "I'll be there to ensure the king doesn't rescind it. Even if he does, I won't publish it in time. We need that decree to remain in effect. We need to fight, we need to win, and we must believe that God has granted us a miracle. We need to have faith in God. Only then will we survive forever."

———≈———

The next day, Esther approached her husband, fell at his feet, and wept. The king's face softened with love as he took her hand and helped her up. "What troubles you, my dear Ishtahr?"

"If it pleases the king, if you love me, and if it is lawful, please rescind HMN's decree to kill the Jews. If my people are eliminated, I won't be able to go on living."

The king regarded her with a stern look. "For this, you cry? I granted you HMN's estate, Mordecai received my signet, and HMN was hanged for raising a hand against the Jews. But, a decree signed by the king's signet must be respected and cannot be rescinded. I thought you could handle it! You are free to write, in my name, any new decree that honors me while respectfully sidestepping HMN's decree."

Satisfied, Esther nodded, smiled, and blew him a kiss.

The king beamed at her.

"Exactly what we wanted," Mordecai said, relief washing over him. "Did you hear what the king said? We have the power to order the Jews to do whatever we want, as long as it is in his favor. There are no limits on time or scope. He has appointed us as joint leaders of the Jews. He has given you your nation, just as you asked."

———✦———

"The king announced that HMN was executed for acting against the Jews," Mordecai reminded Esther. "This might affect the legal status of HMN's sons."

"Are we going after them?" Esther asked.

"We will observe their actions for now. There's no need to decide immediately."

Esther thought for a moment before saying, "The king has prohibited us from changing HMN's killing decree. I believe he is following King Solomon's approach, allowing the two nations to fight it out."

"Interesting," Mordecai contemplated.

"Mordecai," Esther inquired, "HMN's killing decree did not prohibit self-defense. Perhaps we can defend ourselves without issuing a new decree."

"It's going to be a big war," Mordecai declared. "We are merchants, not soldiers. A self-defense decree is essential if we are to have any chance of survival. It will demonstrate that the king is with us, unite us, and boost our confidence."

"How can we achieve that?" Esther asked.

"At the very least, the law-abiding citizens, the governors, and the king's army will refrain from attacking us," Mordecai explained. "We can use HMN's killing decree as a framework."

With this understanding, Esther drafted a new self-defense decree. It did not contradict anything in the killing decree but removed the implication that the king despised the Jews. "Mordecai, here is our new decree," she said, presenting it to him.

The Jews may unite to defend themselves,
destroy, kill, and oppress
anyone who seeks to trouble them,
including their women and children.
They are permitted to seize their spoils
in a single day.

"I chose the word 'trouble' deliberately. It's subjective—any look, sound, or movement could be perceived as a threat, justifying punishment," Esther explained. "People might assume it refers only to a great war, seizures, and massacres, but they would be mistaken."

"You've done an excellent job," Mordecai replied. "I always knew you were clever."

"I learned from the best," Esther smiled. "Please sign it with the king's signet."

"If we are threatened at any point during that day, it will be HMN's fault, and his sons will have to suffer their father's crime. Fortunately for HMN, he won't know about it," Mordecai declared.

"Do you really think we have a chance to win?" Esther asked, worry creasing her brow.

"I believe we do," Mordecai said confidently. "'Loot' is the bait. The mob will be preoccupied with looting rather than killing and destruction."

Esther raised an eyebrow, contemplating his words.

———————≈———————

The new self-defense decree was swiftly dispatched to the provinces, and soon, Jews everywhere began organizing meetings and strategizing their defense plans. Esther instructed Yavin to assign responsibilities to the mature students in the Jewish Academy, training them to manage the impending conflict and serve as defense commanders for their home communities.

Yavin encouraged the students to visualize potential Amalekite attacks, asking them to write down their thoughts based on the two decrees as well as their historical and personal experiences. He used this information to evaluate and prepare for the upcoming conflict. The students received names and addresses of the Amalekite leaders that Mordecai had uncovered in HMN's house, along with details gathered from the freed slaves. Esther guided them on how to conduct their defense and how to treat the attackers and their properties.

"Select commanders for each city," Esther ordered. "Include female students as commanders, dressing them as males."

"Are you sure?" Yavin asked, visibly troubled by the suggestion.

"Do you have a problem with that?" Esther shot back, her eyes fierce.

"No, my queen," Yavin replied quickly.

"See? A willing woman can be a commander," Esther said with a smile.

Yavin returned her smile and bowed his head in respect.

CHAPTER 43

sther then visited the Jewish Academy to meet Sarah and her female students. She settled into a royal chair that had been brought for her. Sarah and about twenty young girls entered, afraid to look directly at the queen. Esther felt A wave of narcissus scent wafted toward her, filling the air with sweetness.

Sarah and her students prostrated themselves before their queen. Curiosity overcame Sarah, and she stole a glance at the Jewish queen, recognizing her as her mistress, Hadassah. Elation and fear flooded her face, leaving her frozen and breathless. Unsure whether she was allowed to disclose this information, Sarah felt a surge of anxiety, fearing she might be punished for making the wrong decision.

Esther saw Sara's distress, rose from the royal chair, and approached her, embracing her warmly and praising her efforts. "You all carry the future of our nation," Esther told the class. "Be proud. You will preserve Jewish traditions in our homes. Your role is as important, if not more so, than that of the men."

In Esther's honor, the students danced and sang Rebekah's beloved song, the "Song of the Sea," celebrating the Israelites' crossing of the Sea of Reeds.

Amid the celebration, Esther noticed a striking woman about her age among the young students, a narcissus flower blooming in her short hair. "Who are you?" Esther asked.

"I am Rebekah, the daughter of Zechariah, the nephew of Gdaliahu Ha-Nasi," she replied proudly.

Esther paused for a moment before saying, "Yes. I believe I should introduce you to Mordecai, if I may."

Rebekah smiled, her lips pressed tightly together, her eyes shining with agreement.

She did not respond verbally, and Esther puzzled over it. *I will take it as consent.*

Sarah then introduced a strong, stocky student with light, short, curly hair and freckles. "This is Dina, the daughter of Zelophehad. She will be the commander of the city of Ozgad."

Moved, Esther embraced Dina warmly. She held her by the shoulders, surveying her with pride. "Be a brave commander!" Esther said, tears sparkling in her eyes. "We depend on you. War is particularly hard on us women. God will bless you. My heart will be with you." She pointed to a strong bodyguard, assigning him as Dina's shadow and protector.

Dina smiled, a mix of confusion and elation on her face, and bowed to Esther.

"You will return her, and you will return him," Esther said, pointing back and forth between them.

After dismissing the students, Sarah requested permission to introduce her family.

"Of course," Esther replied with a smile. "I would be delighted to meet your family."

Sarah bowed and left the room, returning with Michael and two young boys. All bowed to Esther, who felt overwhelmed with joy, shaking her head in disbelief. Rising from her chair, she wiped away a tear and embraced her cousin before kneeling to hug his children, tears glistening in Michael's eyes.

"You got your king," Michael said, a hint of sarcasm in his voice. "I wanted to have you."

"Now I have all of you," Queen Esther replied slowly, her emotions swirling.

"I won a family," Sarah added, smiling as she pulled Michael's hand to her belly.

Sarah then pulled a lock of long, light brown hair from her chest pocket and presented it to Esther. "This is your hair, my queen, when you left for the contest," she said. "What a sad day it was. I've kept it all these years since that awful day. I knew I would find you."

Esther's expression shifted to surprise as she hugged Sarah again. "It's yours. The Queen's hair. Keep it as a memory of our joint past."

———※———

Esther instructed Yavin to arrange a ceremony with the students before their departure to defend their cities. She emphasized, "Remember, we are good people. We will not act harshly as authorized by the self-defense decree. We will not kill the women and *young* children of the thieves."

"But it is God's commandment to eradicate all the Amalekites and their children as well," Yavin argued. "The survivors will carry their evil nature."

"No," Esther replied firmly. "It is not our duty to end that war. We must not act like the Amalekites." She touched her golden dagger and continued, "Even the Prophet Samuel did not eliminate all the heirs of Agag, King of Amalek, who is the ancestor of HMN the Agagite. Killing does not eradicate all evil. Evil can be reborn in all of us if we are not careful. We will eliminate the leaders and their adult children, thereby erasing their criminal enterprise's hidden knowledge."

After a moment of contemplation, she added, "We are permitted to loot the thieves who attack us. We framed the self-defense decree this way to intimidate them, but our intent is not to enrich ourselves. With God's help, if we win, we will recover only the stolen goods found in the Amalekites' homes. The rest of the thieves' property will be delivered to the king in accordance with traditional law."

For the ceremony, Yavin gathered the Jewish students and presented Queen Esther. She addressed them, saying, "Go to your hometowns. Announce to the Jews in my name: 'Stop crying! Rise! Fight, and God will be with us! The predator will become prey. We will write history, and history will be written about us!'"

The students cheered in response.

"Write down my orders," Esther instructed Yavin as she began dictating the rules for training, fighting, collecting, splitting, and distributing the recovered stolen goods.

Yavin bowed respectfully. "So orders the Queen."

In his role as second-in-command to the king, Mordecai sent stern letters to the city mayors and princes, warning them to assist the Jewish commanders or face severe punishment. He also wrote to the Jewish leaders, commanding them to obey the Queen's emissaries and provide all the men, weapons, and supplies they requested. He wished them success in their efforts.

Yavin distributed the Queen's new flags and proclamations to each student, signifying that they were the Queen's emissaries.

CHAPTER 44

Until now, Mordecai had kept a low profile, but with the defense decree published, it was time to assert his full power and authority as second to the king. He made a public appearance, dressed in regal garments of royal blue and white, adorned with an imperial purple silk ribbon and a golden circlet. Taking on the role of chief commander of the imperial armies, one of his first actions was to announce a new tax law. He then dispatched his clerks and officers to the governors and mayors, his men carrying gifts and tax-break notices in one hand and notices of tax audits in the other.

The leaders of the empire and the governors of the provinces were pleased to receive the gifts but were unsettled by the audits. They began to fear and respect Mordecai, flattering him in hopes of winning his favor and securing their positions.

Sarah arranged for her class to visit Mordecai's palace. As they entered, her students bowed to Mordecai, who responded with a nod of acknowledgment. The students then broke into a glorious hymn, celebrating the moment.

> **O LORD, our Lord, how glorious is your name in all the earth!**
> **Out of the mouth of sucking babes, you have established strength,**
> **silencing and avenging your mighty adversaries.**
> **When we behold your universe, the work of your fingers,**
> **the moon and the stars that you have set in place.**
> **What is mankind that you are mindful of?**
> **And the son of man that you care for him?**
> **You have made him to have dominion over the work of your hands.**
> **O LORD, our Lord, how majestic is your name in all the earth!**[10]

---

[10]   A loose translation of Psalm 8.

Mordecai struggled to tear his gaze away from Rebekah. A single tear slipped down his cheek as he glanced at Sarah, nodding in gratitude for granting him this precious glimpse of his beloved fiancée.

———

Esther appointed Yavin as the head commander of the Jewish defense for the empire and in Shushan, the capital of Persia.

Later, Yavin reported to Esther and Mordecai, "The Jews are energized and ready to fight! Hedging their bets, non-Jewish neighbors are contributing money and offering their support. Many are even converting to Judaism to share in our blessings. They understand that if the city is set on fire, their lives and property will be at risk as well.

"And listen to this—*miracle of miracles*! The scattered Ten Tribes of Israel are joining us and merging into the tribe of Judah. Thousands upon thousands of them! We are now united as a single nation. Tribal in-fighting is a thing of the past. We are saving them from extinction, too."

"This is a miracle! Welcome them all for the glory of the Lord!" Mordecai exclaimed. "Invite them to join the IBCE as well."

"You are the first king of the Jews since King Saul to unite all the children of Israel in love! Hallelujah to the king of Israel! God's blessing is upon you; He shares His power with you," Yavin proclaimed with delight.

In humility, Mordecai lowered his head. "I am not exactly the king of Israel, and King David and King Solomon had a shaky united kingdom for a time," he said, blushing. "The Lord gives, and the Lord takes away. Blessed be the name of the Lord forever and ever."

"Parshandatha has not attempted to mend our relationship," Yavin remarked after a moment.

"He doesn't understand that any attack on the Jews on the day of the killing, even an accidental one, will be blamed on his father, and he will face the consequences," Mordecai noted thoughtfully. "Give

Parshandatha, King of Amalek, one last chance to save his life. Ask him to prevent his people from attacking us!"

"I will," Yavin agreed. "But it will be difficult to halt the killing decree. The troublemakers won't listen; they are already salivating at the thought of loot—it's like flies to fresh dung."

"Yes," Mordecai concurred. "I've already spread a few rumors among the Amalekite leaders that the Jews are terrified and will be easy prey for the looters."

The Jews organized local armies and began their training. A few days before the designated killing day, they evacuated women and children from homes that were likely to be the first targets of attack, ensuring their safety in the face of impending danger.

At the king's gate, Yavin announced, "All esteemed leaders and their families are invited to a grand banquet at Queen Esther's palace, beginning on the evening of the twelfth day of Adar and lasting until sunset on the thirteenth. Join us in celebration with Mordecai—may he live long—as the second to the King of Kings and steward of Queen Esther's palace."

This banquet was Mordecai's way of protecting those who had served him and acted as spies against HMN. By hosting them at Esther's palace—formerly HMN's and now confiscated by the king after HMN's execution—Mordecai ensured their safety. Attending the banquet signaled trust, as the guests would be under Mordecai's protection, though essentially placed under house arrest. The sight of the king's lion flag flying above the palace reassured them that no unjust harm would come to them there.

Esther and Yavin visited Parshandatha, HMN's eldest son, advising him to order his people not to attack the Jews. They also extended an invitation for him and his brothers to attend the banquet at Esther's palace. As they spoke, Esther noticed the blue sapphire ring on Parshandatha's finger—it had belonged to her father.

You murdered my father, Esther thought, *and took that ring from his dying hand.*

Though she kept her composure, she awaited Parshandatha's response. He declined the invitation, insisting that the king's decrees must be fulfilled without exception.

As I expected, Esther thought. *He is too proud to accept our offer of peace. His emotions prevent him from joining his father's enemies in the very palace of his father, near the tree that took his life, before even a year has passed. He seeks blood revenge.*

After they left, Esther turned to Yavin and said, "Parshandatha is plotting something."

Yavin paused thoughtfully before replying, "We'll set a trap—bait. We'll make Mordecai an irresistible prey, dangling right before his eyes."

Esther nodded, her eyes hardening. "I saw my father's ring on Parshandatha's finger. He killed him. I want it back," she commanded.

On the day of the attack, many guests arrived at Mordecai's banquet in Esther's palace. Once they entered, they were not permitted to leave until the killing day was over. Lavish food and wine were served, and the guests were encouraged to indulge freely in the luxurious offerings, keeping them preoccupied and under Mordecai's watchful eye.

CHAPTER 45

On the day of the attack, before dawn, Dina, the daughter of Zelophehad, stood on the high roof of her father's palace, scanning the city of Ozgad. As one of Queen Esther's emissaries and commander of the city's defenses, Dina felt the weight of her responsibility. Her father, a wealthy merchant and Jewish leader in Mordecai's IBCE, had instilled in her a strong sense of duty.

She recalled her arrival in Ozgad with her giant bodyguard, Goliath, who had been assigned to her by Queen Esther. Confidently, she marched to the mayor, presented her credentials, and warned him not to cause trouble for the Jews. A smile tugged at her lips as she remembered the mayor bowing, oblivious to the fact that she was a woman beneath her military uniform. The memory of meeting the Jews at the community center was equally satisfying; they had murmured in awe when she boldly declared, "I am the queen's emissary, and now you belong to me!" Goliath's imposing presence had silenced any objections, granting her full authority over the city's defenses.

Time was short. The war was scheduled to start in about six months, and Dina had been tasked with transforming young men—students, apprentices, and shopkeepers—into experienced soldiers.

Now, as she stood on the roof, she spotted a mob of around five hundred aggressive troublemakers closing in on the Jewish neighborhood. They ran and howled like wild hyenas, eager for destruction, armed with mules, donkeys, camels, carts, and wagons, ready to plunder. Stones flew through the air, shattering windows as they rammed doors and stormed into homes, greedily grabbing whatever they could.

Dina waited.

Soon, fires erupted, and a thick, dark cloud rose over the city, filling the air with the smell of burning wood. Flames leaped from house to house, accompanied by the screams of Jews, half-dressed and engulfed in flames, fleeing their burning homes while the thugs laughed and pelted them with stones.

Still, Dina waited.

The mob captured boys and girls, chaining them together as they beat and dragged the terrified children, tearing off their clothes.

Dina waited.

Then, she saw a gang of armed hooligans approach the looters, violently seizing the stolen goods. The thieves begged for mercy, but the hooligans merely laughed, kicked them aside, and ordered them to steal more.

Dina still waited.

Pacing back and forth on the roof with clenched fists and tightened lips, she felt the immense weight of responsibility. Her knees trembled, and her mouth felt dry, knowing so many lives depended on her leadership.

When Queen Esther first commissioned her, many of the men under her command had resisted being led by a woman, but one glare from Goliath quelled their protests. Over the past six months, Dina had trained three hundred Jewish men to fight, tirelessly building their strength and confidence while wielding clubs with sharp metal spikes for initial defense. She taught them to control their horses using only their legs, keeping their hands free for battle. Each man was paired with a partner, working in teams to take down the Amalekite mercenaries.

Dina worried constantly, counting each day as she monitored her soldiers' progress. She felt a deep sense of responsibility to prove herself as a woman in command. Pushing her soldiers harder than most, she always ensured they returned to camp to warm food, clean clothes, and well-fed horses. She also trained them to secure prisoners and protect their property after battles.

Her father made sure the entire community supported their soldiers with weapons, horses, food, shelter, and night guards. He was immensely proud that his only daughter had been entrusted with such a significant role in defending their people.

A few days before the war, Dina allowed her soldiers to ease their training load. She read to them stories of the victories of Abraham, Gideon, Jephthah, Prince Jonathan, and King David, and she did not forget Deborah and Jael.

As the mob of thugs scattered among the houses, robbing as they went through the neighborhood, Dina waited until the arrival rate of new attackers dwindled to a trickle. *Have I trained enough soldiers?* she wondered. *At least the mob is behaving as Esther predicted; they are focusing on looting rather than killing.*

Dina prayed, "Oh great God, please save your children and let us win with minimal losses and injuries." Then, she signaled to begin the defense. Her soldiers moved forward in military formation, their goal to "mark and maim."—'One smash and go to the next' became their motto.

The raiders, spread out in the streets and houses, were unaware of the soldiers' approach. Some robbers, unorganized and in small groups, were caught off guard by the soldiers. While some fled, abandoning their stolen goods, others tried to carry items with them, and a few ill-advised individuals attempted to fight back.

The soldiers were instructed to beat and injure the looters but not to kill them. In no time, the criminals were overwhelmed. Some, bleeding, ran home, while others fled into the countryside or tried to hide among peaceful civilians. However, they were quickly caught, identified, and returned to their homes. Abandoned animals laden with stolen items were followed back to their owners' homes.

In accordance with the king's decree, the Jewish elders demanded that the houses be searched for stolen property. It was difficult for residents to deny any involvement when captured sons, trails of blood, loaded animals, and scattered valuables pointed straight at their doors.

Jews of all ages helped the soldiers subdue the Amalekites and search their homes, even freeing Jewish slaves they found inside. The freed slaves were eager to assist Dina's men in locating the hiding Amalekite leaders and their warehouses and caves filled with stolen goods.

The Jewish soldiers searched for injured thieves, stolen property, and kidnapped children, uncovering troves of stolen items hidden in secret rooms and underground caves. They discovered private prisons and torture chambers, releasing all the prisoners they found.

When the captured Jewish children were freed, they rejoiced and hugged their rescuers. The children cried, cursed, and laughed as they recounted their horrific experiences, while their parents tended to their wounds.

A released Jewish slave identified a young man among the captives as the son of an Amalekite leader. Without delay, Dina summoned the city's mayor to accompany her in searching the palace of the Amalekite leader.

Carrying the queen's flag, Dina approached the fortified palace. She read aloud the self-defense decree, presenting the captured son as evidence of his family's lawbreaking. In desperation, the boy called for his father. When Dina demanded access to search the palace, the Amalekite leader denied the boy was his son, taunted her to kill the "loser," and outright refused to comply.

Seeing no other option, the mayor ordered his soldiers to break down the palace doors, igniting a fierce battle. Amalekite defenders perched on the walls above the gates hurled hot oil and heavy stones down upon the attackers. In response, the mayor's men unleashed a volley of arrows. There were casualties on both sides.

"We can lay siege to the palace and search it later," the mayor suggested.

Dina shook her head. "The self-defense decree gives us only one day. It must be done today."

The mayor considered her words. "I'll pull back my men and continue with archers only."

"That's agreeable," Dina responded, her mind resolute. As the mayor's forces retreated, Dina called to her troops. "This is our battle. The mayor's archers will support us, but we must press on. You've seen what happens if we lose. Be brave, and God will be with us. Pray—the predator will become our prey."

Despite her resolve, Dina made a conscious decision: *I won't use my archers to set the palace ablaze—not yet. There may be women, children, and valuables belonging to the king and the Jews inside.* She kept the option in mind should it become necessary.

After an hour of relentless hammering, the palace door finally collapsed, and Dina's soldiers surged inside. Sensing his impending defeat, the Amalekite leader ordered his men to aim their arrows directly at Dina, his desperation evident in the fear in his voice.

In a last, cowardly attempt to escape, the Amalekite leader seized a group of Jewish female slaves, using them as human shields. Cornered, his men threatened to slaughter the hostages if they were not allowed to flee.

Dina raised her hands and blew a horn to halt the fighting. Her voice echoed through the palace as she declared, "Spoil a slave, be scorched on a stake. Surrender, be spared. Switch sides, and share in the success. If we don't kill you today, the mayor will kill you tomorrow. You are doomed." Her soldiers repeated the chant, spreading the warning to all corners of the palace.

When Dina lowered her hands, the horn blasted again, and the battle resumed.

Overwhelmed by the situation, many Amalekite soldiers laid down their weapons and prostrated themselves. Several foreign mercenaries, recognizing their losing cause, ordered their men to switch sides. However, some Amalekites continued to fight, clinging to their futile hope.

In a final act of brutality, the Amalekite leader beheaded one of the female slaves, swinging her severed head by the hair and hurling it toward Dina. Goliath, Dina's bodyguard, knocked away the grisly missile before it could reach her. Enraged by this savage act, Dina's soldiers roared and charged, quickly overwhelming the Amalekite leader, his lieutenants, chieftains, and adult sons.

With their leaders fallen, the remaining Amalekite soldiers surrendered. Dina signaled for a large victory fire to be lit on the hilltop, a sign to nearby cities that the battle in Ozgad had been won. Reports soon came asking for help. Without hesitation, Dina dispatched half of her troops to assist them.

Gathering her remaining men, Dina offered thanks to God for their triumph. She counted the fallen and sent a detailed report to Esther. Her message read, "The Jews of Ozgad have achieved a great victory. Thirty-two Amalekite men lie dead. The city is now free from their secret, corrupt criminal society."

Outside the city walls, the newly enslaved Amalekites were assembled, grouped by families. Those Amalekite soldiers who had surrendered were permitted to claim their families. Additionally, former Jewish slaves who testified that their masters had treated them fairly secured the release of those particular Amalekites. The rest faced sentences ranging from one to six years of slavery, depending on their involvement in criminal activities.

The Jews were allowed to search the thieves' homes but were instructed to recover only Jewish's stolen belongings. Any remaining property was to be delivered to the king, as required by law regarding lawbreakers' possessions.

In accordance with Esther's order and King David's ancient rule, all recovered stolen goods originally belonging to the Jews were divided equally among the local Jewish families who had participated in the defense—warriors or supporters—regardless of their level of involvement or original ownership. Dina also ensured that non-Jewish supporters and foreign mercenaries who had switched sides were included in the distribution.

As the Jews shared stories of their victory, they distributed gifts to the poor and less fortunate. Each person checked his recovered property, and if the original owner could have been identified, it was returned to the rightful owner, often in exchange for other goods. That night, the Jews celebrated their triumph with great joy, drinking and rejoicing until they could no longer recognize one another.

CHAPTER 46

On the eve of the killing day, Yavin gathered his officers and issued their final orders. Mordecai and the Jewish elders were to be secured inside Esther's palace for the duration of the day.

Yavin then escorted the soldier chosen to act as Mordecai's double to the palace. Upon arrival, the double bowed respectfully to Mordecai, who studied the man closely, evaluating him with a critical eye. The double remained steadfast, unwavering under Mordecai's scrutiny.

"You know you're taking on a dangerous task," Mordecai said. "We'll present you to the enemy, and you'll be the focus of their wrath. All their fury will be directed at you."

With a firm voice, the double replied, "I am a soldier, sir. Yours to command. It is an honor to play a role in this war."

Mordecai extended his hand, gripping the soldier's firmly. "Thank you. May God protect you. I pray we meet again tomorrow night."

As the double departed, Yavin turned to Mordecai and said, "I'll inform Ason Ben Aser that you'll be celebrating safely in your palace."

———≈———

The double, dressed in Mordecai's clothes and adorned with his jewels, left Esther's palace accompanied by soldiers disguised as guests, servants, and guards. Mordecai had instructed his giant personal bodyguard, Joe, to accompany the double to give the impression that Mordecai was with the group. Carrying Mordecai's flag and making a loud commotion, they headed to celebrate at Mordecai's palace.

Yavin had strategically concealed soldiers around the palace. With music and drums filling the air, the double and his companions threw a raucous party. Under the cover of the festivities, a group of Yavin's soldiers danced around the palace while two others quietly hammered iron stakes deep into the ground along the perimeter.

In the morning, Yavin scanned the sky and saw heavy smoke rising from neighboring cities and farms—the Amalekites had launched their attack. The war was raging, but who was winning? How many losses were they suffering? As Yavin watched the smoke billow, a troubling thought crossed his mind: *Is this the end of the Jewish nation?*

———◆———

Also, in the morning, Parshandatha and his nine brothers arrived at Mordecai's palace with their soldiers. They pounded on the door, declaring that, by the king's killing decree, they had come to kill Mordecai the Jew and loot his house. They demanded that he surrender or leave the palace immediately.

When no one answered, they broke down the front door and stormed inside, searching for Mordecai. Meanwhile, the double and his soldiers retreated upstairs to the palace's wooden tower, while releasing pre-arranged heavy rocks and sand down the stairs, barricading the entrance to the tower.

HMN's sons followed the retreating soldiers, attempting to break into the tower. However, when they saw the barricade of rocks, they gave up and set the wooden structure ablaze, smoke rising ominously from the tower's windows.

"How are we going to escape?" asked Joe, Mordecai's giant bodyguard.

"We climb down the hollow column," the double replied.

"It might be too tight for me," Joe grumbled. "I'll stay and fight."

"Fight? The flames?" one soldier scoffed. "You'll end up roasted like a steak!"

"You'll go last," the double said firmly. "Take off your shield and armor and toss them down. If you get stuck, we'll feed you water until you slim down enough to slide out after the war!"

Joe stripped down, and they double-smeared him with oil from a nearby lamp. Using a rope, the soldiers began their escape, sliding down the secret tunnel inside the marble column that led to a safe house a block away. Even Joe managed to squeeze through. Once they were safely out, they ignited a fire at the bottom of the column, burning the rope and sending poisonous smoke up through the tunnel to the top of the tower.

Yavin watched from a distance, amazed at the ten sons' relentless determination to kill Mordecai. The temptation had been too strong. Using a horn, Yavin ordered his men to form a three-man-deep perimeter around Mordecai's palace.

As HMN's sons emerged from the burning building, they carried gold and silver plates, only to be met by Yavin's soldiers, who now surrounded them. Surprised, they dropped their loot and drew their weapons.

Flames roared from the tower's windows, devouring the walls and roof, and casting a yellow glow across the sky. Mordecai's flag burned on its pole, the last shred fluttering upward into the smoke. Yavin and his men saluted the flag until it was fully consumed.

Parshandatha stepped forward and declared, "According to the killing decree, we are permitted to kill Mordecai the Jew, seize everything, destroy his palace, and kill all of you."

"You're mistaken," Yavin shouted back. "That decree has been illegal—your father was hanged for it. You are all condemned under the king's self-defense decree. You will pay for attempting to burn Mordecai alive. There's no escape for you. Surrender now."

Yavin's men, furious at the mention of their fallen leader, prepared for battle.

Parshandatha and his brothers stood with their backs to the blazing palace, flames licking at their feet as burning timbers fell around them. Some of Parshandatha's men broke rank, dropping their weapons and fleeing. Yavin's soldiers didn't pursue them—*they could be planning a counterattack from behind*. Yavin considered the situation carefully.

Parshandatha barked an order, and his remaining men quickly formed a tight column around him and his brothers, leveling their spears as they charged at Yavin's lines.

Yavin's first two lines scattered to the sides, creating an opening in their ranks. Parshandatha's men rushed through without resistance but collided headlong with Yavin's third line. There, shields made of cowhide, stuffed with straw and wood, had been chained to one another and to iron stakes in the ground. The attackers' spears became entangled in the hides, and their advance faltered. The tightly packed soldiers found themselves caged by their own leveled spears, unable to turn or move. Yavin's men surrounded them and attacked from all sides.

Some of Parshandatha's men who had escaped earlier attempted to rejoin the fight, but Yavin's forces swiftly quelled that effort. The battle was fierce yet brief, culminating in the deaths of HMN's ten sons, their blood staining the ground—a testament to their crimes against Mordecai the Jew. In a final act of victory, Yavin yanked Esther's father's ring from Parshandatha's lifeless hand.

Yavin issued swift orders: "Search the homes of HMN's sons. Recover what belongs to us. Eliminate any resistance, but do not harm the women and children. And you, Judah and Moshe," he pointed at two soldiers, "stay with the bodies and preserve them." He sent a messenger to inform Esther of the battle's outcome before joining his men in the search of Parshandatha's house.

Mordecai's palace lay in ruins, reduced to ashes. The roof had collapsed, the walls crumbled, and the stones had cracked. Falling stones damaged the marble floors. Only the chimneys and the marble column of the tower remained intact.

Just wood and stone, Yavin thought, surveying the damage. *It will take time, but we can rebuild.*

CHAPTER 47

sther watched as dark, towering clouds of smoke rose on the horizon, blocking the sun's rays and casting a red glow across the sky. Disturbed by reports of unrest in Shushan, the king summoned his ministers. "Bring Ishtahr," he ordered.

Alarmed, Esther dropped everything. She hurriedly donned her royal attire, including her crown and dagger, and rushed to the royal hall with Hatach. Once inside, she slowed her pace, walking proudly with her head held high, and stood before the king, nodding and smiling at him.

The king regarded her seriously. "In Shushan, the capital of Persia, five hundred men are either missing or dead, and the ten sons of HMN are among the fallen. What has happened in the rest of my provinces? Whatever your petition, it shall be granted, and whatever further request you make, it shall be done."

Esther's blood boiled at the slanderous accusations directed at her by some ministers that day. They sought to topple her, the Jewish queen, causing trouble by exaggerating the death count. In doing so, they signed their own death warrants, but the day was almost over, and they are secured in the king's palace.

Five hundred missing and dead, he said, Esther thought. *I don't believe anyone actually went and counted. Most are surely safely secured in my palace at Mordecai's banquet, while many are simply hiding for the day. They certainly hadn't informed the king that HMN's sons had destroyed Mordecai's palace. Never mind; I will not contradict the king's declarations.*

Though furious, she maintained her composure, holding her head high and refusing to let her gaze wander to the ministers who might revel in her discomfort.

The king's insinuation about the harm done to the Jews in other cities due to HMN's killing decree was clear, Esther thought. *He was subtly indicating that HMN's sons deserved to be executed for their father's offenses and their own attack on the Jews. However, due to their high status, a proper and legal execution must be carried out in according with royal law. By leaving their disgraced bodies out in the street to be devoured by dogs, we disrespected the king. Additionally, the slanderous ministers who attempted to harm me by lying to the king about the death count should face punishment for their actions on the day of the 'defense decree.'*

Without hesitation, she raised her head and spoke confidently, "If it pleases the king, let the Jews in Shushan be granted permission to continue today's work into tomorrow, using the same rules. Let HMN's ten sons be respectfully hanged upon the tree their father made."

All the king's ministers nodded in agreement.

"It shall be done," the king declared immediately.

Esther nodded, satisfied. The king hadn't allowed the slanderous ministers to suggest hanging HMN's sons that night to avoid the second day. *HMN's sons' corpses would remain in the street overnight, disgraced. By the next day, the public would believe the king had justly executed HMN's sons. The extra day would enable Esther to punish the slanderous ministers and the enemies who thought they could hide. They would be stunned to learn about the extension,* she thought.

Harvona informed Esther of the names of the ministers who had slandered her.

Esther then relayed her instructions to Yavin, saying, "Tell Mordecai to extend his banquet for one more day and ensure the safety of his guests. Tomorrow, we will punish the slanderous ministers and the enemies we missed today. Make sure the bodies of HMN's sons are guarded overnight, and hang their corpses on their father's tree at my palace."

On the extra day, the known enemies of the Jews, along with the slanderous ministers, were executed. The remaining ministers dared not voice any complaints to the king again, fully aware that they risked giving Esther a reason to request a third day.

———⟐———

Esther received reports from her commanders, filled with triumphant tales from countless cities and communities. The surviving Jews were celebrating their newfound freedom.

With excitement in her heart, Esther hurried to find Mordecai, who was still in his hidden refuge.

"Look! My father's ring," she exclaimed, her voice brimming with joy. "I'm so happy you're alive!"

"Me too," Mordecai replied, a smile spreading across his face as he embraced her tightly.

———⟐———

Mordecai invited Ason Ben Aser and his father, who had been rescued from Parshandatha's house, to his office. As they entered, Ason and his father prostrated themselves on the floor.

"Ason, you were a backstabber," Mordecai declared sternly.

"True," Ason cried, covering his head with his hands in remorse.

"I understand you couldn't have asked for my help, and we did use you when we learned what you were doing," Mordecai continued.

"Please, have mercy," Ason's father pleaded softly.

"In times of stress, there are always people like you," Mordecai replied. "I found no evidence that you harmed the Jews or that you sought personal gain—other than keeping your father alive. I choose to forgive you. Go home and celebrate our victory; you served us well."

The Jews in Shushan erupted in celebration, rejoicing and dancing throughout the community.

A grand victory party was organized at Esther's palace for the Jewish people of Shushan—men, women, children, and even babies.

Esther brought Rebekah from Sarah's house, instructing her to stand by her side, dressed in her finest clothes.

Esther announced, "We survived! God has given us a miracle! We won! Amen! Glory! Hallelujah! Victory! Success!" The crowd roared in response, jumping, dancing, and hugging one another for several minutes.

As the excitement began to calm, Mordecai raised his hands, calling for silence. He faced the crowd, knelt, and placed his head on the floor for a moment. Rising, he proclaimed, "Blessed be God, ruler of the universe, who granted us excellent leaders: Queen Esther and her general Yavin. Blessed are our brave commanders and soldiers. Bless our nation that fought for our survival and triumphed. Israel lives!" he shouted, his voice ringing with fervor.

The crowd erupted once more in jubilation, chanting, "Israel lives! Israel lives! Israel lives!"

Esther rose and said, "Mordecai, here is your victory gift. Allow me to introduce Gdaliahu Ha-Nasi's great-niece."

Mordecai stood up and walked over to Rebekah, placing his arm around her shoulders. "Thank you for your approval. Let me introduce my bride, Rebekah," he announced proudly.

A few days later, when Zechariah arrived from Egypt, the Jews celebrated once again, this time with the joyous wedding of Mordecai and Rebekah.

CHAPTER 48

Mordecai and Esther wrote a humorous, concise version of their story and published it, declaring a new holiday for the Jews to commemorate their miraculous victory. Each year, they would read the story, give gifts to the poor, exchange presents among themselves, and celebrate.

The children of Israel were filled with joy, grateful for the miraculous victory God had granted them. With open hearts, they embraced Esther and Mordecai's commands, agreeing to celebrate the new holiday for generations to come.

"I fulfilled my promise to my grandfather and accomplished the 'Prosperity and Pain' routes—based on Samson riddle "sweetness came from the strong" . The Jews will not assimilate for thousands of years," Mordecai declared.

Esther replied delightfully. "I lived up to my promise to Gdaliahu Ha-Nasi. I am ready to bring an heir to the king, and you will help me raise him as a Jew."

"Yes, but I am still very disappointed," Mordecai lamented.

"Why? What's wrong?" Esther asked, puzzled.

"We wrote the story as one of miraculous salvation, filled with silly miracles and only a hint of wisdom. Even without mentioning God, future generations will believe we cried and prayed and that God alone brought us victory. This is misleading. I wanted them to understand they can save themselves with wisdom, knowledge, and imagination— Learn, plan, attain gain."

"We all know the economic prosperity you brought will sustain our Jewish identity," Yavin remarked. "But regarding the rest, we had no choice. If we wrote the truth, they might defy you or ignore the importance of maintaining our Jewishness. You told us to keep it a secret."

"But if they learn the wrong lesson, when disasters strike, they'll pray instead of fight. They'll say, 'In Egypt and in Persia, God helped us; why not now?'" Mordecai insisted.

"True, but because we are scattered, some will always survive to carry God's message. When you have a son, teach him the true story," Yavin said with a smile.

"I will do that. It's the least I can do," Mordecai sighed.

In the same month, both Esther and Rebekah became pregnant, giving birth to sons just three days apart. The mothers and their boys became close friends, celebrating Jewish holidays together.

After their victory, merchants saw increased profits. Mordecai instituted a new property and profit tax on merchants and professionals, boosting the king's revenue tenfold and earning him respect from the majority of the people.

CHAPTER 49

"And what happened after that?" my grandchild asked.

"The Jews survived. We are the proof," I replied.

"How?"

"In Babylon and Jerusalem, our Torah was collected and explained, providing a common book and customs that kept us united. Although Mordecai's IBCE office closed, the Jews continued to trade independently across the globe—from China and India to Turkey, Egypt, and Spain. This route became known as the famous Silk Road, bringing prosperity and employment to the Jews for over twenty hundred years while reinforcing their connection to Judaism. Despite facing attacks, they generally enjoyed good living conditions, and their numbers grew into the millions.

"Thanks to the survival of the Jews, both Christianity and Islam emerged, leading to the acceptance of God by more nations.

"The Crusaders sought to establish a competing commercial route to Asia, conquering Jerusalem as a gateway to the East. They killed many rival Jews during their journey, but their efforts ultimately failed, allowing the Jews to resume trade through the Islamic world to Spain.

"In Spain, Queen Isabella conquered Granada, the last Muslim stronghold in Spain, severing the Jews' commercial ties through North Africa to Egypt and the Far East. In 1487, Pero da Covilha traveled to India through Egypt, reporting a potential sea route to India around Africa. Spain and Portugal developed navigational tools and large ships capable of crossing oceans, enabling direct trade with Asia. As a result, the Jews lost their commercial significance. Queen Isabella forced them to convert to Christianity, leave the country, or pay heavy taxes.

"Many Jews fled to Turkey, the Netherlands, and Poland, establishing a new commercial land route from Turkey to Europe, leading to economic success. However, the invention of the train and new rail lines connecting Turkey to Europe diminished Jewish commerce once again.

"The Jews adapted by pursuing higher education and entering universities, becoming professionals and scientists, leading advancements in various fields.

"Trouble began brewing for many Jews along the old, deserted trade routes. Some chose to return to Israel to rebuild their state, while others opted to stay, and still others migrated to the United States.

"Swift and harsh troubles came for the Jews of Europe. Many perished without a fight—women, children, the elderly, and the young. No new Mordecai or Esther rose to lead the nation. The wealthy had the time and resources but failed to prepare the cities. It was a catastrophic disaster. Even their belief in God was shaken. How could He allow this?"

"So we failed?" my grandson asked, concern in his voice.

"We stumbled but did not falter. We survived. God's ways are mysterious. The surviving Jews migrated to the USA and Israel.

"The State of Israel became a center of technology. The knowledge within our community brought us pride and success. We are discovering God's paths of morality and science, and hopefully, this will sustain us forever," I concluded.

"Learn, plan, attain gain," my grandson echoed thoughtfully.

"Amen," I replied, closing our conversation.

Acknowledgments

I am deeply grateful to my dear teacher, Yitzchak Etshalom, whose passion for the Book of Esther ignited my own interest and guided me in understanding the Old Testament more profoundly. I also want to acknowledge the many individuals who have played a significant role in my journey—those who educated me, offered support, challenged my ideas, and even those who may have overlooked me at times. Each of these experiences has shaped my path and contributed to the creation of this book. Thank you all for your invaluable influence and for helping bring this work to life.